TRANQUILITY

Tranquility

ASIN Amazon: B07JVFX24T

ISBN: 978-1-9995059-0-5

2nd Edition November 2018

Cover Design by Kyle Lechner

Formatting by KH Formatting on FB

TRANQUILITY

LAURIE GARDINER

Also By

"Retribution" in A Journey of Words

"Thief" in A Haunting of Words

"Don't Forget Me" in A Contract of Words

Coming Soon

"There's No Sunshine in Hell" in A Flash of Words

For more information and to see all of her works, check out her website.

https://lauriegardiner.me/

Acknowledgements

I'd like to thank Bea Metzgar, Enza Osborn and Jeff Brubacher for sharing their expertise and advice with me. Thanks also to my beta readers, Keith Gardiner, Margaret Chester and Michele Curtis for their input and advice.

CHAPTER 1
EDIE

MY LIFE CHANGED THE DAY Edith MacAdams came into it. I remember it well. It was my first day working in Tranquility's dementia unit and the same day Sam Turner ran streaking buck naked through the halls.

A thin brushstroke of crimson lit up the edge of the dark eastern sky when I pulled into the staff parking lot that morning. Light tendrils of mist danced in my headlights and crept like skeletal fingers around the massive, gray stone building.

I stepped out of the car with coffee in hand and slung my duffle bag over my shoulder. The crunch of fallen leaves stirred underfoot. Breathing in the crisp, clean smell of autumn, I strode into Tranquility, eager for a new beginning after five years of working the nightshift.

The nursing home was eerily quiet so early in the morning. I made my way through the long-term care unit, down a long, gloomy hallway into Dementia, without seeing a soul. As I passed the first hallway, I caught movement from the corner of my eye and turned to look. A tall, lanky man with a shock of white hair hurried down the hall toward me. He wore only black silk boxers covered in bright red lips.

They sagged at the waist, threatening with every step to slide off his slender hips. The shiny fabric hung loosely around his spindly, white legs.

"Hey," he called when he spotted me.

I waited where I was.

He stopped a few feet away and peered at me suspiciously. "Who are you?"

"I'm Sarah. And you are…?"

"Sam. Can't find my damn clothes. Need to go to work."

Sam Turner. I'd been there a few days before, studying my new residents' charts, so I knew he was one of mine. Before I could respond, a petite brunette in scrubs popped her head out of the room behind him. "Sam, you don't have to work today—it's Saturday. Come with me and I'll help you find your clothes."

He shook his head in confusion.

"And your music. Your daughter left music for you."

Sam's eyes lit up. He turned without a word and followed the woman down the hall.

I made my way across the main hall toward the change room, sipping my coffee and studying my surroundings as I went. The walls were a soft, welcoming shade of sunny yellow, the faint aroma of urine not quite masked by the smell of bleach and lemon-scented cleaners. The clock on the wall above the deserted nurse's station said ten after six. I frowned, annoyed with myself for being ridiculously early as usual, and went into the change room.

It was a small room with one wooden bench between two rows of beat-up green lockers. Another room to the left contained two bathroom stalls, a shower stall and a long counter with two sinks. I placed my bag on the bench and sat down beside it to change into my work shoes. I was leaning over, tying my laces when the door flew open with a bang.

"Morning," sang a pretty redhead as she breezed into the room. "You must be Sarah." She continued talking over her shoulder as she pulled a pair of white shoes from a locker. "I'm Tracey. Lucky you, you get to work with me in Hall B."

I wasn't sure how to respond to that.

She smiled much too brightly for the early hour, dropped the shoes on the floor and plunked down on the bench beside them. "Can't wait for you to meet our residents. Man, have you got some characters on your side of the hall."

I thought of Sam and smiled. "I think I met one of them on my way in here. His name was Sam." I picked my sneakers up off the floor and set them in the bottom of a locker.

"Yup, he's yours. Was he wearing anything?"

"He had boxers on. Silk boxers covered in big, red lips."

Tracey chuckled as she tossed her boots into her locker and slammed the door shut. "Must be your lucky day. Usually he's naked first thing in the morning. Key with Sam is to make sure he's always got his music. That's what makes him happy and keeps him out of trouble."

I zipped up my bag and placed it in the locker on top of my shoes. "Thanks, I appreciate it."

"No prob. Some of the residents go out with family on

Saturdays so it might be a light day. You need any help let me know. I'm off to the staff room to grab a quick coffee. Meet you at the nurse's station in five." She waved and was out the door before I could say a word.

The morning passed quickly. Tracey helped me out when she had time and we teamed up after breakfast to make beds.

"So," she said as we pulled the linens down and straightened the bottom sheet of the first bed. "You happy to be off nights?"

"Happy isn't the word. I've been waiting five years to get on days."

"Four for me, but it seemed like forever. I was always so friggin' tired."

"Me too. It was really hard when my daughter was younger. I used to stay up and miss sleep so I could spend time with her."

Tracey stopped working and stared at me. "How old is she?"

"Six. Her name's Kayla."

"Wow, you barely look old enough to have a kid, let alone a six-year-old."

"I'm twenty-five. I'm more than old enough."

"Exactly. You're the same age as me, and I'm so far from ready for kids. Course, I try pretty hard to be immature," she said, grinning impudently.

Later that morning, during my break, I took Edith MacAdams' file into the staff room and studied it. She was due to arrive before lunch and would be taking the empty bed in 8B with Mrs. Sellers whose previous roommate had died.

I was at the nurse's station after my break, replacing the file, when Edie arrived.

A thin, sharp-featured woman strode purposefully through the doors, pushing a woman in a wheelchair. She glanced around the main hall with a frown, and I wondered if the deep furrow between her brows was permanent. The woman in the chair, head down, hands wound together tightly atop the small bag on her lap, looked tiny and frail in the oversized coat she wore. Trailing slowly behind was a small, timid-looking man. His eyes darted around the room nervously as he pushed his glasses up higher onto his nose with one hand and struggled to pull a large wheeled suitcase with the other.

I stepped out from behind the nurse's station to greet them. "Hello," I said, crouching down in front of the wheelchair. "Are you Mrs. MacAdams?"

She lifted her gaze to my face. Her eyes were unexpectedly clear and bright and full of fire. "I am."

"It's nice to meet you. I'm Sarah Scott, one of the personal support workers in Hall B. Welcome to Tranquility."

"Thank you, lass. You can call me Edie."

I heard an impatient sigh above me and stood up. "Hi, it's—"

"We heard you," the woman said, looking down her beak-like nose at me. "This is Tom, her son." She jerked a thumb over her shoulder at him. "I'm his wife, Anne. We're in a hurry. Is there anything we need to do before we go?"

Ignoring her brisk, bossy tone, I nodded stiffly and said,

"Just the last of the paperwork to finish up. I'll take Edie to her room and you can join us when you're done." I gave Tom and Anne directions to the room before wheeling Edie down the hall. "This is the dining room." I stopped in the doorway to let her have a look. "Lunch is in half an hour. If you like I can bring you down and help you find a seat."

"No need, lass. I'm sure I can find my way."

Across from the dining room was the lounge; a big room full of comfortable furniture and a large flat screen TV. Two women reclined on the sofa watching an old black and white movie. Another was slumped over in her wheelchair in the corner, snoring softly. A trail of drool ran down her chin into the creases of her neck. Sam was in the corner...pulling down his pants!

"Sam! I'll be right back, Edie." I hurried over to the corner as his pants dropped to his ankles. "Do you need to use the bathroom, Sam?" I asked quietly.

He nodded.

"Okay. Pull your pants up and come with me, please. I'll take you to your room."

He shrugged nonchalantly, pulled up his pants and followed me into the hall. I apologized to Edie and we continued on to Hall B with Sam in tow. Edie waited patiently outside Sam's room while I went in and made sure he used the toilet. I left him with instructions to pull up his pants and wash his hands, and then took Edie to her room.

Tom and Anne came into the room as Edie and I unpacked her small bag. Anne stood over Edie, who still sat in her wheelchair. "Goodbye, Mother. Be sure to listen to the nurses and take your meds on time every day." She looked at me and whispered loudly over Edie's head, "She can be very stubborn at times. Don't be afraid to be stern with her."

"I'm sure she'll be fine." My tone was pleasant, but I wanted to slap her.

Anne turned to Tom. "Say your goodbyes quickly, Tom, and let's go. We have things to do."

Tom put a hand on Edie's shoulder. He bent down, kissed her cheek and spoke into her ear softly. "I'll see you soon, Mom. Don't worry, you'll be fine."

Edie raised a trembling hand to clutch at Tom's.

Anne took hold of her husband's arm and gave an impatient tug. "Enough! Good Lord, it's not forever. We'll be in to visit next weekend. Let's go!" She stalked out of the room as though expecting him to follow.

Tom smiled apologetically at his mother and turned to leave as a scream echoed through the hallway. He and I looked at each other and rushed to the door in time to see Sam streak past. He was naked and grinning from ear to ear. I peeked around the corner. Anne stood flattened against the wall with her eyes tightly shut, muttering "Oh, my God" over and over. Lily and Beth, the inseparable twin sisters, were at the other end of the hall giggling like giddy schoolgirls.

Sam stopped, turned around, spread his arms wide and did a little dance. "Come and get it girls!" he yelled at the twins as his parts dangled and swayed between his legs.

They covered their eyes with their hands and giggled even harder as they peeked at him through their fingers. Tracey came out of a room at the end of the hall near Sam.

She grinned widely when she spotted me with Tom and gave me a wave and a wink before turning to take Sam by the arm and lead him into his room.

I turned to Tom. "Sorry, apparently he does this every so often. I'm sure he's harmless."

Tom simply nodded and smiled, but there was a twinkle in his eye. He went to his wife, who was still pressed against the wall looking horrified. She ranted at poor Tom as she rushed away, as though the whole episode were his fault. He followed silently after her.

Shaking my head, I turned to speak to Edie and was startled to find her standing behind me. "Well," I said, trying to hide my surprise, "it's too bad they couldn't stay a little longer."

"Och, Lass," Edie scoffed, "I'll be better off without the both o' them." She continued unpacking, moving quickly between the bed and the wardrobe as she spoke. "That woman is a tyrant and has been a pain in my arse since the day they met. And Tom, well, he's my son and I love him, but he has nae backbone. He has nae stood up to that woman once in the all the years they've been married."

She paused and took a deep breath before she continued. "I'm sorry, lass. I tend to revert to my Scottish roots when I'm angry." She hung her head and her shoulders slumped. "Being here is not my choice, you know. It's Anne's doing. I used to stand up to her when I was younger and stronger. I guess I had more fight in me then. Now, it's easier to stay quiet. She's worn me down for too long and I'm tired."

"No need to apologize, Edie," I said, taking the clothes

from her and hanging them in the wardrobe. "You have every right to be angry."

We worked in silence for a few minutes before she asked, "That man who was running down the hall naked, why does he do that?"

"Sam? I'm not sure. I think it's the type of illness he has that causes him to do…strange things. It's my first day, too. I worked upstairs in the palliative care unit until a couple of days ago, so I'm still getting to know everyone."

"Well," Edie said with a grin, "I've a feeling he'll be keeping us entertained."

We continued unpacking. Edie talked and I listened. As for the wheelchair, I helped her fold it up and tuck it away in the corner, and that's where it stayed.

* * *

I found myself thinking about Edie on the drive home later that day. There'd been an instant connection between us and I looked forward to getting to know her better. She reminded me of my grandmother, with her sharp wit and straightforward, no-nonsense way of speaking.

My daughter, Kayla, had been home all day with my mom and grandmother. She ran to the door and flung herself into my arms when I walked into the house. I scooped her up, hugged her tight and breathed her in. "I missed you, munchkin."

"I missed you too, Mommy." She wriggled out of my arms impatiently and scampered back into the living room yelling, "Nana, Gran, Mommy's home!"

She was a non-stop bundle of energy and had her dad's carefree, happy nature. How different would her life be if he were still alive? She was missing out on everything I remembered so fondly about my own dad; weekends at the trailer, fishing, long talks under the stars at the campfire. I closed my eyes and could almost hear the deep rumble of his voice against my cheek as I snuggled on his lap, the smell of wood smoke filling my nostrils as I breathed him in. Kayla had only been a baby when her dad had died and would never have memories of him to keep close. The lack of a father figure in her life bothered me, despite how well-adjusted and happy she seemed, but being a single mom and working full-time left little time for dating.

I went down the hall to the living room to join my family. Four generations of women had lived under the same roof since my grandmother's stroke two years earlier. I stood in the doorway watching the three of them play rummy. Mom and Kayla sat together on the couch, the similarities between them so obvious; the dark hair, brown eyes and small turned up noses. I'd always looked more like my dad with my blonde hair and blue eyes.

My grandmother sat across from them in the armchair, looking put together as usual and much younger than her years. Her hair, always dyed a deep chestnut to hide the gray, was pulled into a neat bun at the base of her neck. Ruby red polish flashed at her fingertips as she shuffled the cards. It matched her lipstick and high heels perfectly.

My chest tightened and my hand went to the heart pendant at my throat. I stroked it with my thumb. It was the last birthday gift my dad had given me before he'd died. These three people were all I had left in the world.

Mom looked up. She smiled and patted the seat beside

her. “Come play a game with us, Sarah, and tell us about your first day in the new unit.”

“I wonned a game, Mommy!” Kayla yelled, bouncing up and down in her seat.

“You won, sweetie. Won, not wonned,” Mom corrected gently.

“Don’t nag the poor child, Brenda,” Gran said mildly. “She has her whole life to learn grammar.”

I sat on the couch beside Mom. Kayla climbed onto my lap and kissed my cheek. “I’m glad you’re home, Mommy.”

“Me too, munchkin. Will you let me win this game?”

“No way. You haffta win fair ‘n square.”

“Oh? Who says?” I leaned down and planted quick little kisses all over her face.

A few minutes later Kayla was back in her own seat, still a little breathless from the laughter and shrieks of joy.

“So,” I began, picking up a card and tossing it immediately onto the discard pile, “I think I’m going to like working in Dementia. One of my residents went streaking today.”

CHAPTER 2
THE SOUP INCIDENT

I WENT INTO EDIE'S ROOM shortly after six-thirty the next morning. She was already awake, sitting in her armchair in the dark, staring out the window. The sky was beginning to lighten. It had rained sometime through the night and a light mist hung over the courtyard, muffling the sound of birds chirping at the feeders.

I turned on the small lamp beside her bed and spoke quietly, as to not disturb her roommate, Mrs. Sellers. "Morning, Edie. How did you sleep?"

"I tossed and turned most of the night. It'll take some time to get used to being here."

I pulled the bedding back on her bed to let it air out, then went to her wardrobe and unlocked it.

"I was wondering why my things are locked up," Edie said. "I wanted to read last night before bed, but my book was in there."

"It's not to keep you out, Edie. It's to keep your things safe."

"Are you saying someone might steal from me?"

"It's not that." I shifted from one foot to the other, unsure of how to explain. "Sometimes the residents forget where their rooms are and may wander in here. I'm sorry if it's an inconvenience."

"No need to apologize, lass. I know you're just doing your job."

I smiled gratefully. "Will you need help getting washed and dressed?"

She raised an eyebrow. "Of course not. I'm quite capable of washing and dressing myself, despite what Anne may have told you."

"I'm sure you are, but I had to offer. If you do need help with anything, I'll be down the hall waking the other residents. Come find me if you need me."

I went down the hall to Sam's room. His roommate, Albert, was still asleep. Sam paced back and forth in front of the window. He looked up accusingly when I walked in. "Who the hell are you?"

"Hi, Sam, my name's Sarah. Jan asked me to help you this morning."

He eyed me suspiciously, but relaxed at the sound of his daughter's name. "Oh, she did, did she? She coming to get me today? I want out of this place."

I unlocked his wardrobe and took his iPod down from the top shelf. "She's coming later. She sent some music for you." I went to him, and knowing he might not remember doing the exact same thing the morning before, explained what I was about to do. "This is an iPod. It's a new gadget that has music on it, the same as a record or a cassette. These go in your ears so you can hear it." He watched me warily, but didn't resist as I put the ear buds in place. I turned the iPod on and tucked it into his shirt pocket. His face lit up and he began to hum along to Johnny Cash as I led him to the bathroom.

Ten minutes later, Sam was washed, shaved and dressed, still humming as he sat in his recliner near the window, watching the birds flit in and out of the feeder.

I woke Albert, who was already stirring, and took him into the bathroom. He stared at me blankly. "Do you need to use the toilet, Albert?"

His eyes moved to my chest. "Nice knockers," he said in a heavy British accent, lifting his hands as though to grab them. He'd been diagnosed with Pick's disease, a rare form of dementia that sometimes caused him to say and do sexually inappropriate things. Sam was often inappropriate as well, but he did it with intent, with a lecherous smile and a gleam in his eye that led me to believe he'd been inappropriate long before he had dementia.

I took Albert's hands and held them gently in mine. "Albert," I said, speaking slowly and clearly. "I want you to use the toilet, please."

He forgot about my chest. "Hairball!" he called, looking around the room.

According to his charts, he'd once owned a cat named Hairball and now spent much of his time walking round and round the racetrack-like halls looking for it. I spent the next five minutes trying to distract him from finding his cat and finally managed to get him ready for breakfast.

I left Albert circling the halls and moved on to the twins' room. I switched on the dim fluorescent lights on the wall behind the beds as I greeted them.

Lily and Beth stretched and yawned as they sat up in

bed. "Morning, Aunt Helen," Beth mumbled, rubbing sleep from her eyes.

Helen had helped them care for their mother, who had developed early-onset Alzheimer's in her fifties. The twins had spent most of their early adult years looking after her and never left home, married, or had children.

I gathered clothes from the wardrobe for Lily, who had a bath scheduled for seven. After helping them into their robes and slippers, I sent Beth into the washroom and escorted Lily down the hall to the bathing room. "I'm going to leave you with Sheila for a bit," I explained. "She'll help you with your bath. When you're done, I'll take you to the dining room for breakfast."

"She'll see me naked." She whispered the last word as though it were naughty, put her hand over her mouth and giggled.

"It's okay, Lily. She's a girl too, so it's nothing she hasn't seen before." I left her sitting on a bench outside the bathing room and strode back to Hall B. As I came around the corner, I heard Sam's raised voice and hurried into his room.

Sam had Albert cornered and was reaching for something in Albert's hand. "Give it to me," Sam said.

Albert clutched it tightly and hid his hand behind his back. "You're snookered. Off your trolley, old chap."

"Sam, Albert, what's the problem?"

Sam swung around. "He has my music!"

That explained it all. "Albert, can I see what's in your hand, please?"

He shook his head and slipped past Sam to his nightstand. He opened the drawer, placed the item inside and slid it shut carefully. Sam tried to get around him, but Albert stood, unmoving, with his back to the drawer as though guarding it.

I went to Sam's side, took him by the arm and spoke softly into his ear. "Sam, come with me. I'll get your music back, I promise."

He hesitated.

I pulled gently on his sleeve. "Come on, Sam. I'll take you to the lounge to wait for breakfast. Maybe the ladies will be there."

That piqued his interest and he went along willingly. I left him in the lounge in front of the TV and rushed back to the room to deal with Albert. He was gone. I opened the drawer to find the iPod there along with a variety of other items. I looked through them quickly and spotted the comb that had gone missing from the twins' bathroom the day before, a tube of lipstick, a few packages of crackers and half a moldy sandwich.

I pulled Sam's iPod out and slid it into my pocket. The rest I'd have to deal with later.

When I went to collect Lily from her bath, she was dressed, sitting outside the bathing room on a bench, looking miserable. I crouched down so I was eye-level with her. "How was your bath, Lily?"

"She's a miserable cow." An indignant look came over her face. "She calls it a 'fish'," she whispered, pointing at her crotch.

I blinked in surprise. "Oh, Lily. I'm sorry she made you uncomfortable."

Tears sprang to her eyes and she pushed her bottom lip

out slightly. "And I hurt my arm, too."

I looked down to see her rubbing her wrist gingerly. "May I see, please?"

She hesitated, but held her arm out for inspection. Her wrist was slightly red. I turned it over. It was red underneath as well.

"How did you hurt it, Lily?"

She looked confused then, and stared off into the distance as though struggling to remember. "I-I'm not sure. I think she was mad at me, but I don't know why."

"Sheila was mad at you?" I glanced around and lowered my voice. "Did she hurt you?"

Her brow wrinkled in confusion. "Hurt me? I don't think…I can't remember."

"It's okay, Lily." I pulled a tube of lipstick out of my pocket. Her eyes lit up and she pursed her lips so I could apply the deep red color to them.

* * *

I caught up to Edie as we left the dining room after breakfast. "I'll be taking some of the residents to the auditorium shortly for the church service if you'd like to join us."

She looked amused by my offer. "If I decide to go, I'm sure I can find my own way, lass. I have the map you gave me yesterday and I did some exploring last night, so I know my way around. I have the schedule as well, so I know all about the activities this week." She stopped outside the lounge, turned to me and put her hand on my arm. "I'll not be acting helpless just because Anne has decided I am. And you won't need to be catering to me, my dear." She gave my arm a pat, turned and walked into the lounge before I could say a word.

I left a few of my residents in the auditorium singing hymns and went to help Tracey make beds. The incident with Lily had bothered me all morning and I'd decided to talk to Tracey about it. She was already making beds when I found her.

"Hey, how's it going?" she asked when I walked in.

I went to the other side of the bed to help. "It's okay. It's a little faster pace than I'm used to."

"A little? I've been in Palliative. My God, it's like a friggin' morgue up there at night. Don't worry. Once you get into the routine, it'll get easier. And it's never boring."

We moved on to the next bed and worked in silence for a few moments while I debated whether I should say anything about Lily. Finally, I glanced over my shoulder at the door and said in a hushed voice, "Lily told me something after her bath today."

"Uh-huh."

"She said she hurt her arm. Her wrist was red all the way around as though…."

Tracey stopped working and stared at me. "As though someone grabbed it?"

I nodded. "When I asked her how she hurt it, she said she didn't remember, but she thought Sheila was mad at her."

Tracey's face darkened. "What do you know about Sheila?"

"Not much. I've heard rumors from people in Palliative who've worked with her over the years. I know they call her the 'Bath Lady' and she's been here a long time."

"Too long. Since Tranquility opened thirty years ago. Abby might be head nurse, but she pretty much lets Sheila do what she wants and Sheila acts like she owns the place. Even has the nurses under her thumb." She leaned across the bed and whispered, "And believe me, she gets called a lot more than the 'Bath Lady'. She's a nasty old bitch."

"Why is she still here?"

She snorted. "Are you kidding? The rest of them have been here almost as long as her. They all have their place in the pecking order and she's at the top."

"Are you saying I shouldn't do anything about Lily?"

"No. Record it. Report it to Abby, but be careful how you word it. She's worked with Sheila a long time."

"But Abby's the supervisor. If someone reports abuse she can't ignore it."

"Not how it works around here. She's probably just as afraid of Sheila as everyone else."

"Why would people be afraid of Sheila?"

Tracey rolled her eyes. "You obviously haven't had a run-in with her yet. Don't cross her whatever you do. She'll make your life hell."

I found Abby in the nurse's supply room just before lunch, stocking her cart with lunchtime medications. Her long brown hair was pulled tightly into a ponytail, giving her face a severe look. I wondered, as I stood in the doorway watching her bustle back and forth between the cart and the shelves, how she kept her white scrubs so clean.

A moment passed and she still hadn't looked up. I cleared my throat and she glanced my way. "Sarah," she said with a nod of acknowledgement. "Can I help you?"

"I, uh, just wanted to let you know about an incident this morning."

"Okay, go ahead." She continued working as I explained.

"When I picked Lily up from her bath this morning, she told me she hurt her arm. I checked it and I didn't see any bruises, but it was a little red."

Abby barely looked up. "Where?"

"Around the wrist, all the way around, on both sides."

"Did she say how it happened?"

"She didn't remember."

Abby straightened up and pushed the cart out of the room. She turned her back and continued speaking as she locked the door. "I appreciate you coming to me, Sarah, but an incident this minor really doesn't need to be reported. It sounds like her wrist was sore or itchy and she was rubbing it."

"But she said Shei-" I remembered Tracey's warning. "She said she hurt it."

Abby turned and took hold of the cart. "I'm sure it's nothing serious. Record it in the support worker binder if it makes you feel better. I have work to do and I'm sure you do as well." She marched away, pushing the cart toward the nurse's station.

* * *

With Tracey's help, I managed to get all my residents to the dining room in time for lunch. I pushed Mrs. Sellers up to a nearby table and directed Albert to a chair beside her. He rubbed his bald head in confusion and looked around the room.

I leaned down to eye level. "We're here for lunch, Albert. Would you like some tea, or coffee, or a glass of juice?"

He looked me straight in the eyes with a smile on his face and said, "Sod off."

I smiled in return, as though he'd wished me a good day, and went to get him a cup of tea.

Edie was sitting at a table with another of my residents, Rose, a sweet, gentle woman in her fifties with Down syndrome and Alzheimer's. Across from them sat Mrs. Wojciechowski, who, for obvious reasons, everyone called Mrs. W. She was in the later stages of dementia and had recently developed problems with muscle control, including swallowing.

Sheila was sitting beside Mrs. W, feeding her.

I sat down between Albert and Mrs. Sellers and helped Albert fix his tea. Sam was across the table from me. Lily and Beth, the twins, stood to my right, bickering over who should get to sit beside him. Beth had reached the chair beside Sam first, pulled it out from the table and prepared to sit, but Lily shoved past her sister and slid into the seat first.

Beth made a sound of outrage and pushed her bottom lip out in a hot pink lipstick pout. "I was here first, Lily."

"No you weren't," Lily said nonchalantly. She picked up her napkin, flicked it open and smoothed it across her lap.

Beth's eyes narrowed in anger and she moved around the chair to look down at her sister. "I'm telling Mother."

I patted the seat of the chair beside me. "Beth, come sit with me and tell me about the boy you like." I'd overheard

Beth talking to Lily the day before about her high school sweetheart and hoped I could distract her from the argument with her sister.

."You mean Paul?"

"Yes. I want to hear all about him."

She smiled indulgently and sat down to tell me about him. I placed her soupspoon in her hand and she soon became distracted from her stories by the food in front of her.

Mrs. W was having a hard time that day. She choked and coughed with the first spoonful. Soup trickled down her chin and neck, soaking her apron before Sheila impatiently swiped at it with a napkin.

Mrs. Sellers tried to push her wheelchair away from the table. I pulled her back in, moved the half-empty soup bowl away and placed a ham and cheese sandwich in front of her. "Here, Mrs. Sellers, here's a sandwich for you." That piqued her interest and she began to eat again.

Lily giggled and I looked over to see her with a sandwich in one hand and the other on Sam's crotch. Sam had a huge grin on his face. I turned back to Mrs. Sellers with a smile. She was still engrossed in her sandwich and oblivious to the antics across the table.

Sheila's loud, shrill voice rang out. "Open your mouth now, dear. You have to eat."

"Open your mouth, dear," parroted Lily. She and Beth giggled, oblivious to Sheila's angry glare.

There were a few other snickers throughout the room, no doubt because Lily had sounded so much like Sheila, condescending tone and all.

My eyes met Tracey's as I looked around the room. She raised an eyebrow and shook her head in disgust. We both looked back at Sheila as her power struggle with Mrs. W continued.

Mrs. W clamped her mouth shut as she turned her head from side to side in an attempt to get away from the spoon. Sheila leaned forward and caught Mrs. W's chin in one hand. She held her head still and forced the spoon between her lips. "You. Need. To eat!"

The force of the spoon pried Mrs. W's lips open and in went a mouthful of soup. Sheila sat up taller and looked around for approval, but all eyes were on Mrs. W's face as she prepared to empty her mouth. Her eyes shot daggers at Sheila as she puffed out her cheeks and took a deep breath in through her nose. Sheila had finished gloating and was turning back toward the table when Mrs. W expelled her breath forcefully. Soup and spit flew from her mouth and hit Sheila full in the face.

There was a collective gasp before the dining room fell silent. For a moment, no one spoke or moved as we all watched and waited for Sheila's reaction. But even she seemed shocked into silence. Finally, she sputtered and reached for a napkin.

Edie, who had been staring at Sheila as though mesmerized by the globs of slimy soup dripping off her face, now glanced at me. My hand had gone automatically to my mouth when the soup flew. I saw the glint in Edie's eye and realized that, behind my hand, I was smirking. I shook my head violently at her, but it was too late.

Edie chuckled. Lily and Beth, upon hearing Edie's

laughter, both snorted loudly and were soon laughing as well. Sam and Albert were oblivious to it all and continued to eat as though nothing had happened.

Sheila's expression was murderous. She eyed Edie from across the table as she wiped her face with the napkin. Her angry glare only made Edie laugh harder. It was contagious and soon most of the residents joined in. Staff members turned away to hide their grins. Tracey hid her face behind her hand, but her shoulders were shaking.

Sheila remained silent, but I could tell by her stiff movements and the set of her jaw that she was quietly seething. She finished cleaning her face as well as she could with the napkin, and then went to the sink to wash properly. She came back to the table and proceeded to feed Mrs. W her pudding, which she ate willingly.

The laughter died down and everyone went back to eating as though nothing had happened. Everyone but Sheila. The dark looks she gave Edie, her rigid posture and silence, said more than any angry words could have.

My "Sheila-watching" days had just begun.

CHAPTER 3
FORGOTTEN MEMORIES

WATCHING SHEILA WAS A challenge since she spent most of her time alone in the bathing room with residents. While she was bathing them, the rest of us were busy helping people get up and ready for breakfast. I simply didn't have time to "spy" on her. I had no proof that Sheila was mistreating anyone. My suspicions were based on intuition and rumors. The thought of anyone mistreating the residents outraged me, especially in the dementia unit, where people were so much more vulnerable because they were often unaware and unable to communicate.

In the week following the soup incident, I became almost obsessed with catching Sheila in the act. Whenever I had a moment, I listened outside the bathing room door, or found an excuse to go in. I plied my residents subtly for information, bringing Sheila's name into the middle of a conversation, asking how they'd enjoyed their bath that day, listening and observing their reactions. Problem was, they all had some form of dementia. Some of them didn't even remember they'd had a bath an hour ago. The small bits of information I managed to gather were weak at best and offered no solid proof of abuse.

I even spoke to Mr. Gallo, a kind, soft-spoken Italian man who, despite his own struggles with Parkinson's, got on a bus every morning and came to Tranquility to spend the day with his wife. He helped her eat her lunch and later, sat reading in the chair beside her bed while she napped.

It was no secret that Mr. Gallo did not care for Sheila. In fact, he disliked and mistrusted her so much that he insisted she not bathe his wife unless he was present. When I asked him why he didn't want to leave his wife alone with Sheila he said simply, "She no good," but the tightness of his jaw and the slight trembling of his hand were telling enough of his feelings.

Edie, however, was more than willing to talk and had a memory better than my own. She stood out like a lone star in the dark night sky at Tranquility. She was sharp and quick to remember what had happened an hour or a week ago. I had begun to question whether she had dementia at all.

I went into her room one afternoon before leaving for the day. She was sitting in her chair with a book open on her lap, but she wasn't reading, she was staring out the window with a gloomy expression on her face.

"Edie?"

She looked up in surprise. "Sarah. Why aren't you on your way home?"

Mrs. Sellers moaned and stirred in the bed beside us. I pulled the curtain across between the beds and said in a hushed voice, "I wanted to talk to you about something."

Edie watched me curiously as I pulled myself up to sit on the wide ledge below the window. "Is it about the Dragon?" she asked.

"The what?"

She leaned forward and whispered, "You know, that woman."

"Oh. Yes, it is. I want to ask you about your baths."

"Ah, I thought as much. Unfortunately, there's not much to tell. I know she doesn't like me, but she's careful and a little too nice, if that makes sense at all."

"It does. It's nauseating sometimes, how nice she acts. I have a bad feeling about her, Edie, but I'm new here, so I have to be careful. And the other residents don't always remember as well as you do."

"Are you asking for my help then?"

"I'm just asking you to let me know if you see or hear her do anything inappropriate. Come straight to me, though. Don't confront her, whatever you do. I don't want you to make her angry."

Edie gave a short bark of laughter. "It's too late for that, I'm thinking. She's had it in for me since that day I laughed at her in the dining room. Besides, she's more likely to do something if she's angry, don't you think?"

I was starting to wish I'd never said a word. I jumped down off the ledge and put my hand on her shoulder. "Edie, please don't *try* to make her angry."

She reached up and patted my hand reassuringly. "Don't worry yourself, lass. I'll not do anything foolish."

I turned to leave, stopped, and asked, "Are you okay? You looked a little down when I came in."

She smiled, but her bottom lip trembled slightly. "I get that way every so often. The doctor says it's the depression. I appreciate the concern, but it's nothing to worry yourself about."

* * *

My suspicions about Edie not having dementia were confirmed by a conversation I had with her a few days later. We were sitting together in the lounge one afternoon right before my shift ended, watching some of the residents dance to the Rolling Stones. Mr. Gallo sat beside me with Mrs. Gallo next to him in her wheelchair. He held her hand and tapped his toe to the music as she dozed.

Edie was telling me about her second husband. "Ian was a Scot. I suppose that's why we hit it off. He was a cop, a good one, and a good man too. I was fifty years old and he made me feel like a schoolgirl again."

"I can see that," I said. "You still glow when you talk about him."

"I know it. I married Tom's father out of duty, but I did it right the second time round. Ian was for love." She sighed. "I still miss that man."

"So, when you say you married out of duty do you mean…?"

Edie chuckled and patted my hand. "Don't be so surprised, lass. It happened more than you know. My first marriage was a perfect example of why wee ones are not a good reason for marrying."

Sam gyrated his hips wildly to "Satisfaction". He was surprisingly handsome at seventy-three with his thick, white hair, bright blue eyes and tall, lean frame. Lily and Beth, who had been dancing happily beside Sam earlier, began to argue when a slow song came on.

"You have a boyfriend already, Beth," Lily said, flipping

her blonde hair in annoyance.

"Well, he's not here right now," Beth replied, "and besides, I like *him*." She jerked a thumb toward Sam.

"Well, I like him *too*, and I saw him *first*!" Lily gave Beth a shove that nearly sent her toppling onto Mrs. Gallo's lap.

Mr. Gallo grunted in surprise and moved to get up. I put my hand on his knee to stop him, jumped up and put myself between the twins and Mrs. Gallo. "Ladies, I'm sure Sam will be happy to dance with both of you."

Lily was having none of it. "No, I saw him first. Beth can find her own partner."

Beth's lower lip came out in a pout. "I'm telling Mother when we get home!" she said, flouncing off to sit by herself in the corner.

I went back to my seat beside Mr. Gallo. He was leaning over speaking to his wife in Italian, his voice soft and reassuring. Only the slight tremor in his hand gave away his upset. I watched Lily smooth her hair and make her way back to Sam who was still dancing obliviously.

Edie turned to me in disbelief. "What is wrong with these people? Are they *all* crazy?" She glanced at Mr. Gallo apologetically. "I'm sorry. No offense intended."

He shook his head sadly. "No, no, is okay." He leaned closer and said in a hushed voice, "Is not their fault. Is the disease. It make them crazy."

"What disease? Are you saying all these people have the same disease?"

"Dementia, Edie," I said. "Everyone here has some type of dementia, like Alzheimer's. This is the dementia unit."

Edie paled instantly and her hand went to her mouth. She looked away and was silent for a moment. Her eyes flew back to my face and she flushed red with anger as the realization set in. "Sae, that's why that bitch made me go tae the doctor tae get all those tests done!"

I glanced at Mr. Gallo. He cleared his throat and turned away to rearrange the blanket on Mrs. Gallo's lap. I turned back to Edie. "What tests?" I asked.

She twisted her hands in her lap. "Some sort of clock test, and others—memory tests, I think. They asked me all sorts of questions. I don't remember much, but I know I didn't do well. I overheard Anne later, telling Tom I'd failed."

She said it so dejectedly that I was sure she thought by failing those tests she had sealed her own fate. I put my hand over hers reassuringly. "It's not your fault, Edie. There must have been some reason why you didn't do well."

"I don't know. My mind…it was muddled. I couldn't understand what was going on. I felt confused all the time and I was forgetting things, like what day it was, and why I was living with Tom. I didn't understand why I couldn't go home. I'd forgotten my house had been sold because Anne didn't think I should be living alone anymore."

Edie hung her head and swallowed hard before she continued. "Anne said I became 'violent'. The ambulance came and they strapped me down and sedated me. I'm not even sure how long I was in the hospital. It felt like months, but they had me so drugged up, I couldn't think straight. Finally, Tom came and took me home. Anne was there with me all the time. I couldn't even piss without her knowing about it!" She spat the words in disgust. "Then she took me for the tests, and not long after that they brought me here. They told me it was a retirement home!" Edie sat back in her chair and angrily swiped a tear from her cheek.

I was silent for a moment as I digested it all. Edie would pass any memory test now, I was sure of it. Could it have been an illness that had caused her confusion? Or maybe it had been drug-induced. "Were you sick at all, Edie, besides being muddled and forgetful before you went to the hospital?"

She shook her head.

"Were you taking any drugs then that you aren't taking now?"

She shrugged her shoulders. "I've no idea. I don't think I knew my name half the time, let alone what drugs I was taking."

I watched Lily stalk off the dance floor in a huff. She sat down hard, crossed her arms over her voluptuous chest and stuck her ruby-red bottom lip out as far as it would go. She then proceeded to glare at Beth and Sam as they slow-danced to Elvis's "Are you Lonesome Tonight."

I smiled as Sam's hand inched slowly downward until it rested on Beth's ample, purple polyester-covered cheek. I squeezed Edie's hand reassuringly. "Try not to worry, Edie. We'll figure this out."

* * *

Tracey caught up with me as I was leaving for the day. "Hey, Sarah, wanna go for coffee?"

"Sorry, I can't. I have to pick Kayla up from school soon," I said, punching in the code to open the door.

We walked through a long hallway with a wall of windows looking out onto the courtyard. I glanced at her. She looked disappointed and I felt a twinge of guilt. It was only a five-minute walk from the house to the school and I knew Gran would have been happy to pick Kayla up. "How about we plan it for another time? If I know ahead, I can arrange for my grandmother to pick her up for me."

"Sure, sounds good."

We went through another set of doors into Long Term Care. The unit was a buzz of activity. The sheer number of residents with varying needs, as well as the array of nurses, doctors and various other staff, meant non-stop activity throughout the day. The weekends were even busier, with a constant stream of visitors coming and going all day and into the evening.

We waved at Marg, the receptionist. She peered at us over her glasses and gave a stiff nod before returning to her work. Tracey punched in another code and we exited the back door into the staff parking lot.

"I won't forget, you know. We're going out soon. I'm holding you to it," she called as she sauntered off.

I turned my face to the sun as I strolled to my car. It had been a dreary, rainy autumn so far and the heat of the sun was a welcome change. Fall had always been my favorite time of year, and my dad's as well. Now, the cool nights and changing colors brought only bittersweet memories. Every fall, Dad and I had raked leaves together. As soon as we had a pile big enough to cover me, I'd burrow beneath them. Dad would continue raking, whistling as though oblivious to my antics. When I was out of sight, he'd drop the rake and run around the yard calling my name, pretending to look for me as I tried not to giggle. He'd stop, close enough that I could peek out and see his feet, and say, "Sarah? Is that you?" I'd jump out, yelling and throwing handfuls of leaves at him until he scooped me up, tossed me back into the leaves, and tickled me until we both lay breathless.

It had been nearly ten years since he'd died. Sometimes I'd hear a deep, gravelly voice, or smell cigar smoke and turn, expecting to see him, yet there were times when I could barely recall his face, and that scared me. Memories were all I had left of him. Losing them would be like losing him all over again.

* * *

I went home to shower and change before going to the school to get Kayla. I heard Gran's voice from the living room and peeked in to see who she was talking to. She was sitting in the recliner, scowling at the laptop in front of her, talking to herself.

"Gran? Is that yours?"

She barely looked up. "Yes, it is. I'm debating whether to return it or throw it out the window."

I crossed the room and stood looking over her shoulder. "When did you get a laptop?"

"Today. I'm taking a computer class at the seniors' center."

I leaned down and kissed her on the cheek. "I'm impressed. Do you want help with it?"

She cupped my chin in her hand and kissed me in return before I straightened up. "No, no. You go have your shower. I'll take it to the next class with me and they'll help me figure it out." She snapped it shut, placed it on the coffee table and pushed herself wearily out of the chair. She staggered as she stood and would have stumbled forward if she hadn't caught hold of my arm as I reached for her.

"Are you okay? Do you need to sit down again?"

"I'm fine." She removed her hand from my arm and stood on her own as if to prove it to me. "I stood up too quickly, is all."

"Hmm, into the wine again this afternoon, were you?"

"No," she said with a laugh. "But, it's an idea. I think I'll pour myself a glass of red. Would you like one?" She teetered toward the kitchen, still a little unsteady on her feet.

I hesitated. I had half an hour before I had to be at the school. I could have a shower later. "Well," I said, following her into the kitchen. "I can't very well let you drink alone, can I?"

CHAPTER 4
THE NEW GUY

LATER THAT WEEK, I SAT down during my lunch break and went through Edie's medical charts. I compared her previous and current medications and read through the doctor's notes. She occasionally took an over- the-counter sleep aid and was on anti-cholesterol medication. There had been no reference made to memory loss, confusion, or any other signs of dementia, until nearly two months before Edie came to Tranquility. A few weeks before that, the doctor had prescribed anti-depressants.

I jotted down some information and made a mental note to do some research on drug interactions after my shift. I'd also speak to Abby.

On my way to find Abby later that afternoon, I heard a commotion coming from Hall A. An unfamiliar voice roared in anger and a slew of curse words followed. I hurried down the hall toward the voice. Rose paced back and forth outside the room, shaking her head and mumbling under her breath. Her round face was crumpled with worry.

I hurried to the doorway. "What's wrong, Rose?" I placed a gentle hand on her back as I took in the scene inside the room. Rose stopped pacing, but barely acknowledged me as she continued to mumble. I could feel her plump body trembling beneath my hand. A few other residents emerged from their rooms, eager for a little afternoon entertainment. Luckily, most residents were either napping or watching *Bringing Up Baby* in the lounge.

The room was a mess. The beds had been ripped apart, sheets and pillows thrown in a heap on the floor. A door on one wardrobe hung at an awkward angle. Clothes were strewn everywhere.

I didn't know the angry, frustrated man standing in the middle of the room yelling and gesturing violently. One of Carol's residents had recently been moved to Palliative, so I assumed this was his replacement.

Carol and Tina, the dayshift support workers in Hall A, were in the room, but keeping their distance from the man as he raged. Carol, a crusty, middle-aged woman who rarely smiled, had worked at Tranquility nearly as long as Sheila and was almost as bossy and intimidating. Tina was slightly younger, petite and unfailingly cheerful. It seemed an unlikely partnership, but they had worked together in Hall A for years.

Carol's face was red with frustration. She barked orders in her usual gruff manner as though that would help the situation. In fact, every time she spoke, the man became more agitated. Tina had put the bed between herself and the angry man. She occasionally uttered a soft "There, there, dear" but could barely be heard over Carol's booming voice.

The man paced erratically in front of the window. His eyes twitched and flickered back and forth nervously as he yelled, "Where are you?" and "Stupid bitch" among other things.

I spoke quietly, hoping not to disturb the man further. "What's going on?"

Carol glanced over and replied, "He has schizophrenia and dementia. That's all I know about him. His wife dropped him off a couple hours ago. He seemed okay so I went to have my break. When I came back he was like this. We need Abby. She's going to have to sedate him."

"What's his name?"

"John."

I looked at Tina questioningly. She took the opportunity to move closer to me and the doorway. "Any idea what set him off?" I asked.

She shook her head nervously and blew her long brown bangs out of her eyes. "I heard yelling and came running. Rose was just leaving his room…." She trailed off as we looked at Rose.

Rose appeared decidedly guilty. Her eyes shimmered with unshed tears. She began to pace again and wring her hands with worry. "Ju…just… wanted to say hello," she muttered.

Tina and I exchanged a knowing look. "You take Rose with you and go get Abby," I instructed. She nodded, took Rose by the arm and hurried away as fast as Rose's shuffling gait would allow.

"John," I said, entering the room cautiously, "do you want to tell me what's wrong?" No response. I kept my distance, but continued to speak to him soothingly. "No one's going to hurt you, John, we're here to help you." Gradually the yelling decreased, but he continued to pace and watch us suspiciously. I couldn't get too near him and chance getting hurt. All I could do was continue speaking in the same soft, soothing tone and hope for Abby to arrive soon.

Carol had finally shut up and now made her way closer to the door. "I'll watch for Abby," she mumbled as she leaned against the doorframe and peered around the corner.

John paced faster. He seemed to be going off again into his own world where the sound of my voice had become an annoyance. He muttered and shook his hands violently, as though to rid them of something evil.

Where the hell is Tina with Abby? No sooner had I thought it, I heard voices. It was Tracey however, not the nurse. I kept my eyes on John and backed slowly toward the door.

"New resident?" Tracey asked.

I nodded. "His name's John."

"I could hear him all the way to the nurse's station. Where's Abby?"

"Tina went—"

"Mary?" John had stopped pacing and was looking at Tracey. The change in him was immediate and amazing. His face lit up and all the tension and aggression left his body. "Oh my God, Mary, where have you been?" He rushed toward her and lowered his voice to a near whisper. "They took everything. My wallet, my clothes, everything's gone." He grabbed her arm. "Why did you leave me here?"

Tracey quickly fell into the role of Mary. "Shhh, John, it's okay. I have all your things safe at home."

"Did you come to take me home?" John asked. "Please,

take me home with you."

I watched Tracey put her hand over John's. She lifted it from her arm, but continued to hold it as she led him to the chair in the corner and helped him sit. Crouching down in front of him, she said gently, "I can't take you home yet, John, you need to get better first. These people are here to help you."

When he tried to protest she shushed him again and assured him, "I'll be right here with you. I'm not leaving and I won't let anybody hurt you." That appeased him for the time being and he seemed content to sit holding her hands quietly.

Now that John seemed more relaxed, I began picking clothes up off the floor and hanging them in the wardrobe. While I worked, I listened to Tracey, her voice low and soothing as she continued to speak to John. I was impressed with how she'd diffused the situation and calmed him so quickly.

Abby came rushing into the room a few minutes later. She moved quickly and efficiently, checking John's pulse and blood pressure. "What happened?" she asked as she worked.

Carol filled her in while I continued to tidy the room.

When Abby finished with John, she stood and pulled Carol aside. "You're going to have to keep a closer eye on him, at least until he settles in. We can't have this happening again."

"I can't be with him every second of the day. I was on break."

"Then you should have asked Tina to keep an eye on

him. If he becomes aggressive again let me know right away," Abby said as she turned to leave.

I couldn't let her go without trying to talk to her. "Abby?"

She stopped and looked at me, eyebrows raised. "Yes, Sarah. What is it?"

"I need to talk to you about Edith MacAdams. Do you have a few minutes?"

"Not right now. It's been a busy day. Come to the nurse's station at the end of the shift. If I'm there, we'll talk," she said over her shoulder as she strode out of the room.

John's shoulders were slumped with exhaustion after his tirade and he went willingly to the relaxation room with Tracey. Napping in his room was not an option in its current state.

Carol and I finished cleaning up the mess. I picked clothes up off the floor and hung them in John's wardrobe while Carol made the beds. Her rigid posture and terse movements were telling of her mood and we worked in silence for a few moments.

"Do you know who Mary is?" I asked finally.

Carol glanced up, but continued working as she spoke. Despite her size, she moved quickly, with the mindless efficiency of someone who had made thousands of beds. "She's his wife. She dropped him off here earlier. Could be Tracey's mother, they look so much alike."

The incident with John put me behind. By the time I caught up and went to the nurse's station, it was after two-thirty and Abby was gone. Our talk would have to wait.

CHAPTER 5
THE MESS

I ARRIVED AT WORK THE next morning determined to find time to speak to Abby before the end of my shift. It would have to be after lunch; mornings in Dementia were nothing short of chaotic. From the moment our shift began, it was a rush to get the residents up and ready for breakfast on time. The rest of the morning was filled with changing sheets, making beds, gathering laundry and taking residents to morning activities such as exercise class and hair appointments.

After lunch, when personal needs were again looked after, some of the residents would settle in for a nap or an afternoon movie. If we were lucky, that left us with a few minutes to do the required documentation and fill the afternoon shift in on any issues before we left for the day.

I started my routine as usual that morning and turned on the dim light beside Edie's bed shortly after six-thirty. From there I moved on to Sam and Albert, then the twins, and finally into Rose's room. She and Mrs. Gallo were still asleep. I woke Rose gently and directed her to the bathroom where I helped her get washed and dressed.

When I took her to the lounge ten minutes later, she

glanced shyly around the room, wringing her hands nervously. I led her to the sofa where Sam lounged, pried my hand from her tight grip and sat her down beside him. He moved closer, so close their legs touched, and stretched his arm across the back of the sofa behind her. He smiled and winked at her. Rose smiled in return and settled back into the couch.

I hurried back to Hall B to help Tracey get her resident, Mrs. Amaral, out of the lift and into her wheelchair. I smiled down at the large woman affectionately. She spoke almost no English, so Tracey had taught me how to say hello in Portuguese. "Bom dia, Mrs. Amaral."

It was hard not to favor her. No matter how she was feeling, she always had a smile and a kind word to offer. She suffered from congestive heart failure and needed constant oxygen. Her size and worsening condition had also left her wheelchair bound.

A smile spread across her face until her neck disappeared beneath the many folds of her chin. The prongs of the oxygen tube were pressed farther into her nostrils when her lips curled. She clutched at my hand as she gasped for enough air to speak. "Bom dia, belo," she wheezed.

Once Mrs. Amaral was settled in her chair, I went down the hall to Mrs. Gallo's room and opened the curtain between the beds to let a little light in. I didn't dare turn on her light, or try to wake her too early. She loved her bed and her sleep and didn't appreciate being woken before she was ready. Mr. Gallo had made it clear to me that she was to be allowed to sleep as late as she wished. If she missed breakfast, that was fine. He would be there to make sure she ate lunch.

I pulled Rose's bedding back and locked the wardrobe. Tracey came to the door to see if I needed help with Mrs. Gallo's lift. I glanced at the bed. The covers moved gently up and down with each breath, but Mrs. Gallo didn't stir. I shook my head, indicating we would come back after breakfast. Tracey looked relieved. She gave me a quick wave and hurried away.

I was sure some of the staff disapproved of the way I did my job. I didn't always follow the routine and would break protocol if I felt it was best for my residents.

Tranquility had opened in the eighties when nursing homes were still run as institutions with rigid schedules and strict rules. I doubted much had changed in the past thirty years. It was still under the same management and the practices and principles had not kept up with the changing face of elder care.

I understood that, especially when caring for people with dementia, there were times when residents needed help with decision-making. They also needed to be encouraged to eat and exercise and sleep regularly. But, I had a problem with making anyone do anything against their will, especially if it upset them to the point of needing to be sedated.

* * *

I was wheeling Mrs. Sellers out of the dining room after breakfast, when I heard raised voices coming from Hall A. I left Mrs. Sellers sitting beside the aquarium and hurried down the hall. As I got closer I recognized John's voice. The smell hit me before I even stepped into the room. I turned quickly to get a mask and gown from the cart in the hallway. I pulled on a pair of shoe covers, shoved an extra pair into my pocket, and shrugged into the gown as I hurried back to the room.

I stood in the doorway looking around the room as I put on the mask and a pair of gloves. The smell was overwhelming. John's bed, the floor in front of the bed, and the wall beside it, were covered in feces. John, still in his pajamas, was covered in it as well.

Carol was in the room. She had gloves on, but no mask or gown. She hadn't noticed me yet. She tried to grab John's hands, then ducked to avoid being hit by his wildly swinging arms. "John, stop it. Stop it right now!" she cried. Her voice was tense and raised in frustration and only seemed to make him more frantic.

I heard voices and turned to see Tina pushing her resident, Mrs. Baker, down the hall in her wheelchair. The smile on Tina's face disappeared the moment the smell hit her. She wrinkled her nose and peeked around the doorway into the room. Her hand flew to her mouth as she exclaimed in horror, "Oh, my God!"

"We're going to need Abby," I said. "And Tracey. Find Tracey, please, and tell her we need her here."

Tina jumped at the opportunity to leave and wheeled Mrs. Baker down the hall at a near run.

I walked hesitantly into the room and stopped short of the mess on the floor. "Carol?"

She glanced quickly over her shoulder. Relief flooded her face when she saw me. "Thank God," she sighed.

She turned and took a step toward me. I quickly took a step back. The look of revulsion on my face must have brought her to her senses. She looked down at herself and cringed.

John calmed down as soon as Carol turned her attention elsewhere. He paced back and forth in front of the window, muttering.

I motioned Carol away from the bed. "Why don't you go get cleaned up? Tina went to get help. I'm sure they'll be here any minute."

She glanced indecisively between John and the door.

"Carol," I said firmly, before she could say anything that might upset him again. "He's okay. We'll take care of him. Go, get cleaned up."

"Fine. Be back as soon as I can."

"Uh, you might want to put these on before you leave." I pulled the shoe covers out of my pocket and held them out to her.

Carol looked down at her feet, then behind her at the mess she'd left. She uttered a sound of disgust. "Thanks," she mumbled, reaching for them. She stopped when she realized her gloves were covered in feces as well.

I grabbed the wastebasket from beside John's bed and held it out as she carefully peeled off the gloves.

She dropped them gingerly from her fingertips, lips pressed together tightly, and I handed her a fresh pair of gloves. She put them on, took the shoe covers from me, bent down and pulled them over her shoes. After one last look at John, she hurried from the room.

John was still pacing and mumbling incoherently. His pajama pants were sagging at the back where the worst of the mess had soaked through the flannel. His hands were covered in it as well and I cringed every time he rubbed his face or ran a hand through his thin grey hair. There was no sense trying to talk to him or calm him further. He'd only been agitated by Carol's attempts to do so and I had no reason to believe it would be any different for me. All I could do was stay with him until help arrived, which it soon did.

Tina must have briefed Tracey about the situation. She entered the room wearing full protective gear, stood beside me and asked, "Think it's safe to go near him?"

"He's a lot calmer than he was when I came in, but I wouldn't get too close."

She nodded and took a few cautious steps toward John. He looked up as she approached and immediately became more agitated. "Stay away from me. You hear? Stay away!" he yelled.

Tracey immediately pulled the mask down, away from her face and spoke to him urgently. "John, it's okay, it's me."

He looked confused. "M-Mary? What are you wearing?"

"You had an accident, John. I need to clean it up."

He looked around the room and grimaced in disgust as though noticing the mess for the first time. His eyes welled up with tears and he lowered his head in shame. "I'm sorry," he whispered.

"Oh, no, John. It's not your fault. It was an accident," Tracey assured him.

He remained silent and continued to stare at the floor, clearly mortified by what he had done.

Tracey took his hand. "It's okay, John. We'll get you cleaned up." She looked back at me. "Sarah, would you grab a gown and some shoe covers for John, please?"

I hurried from the room as Abby came down the hall. "Is he okay?" she asked.

"He was pretty upset, but Tracey seems to have calmed him down," I said, stopping at the supply cart.

Abby poked her head into the room. She drew back quickly, grimacing at the smell. "He seems fine now. I don't think I need to sedate him."

I grabbed shoe covers from the top shelf of the cart and stuffed them in my pocket. "He seems to respond really well to Tracey." Afraid Abby had forgotten my request, I quickly added, "Will you have time to talk about Edie today?"

She shook her head and started down the hallway. "I don't know. I have to finish giving out meds. Maybe later."

Tracey and I worked together to clean John up enough to take him down the hall to the bathing room without leaving a smelly mess in our wake. I pushed the door open and held it wide for Tracey as she led John through. Sheila was crouched beside one of Tina's residents. The woman sat on the seat of her walker grimacing as Sheila shoved shoes onto her feet. Sheila glanced over her shoulder and asked, "What's going on?"

John followed Tracey into the shower area and I filled Sheila in as she stood and pulled a comb roughly through the woman's hair. Before I left, I peeked into the shower room. John sat calmly on the bench, while Tracey soaped up a cloth and began washing him.

"Trace," I called over the noise of the running water. She glanced up and I continued. "I'm going back to John's room to help clean up." She gave me a thumbs-up. I closed the door gently and headed back to Hall A.

I passed a cleaning cart in the hallway outside the staff room and popped my head inside to break the news to Lois from housekeeping. She had her head down, busily mopping the floor. "Morning, Lois," I said.

She looked up suspiciously. "Oh, no," she groaned. "I know that tone. What happened now?"

"I know, I'm sorry. It's room 3A. John Lindquist had a big, nasty accident." Poor Lois looked so crestfallen by the news that I hurried to appease her. "I'm on my way there now. I'll gather all the dirty clothing and bedding, bag them as contaminated and take them to the laundry room. We just need you to wipe down and sanitize everything."

She sighed in resignation. "Okay, I'll be right there."

Tracey walked into John's room shortly after I got there. I looked up in surprise. "You're done already? Where's John?"

"Sheila kicked me out. Said she had a few minutes before the next bath, so she'd finish cleaning John up."

That was a fight waiting to happen. "Are you sure that's a good idea? It's like putting two ticking time bombs in the same room together."

"Hey," Tracey said with a shrug. "She insisted. Practically kicked me out. It's her room, her domain. Who am I to argue?"

Lois came in with a cart full of cleaning supplies and went to work. Tracey gathered up the bags of dirty bedding and curtains and took them to the laundry room. I hurried back to Hall B and into Mrs. Gallo's room, relieved to find her still asleep. She stirred and woke as I moved about beside her, making Rose's bed. Tracey arrived shortly after, as I was readying the lift.

"Can't say our jobs are boring, can we?" she said, grinning widely as we secured Mrs. Gallo into the sling.

I rolled my eyes. "I'd rather boring over that any day."

Tracey worked the lift as I guided Mrs. Gallo, suspended from the ceiling lift, into the bathroom. We'd just lowered her onto the toilet when the sound of raised voices came from the hall. Tracey and I looked at each other knowingly. "Uh-oh," Tracey said. "I'll go see what's going on."

Ten minutes later she still wasn't back. Mrs. Gallo was finished on the toilet and I'd helped her wash, brush her teeth and comb her hair. Mr. Gallo would be there soon and she wasn't even dressed yet. I needed help with the lift, but I couldn't leave Mrs. Gallo sitting on the toilet alone to go find someone. Just as I reached for the call bell, Tracey ran into the room.

"Sorry," she said, struggling to catch her breath as she went to the other side of the lift.

"What happened?" I asked as we guided Mrs. Gallo out of the bathroom.

"I don't know much because while Sheila was ranting about it to Abby, I took John back to his room to calm down, but he had a fat lip."

"What!"

"I know. I'm thinking the same thing you are. Don't worry, I'll find out more later.

I had no doubt she would. Tracey was good at digging up gossip. No one but Tracey told me anything, I suppose because I kept to myself too much.

We lowered Mrs. Gallo into her chair and began to dress her.

"So," Tracey said as she pulled a sweater over Mrs. Gallo's head, "wanna meet for coffee tonight?"

"I don't know—"

"I know, I know, I was supposed to plan it with you ahead of time, but I'm more of a 'fly by the seat of your pants' kind of girl. C'mon, please? I need to get out of my apartment."

I thought about it for a moment and realized Mom would be ecstatic that I was taking her advice and going out. She and Gran would be more than willing to watch Kayla. "Sure, I'll meet you at the coffee shop on Main at seven."

* * *

I went home for a quick shower before going to the school to get Kayla. The house was silent, but Gran's coat and purse were in the hall closet. She usually watched *Dr. Phil* at three, but I didn't hear the TV. I frowned and headed into the living room. I'd been worried about her since her dizzy spell earlier that week. Who was I kidding? I'd been worried about her since the stroke two years ago.

It had been painful watching Gran struggle to recover. When I was growing up, she'd always seemed so much larger than life and invincible. Her short hair was always perfectly styled, dark and glossy with no hint of grey. She never left home without makeup on and lipstick in her bag. She strode into every room with purpose and exuded confidence. She was full of life, laughter and crazy, wonderful ideas.

"Let's go for a car ride," she'd say.

I'd clap my hands in excitement and squeal as she swept

me up and carried me to the car. I'd wrap my arms tightly around her neck and breathe in her sweet, musky perfume. "Where should we go, Gran?" I always asked, even though I knew the answer.

"Anywhere we want!" she'd say, smothering my face with kisses.

Gran drove, sometimes for hours, with no direction or particular destination in mind. We tore down country roads with the top of her little, white convertible down and dust from the dirt roads flying up for miles behind us. We explored roadside stands and obscure little junk shops. The ice cream parlor was always the last stop before Gran took me home, dusty, sticky, exhausted and deliriously happy.

She'd always been there. After Dad died, I cried every night for weeks. Mom sank into a deep depression and barely left her bed for months. Beneath my hurt, anger festered and grew. I was angry with Dad for leaving us and with my mother for being weak and, because she was the only other person in my life and she could handle it, I lashed out at Gran. She took every angry word I threw at her and gave me only love and support in return.

I'd been devastated when she had the stroke, and terrified that she'd leave me the way Dad had. But Gran had other ideas. She was strong and stubborn and within six months had fought her way back to near-normal health. Despite that, she continued to suffer from depression long after the stroke. We were told it was normal. She just needed time. It turned out what she needed was Kayla. Somehow, amid the chaos of Gran's rehabilitation and the rebuilding of our lives, a four-year old girl and an eighty-two year old woman had become the best of friends.

Everything's fine, I told myself as I hurried into the living room, but I had visions of Gran lying on the floor. I pulled up short in the doorway when I saw her curled up on the couch under a blanket.

She stirred and looked up. "Sarah," she said, stifling a yawn. "What time is it?"

"It's three. I just got home." I crossed the room and sat in the chair beside her. "Are you okay?"

She sat up and stretched. She had no makeup on and her nail polish was chipped and faded. "I'm fine. It's just been one of those days. I didn't feel like getting out of bed this morning and, when I sat down after lunch to read, I could barely keep my eyes open."

"Can I make you a cup of tea?" I asked. My shower could wait until after I picked Kayla up from school.

"Only if you have one with me."

Gran came into the kitchen and sat at the island as I was pouring the tea. I left it to steep and went to the fridge for milk. When I turned around Gran was sitting with her elbows on the counter, holding her head in her hands. I set the milk in front of her. "Do you have a headache?"

She looked up and gave me a weak smile. "I do. I woke up with it this morning. I was hoping the nap would help."

"You've been tired all week and now you have a headache. Do you think maybe you should make a doctor's appointment?"

"I'm sure it's nothing, but I suppose it couldn't hurt. Have you heard back from the university yet?"

I smiled and shook my head in resignation. Gran was

good at changing the subject when she didn't want to talk about something.

Shortly before transferring to Dementia I'd applied to nursing school. Working at Tranquility had made me realize how much I loved helping people. It made me feel good to go home at the end of the day knowing I'd made someone's life a little better. This discovery had led me to the decision to go back to school to get my nursing degree and specialize in gerontology.

"No," I said, "I may not hear back for a few months."

Gran reached for my hand. "You make me so proud. You're beautiful and smart and such a good mother to that little imp of ours." Her eyes shone with tears suddenly.

"That," I said, giving her hand a squeeze, "is because I take after you."

* * *

I got to the coffee shop at seven sharp, ordered a decaf mocha and sat down at a quiet table in the corner to wait for Tracey. She sauntered in ten minutes later, waved and went to the counter to order.

She sat down across from me a few minutes later. "Sorry," she said, stripping off her jacket. "Lost track of time. I'm notoriously late for everything."

"That's okay. I would have bought you a coffee, but I didn't know what you'd want."

She lifted her cup. "Vanilla latte," she said before she took a sip. "I like to try a different one each time. Kind of like men."

I choked on my mocha.

Tracey smiled innocently before she looked around the

room and leaned across the table. "I found out more about what happened today."

I took a napkin and wiped the spots of coffee off the table where I'd spewed in surprise. "And?"

"Tina said she overheard Sheila tell Abby that she "accidentally" hit John in the mouth."

"Oh, c'mon. Does she seriously expect anyone to believe that? She would have been better off saying he fell and banged it."

"Right? But get this—she said John got angry and grabbed her arm when she tried to dry his privates, and when she tried to pull away, he let go and her arm hit him in the face."

I shook my head in disbelief. "Wow. If Abby believes that, then what hope is there of ever convincing her that Sheila's mistreating people?"

"Oh, don't you worry. Sheila's so bitter and burnt out she'll probably end up doing something so stupid that even Abby won't be able to sweep it under the rug."

"I know. That's what I'm afraid of."

"So, no more talking about Sheila. It's way too depressing. Tell me what you think of Dementia so far?"

"I like it. And you were right, I do have some characters."

"Right? They're hilarious. Has Albert molested you yet?"

"Albert? I'd be more worried about Sam. He actually knows what he's doing."

Tracey nodded her agreement. "True."

I folded the napkin carefully and placed it under my

cup. “So,” I said slowly, “what do you think of Edie?”

“Sweet lady. Seems kind of sad sometimes.”

“I think she is, but then a lot of the residents are. Have you noticed how on the ball she is?”

“Hmm, she’s pretty quiet, but yeah, now that I think of it, she’s pretty with it.”

“She’s quiet until you get her one on one, then she’ll talk your ear off. I checked her chart. She was diagnosed with Alzheimer’s a few months ago, but they had her on meds that can interact and cause confusion and hallucinations. She’s awake early every morning when I go in, just sitting in her chair waiting. She doesn’t wander or get confused and I never have to remind her to do anything. I think she may have been misdiagnosed.”

“And if she was,” Tracey added, “she doesn’t belong in Dementia. You talk to Abby about this?”

“No, not yet. I was planning to today, but dealing with the mess put me behind. By the time I went to the nurse’s station she was gone.”

“Do it. Soon. And I hope Abby does something about it. Poor Edie. No wonder she’s sad.”

CHAPTER 6
THE FIGHT

DECEMBER BROUGHT SNOW AND THOUGHTS of Christmas. I was off work two days in a row for the first time in a long time. Mom had Monday off as well, so we spent a good part of the day Christmas shopping.

We were sitting in the food court at the mall eating lunch. I'd just finished telling Mom and Gran about the soup incident. We were still chuckling and wiping tears from our eyes, when a tall, distinguished-looking, grey-haired man walked up to our table and put his hand on Mom's shoulder. "Brenda?"

She looked up in surprise. "Andrew, how nice to see you. This is my daughter, Sarah, and my mother, Elaine."

He nodded at us. "Nice to meet you."

"Would you like to sit?" Gran asked.

"No, thank you, I'm on my way home." He held up his shopping bags. "I finished it all this morning, so I won't need to come back. This place is getting crazy."

"It is," Mom agreed. "And it's only going to get worse. How have you been keeping since…?"

"I'm doing okay. The kids and grandkids keep me busy. It's a hard time of year to get through, but I don't need to tell you that. I'll leave you ladies to your lunch now. Have a good Christmas." He smiled down at Mom and gave her shoulder an affectionate squeeze. "It was nice seeing you, Brenda. We should meet up sometime for coffee."

"He seemed very nice," I said, watching him walk away. I shot Gran a conspiring look.

"Very," said Gran. "And about your age I'd say, Brenda."

Mom had gone back to eating, seemingly oblivious to what we implied. "He's a couple years older I believe. His wife just passed away last January."

"Nice looking guy, too," I added with a mischievous grin.

Mom looked up from her food. She glanced from me to Gran suspiciously. "What are you two up to? My God, his wife hasn't even been gone a year."

"Mom, he asked you out for coffee. It wasn't a marriage proposal."

"He did *not* ask me out for coffee. He suggested we should meet for coffee sometime. There's a difference. And he was only being polite."

"I don't know," I said, "he seemed interested to me. He didn't take his hand off your shoulder the whole time he was here."

"Brenda," Gran said. "There's no harm in meeting the man for coffee. You know as well as I do, the older we get, the faster time goes. You have to take these opportunities as they come."

Mom gave an exasperated sigh and said with firm finality, "Enough, both of you. You know I have no interest in dating."

Gran looked at me, shook her head in disappointment, but wisely said nothing.

"Okay, then," I said too brightly. "I think we should go home and take the Christmas decorations out of the attic so we can decorate the tree tonight."

* * *

We kept Mom busy getting the house ready for Christmas, but, despite how we tried to distract her, I could see the sadness creeping back into her eyes. It was a hard time of year for both of us. Dad had been diagnosed with stage-three pancreatic cancer in July ten years earlier. The treatments had only prolonged the inevitable and by November he was in the hospital. He never came home. Three weeks before Christmas, he died.

Mom and I went to the cemetery together on the evening of the tenth anniversary of his death. I stood back and watched as she knelt down and placed a wreath on the grave. She put her hand against the cold earth, bent her head and began to cry.

I wandered to a nearby bench and sat shivering as I waited. I'd learned long ago that my mother was inconsolable in her grief. I closed my eyes against the cold sting of December's first snowfall. The sound of my mother's sobs conjured up memories of the funeral.

Mom had sat in stony silence throughout the service. I hadn't heard or seen her cry once when he died, but when she walked up to the casket, she broke down and collapsed onto the floor, sobbing uncontrollably. The minister helped Gran pick her up and they led her away to another room. I stood alone beside the casket as friends of my parents and people I'd never met filed past somberly. Some barely looked at me as they mumbled awkward words of sympathy. Others reached out, took my cold hands in theirs and tried to offer comfort. But it was not comfort I needed. It was my mother.

I'd lost both my parents the day my dad died. It wasn't until three years later, when I told my mother I was pregnant, that I finally saw a faint spark of hope in her eyes. The first time my mother held Kayla in her arms she'd cried tears of joy and wonder. Kayla had filled a hole in my mother's heart and made her happy in a way I hadn't been able to since my dad's death.

It was impossible to be depressed with Kayla around. Her excitement and laughter were contagious. She and Mom spent hours baking and making homemade decorations. They sang along to Christmas carols and watched Christmas movies. Thanks to Kayla, the glimmer of sadness in Mom's eyes remained just a glimmer.

* * *

Three days after John's accident, I was back at work, still trying to get images of the mess out of my head, and hoping for a typical day with no surprises.

Tranquility, however, was rarely boring. I'd only been back to work for a few hours when the fight started.

I'd taken a group of animal lovers to the auditorium for Pet Therapy after breakfast and was on my way to Hall B to start making beds, when I heard raised voices. I followed the sound to the lounge.

Sam was sprawled on a loveseat, humming along to his iPod. He seemed oblivious to the drama unfolding in front of him. Beth was beside him, sitting on the edge of her seat, wringing her hands anxiously. A few other residents were scattered throughout the room, watching in fascination as Lily and Mrs. W battled over the large flat screen TV in the far corner.

Mrs. W leaned precariously out and to one side of her wheelchair. She stretched her hands frantically toward the control buttons on the TV as she shouted in a hoarse voice, "Zamknij sie." It was a phrase she said often when she was angry. It meant simply "Shut up."

Lily jumped in front of Mrs. W and grabbed her hands. Her whole body trembled with rage as she squeezed them tightly. "I. Want. It. On."

Mrs. W winced in pain. I rushed toward them as Mrs. W let out one angry, terrifying roar, pulled a hand loose and struck Lily across the face. Lily dropped Mrs. W's other hand, took a quick step back and touched her cheek in disbelief. Her face crumpled and she began to cry.

I moved quickly across the room as Mrs. W turned her chair toward Lily and prepared to charge. The images that flashed on the screen behind them were horrific; World War II footage of hundreds of emaciated bodies in mass graves.

I choked back the bitter taste of revulsion that rose in my throat. I could hear the narration now that I was closer. "…occupation that lasted more than five years. The Nazis were eager to implement policies against people classified as 'racially inferior.' Entire Polish villages were set fire. Those still alive were taken hostage or executed."

I grabbed the handles of Mrs. W's chair before she could use it as a weapon. "Lily, it's okay," I said gently. "Go sit down, please." I nodded to a nearby chair.

Lily sat obediently, pulled a handkerchief from inside her shirtsleeve and blew her nose loudly. Beth rushed to her side and rubbed her arm consolingly as she spoke to her in a low voice.

The narrator's somber voice droned on tirelessly. "The Nazis' goal was to turn Poland into a nation of slaves. By the fall of nineteen-forty, half a million Poles were crammed into the Warsaw ghetto. Starvation and infectious diseases were killing more than five thousand people every month."

Mrs. W made a pitiful, heart-wrenching sound of despair. She covered her eyes as she rocked in her chair, crying softly over and over, "Zamknij sie."

I came out from behind her chair and hit the power button with firm resolution. The image, of children, barefoot, half-naked and filthy, sitting, huddled against the high wall that imprisoned them, faded. The children were skeletal shells of the people they had once been. Empty, hopeless eyes stared out at me, through me. Dead eyes.

The room became eerily quiet save the quiet whimpers and sniffling of both women.

I crouched down in front of the shelf unit beneath the TV and pushed the channel button on the digital box. I left it on the channel it was normally on, that showed old movies and TV shows from the fifties and sixties.

"Who," I wondered aloud, "would have left it on the History Channel?" I shook my head at the thought and turned back to Mrs. W.

She had stopped crying and was slouched in her chair, muttering forlornly in Polish. Her hands lay limply in her lap. Her eyes drooped with exhaustion. Streaks of drying tears lined her face.

I pulled a tissue from a box nearby, bent down in front of her and gently wiped the dampness from her cheeks and nose. I tucked her lap blanket around her legs as I spoke in a soothing voice. “You’re safe now. No one’s going to hurt you.” I put my hands over hers comfortingly and looked up at her weary face. Her pale blue eyes were filled with the pain of remembering. She nodded her head in understanding and sighed heavily.

I straightened up and looked over at the twins. Beth had a comforting arm around Lily’s shoulders. Her face was lined with worry as she fussed over her sister. Lily’s cheek was a little red where Mrs. W’s hand had connected, but she seemed to enjoy the attention and made a show of dabbing at her tears.

I went to where they sat and crouched on my heels in front of them. “Are you okay, Lily?”

She sniffed once more and sighed loudly as she tried to look pitiful, then nodded hesitantly and gave me a weak, trembling smile in return.

“Good. I’ll be back in a few minutes with some ice for your cheek.” I smiled at Beth as well and gave her hand a reassuring squeeze before I stood and walked back to Mrs. W. I wheeled her past the TV, pushing the power button as I passed. Ingrid Bergman’s striking face lit up the screen as I continued out of the room, pushing Mrs. W in the wheelchair ahead of me. I took her to the relaxation room at the far end of the hall, away from the noise of the lounge and dining room. I turned her chair so she faced the projector screen. She lifted her head wearily to look around.

"Would you like to listen to some music, Mrs. W? Nice soft music. And you can stay here where no one will bother you and have a nap if you like."

She nodded. Her body sagged with relief.

I turned on the projector and flicked off the lights. The room was at once dark and filled with the glow of hundreds of twinkling stars on the walls and ceiling. At the push of another button, the soft, soothing sound of flutes and harps flooded the room. The stars danced and swayed gently across the room as though keeping time to the music.

I sat in the recliner closest to Mrs. W, took her hand in mine and watched as her body relaxed. The tension slowly left her face and her eyes drifted shut. Her head lolled back and forth and finally settled into the headrest behind it. I waited a few more minutes, until she began to lightly snore, then I pulled my hand gently from hers and left quietly, leaving the door open so she could easily leave the room if she woke.

In the staff room, I wrapped a small ice pack in a paper towel and took it to Lily in the lounge. She held it to her face like a trophy and looked proudly around the room.

I went to the nurse's station to fill out an incident report. It wasn't much of a fight, even for a nursing home, but it was a fight nonetheless.

CHAPTER 7
BUSTED

THE FIGHT THAT MORNING PUT me behind in my routine, but with a little extra help from Tracey, I managed to get caught up. Most of the residents who weren't napping that afternoon had gone to the auditorium for a sing-a-long, so the halls were unusually quiet.

It was near the end of my shift and I was on my way to the nurse's station to do my recording for the day. I hoped to find Abby there as well, so I could finally speak to her about Edie. I glanced down Hall B as I passed by and spotted a familiar figure entering Dementia through the door at the far end of the hall.

Edie was bundled up in her winter coat. It was one I recognized as a cast-off from Anne and was ridiculously big on her. She also wore a knitted wool hat and a scarf, which she had wound around her face so only her eyes and the top of her nose showed. She peeked around the door as she opened it and darted into her room at the far end of the hall nearest the exit.

I stood in the hallway frowning. Where in the world had Edie been? More importantly, how had she gotten out?

Dementia was a locked unit. Staff and visitors had to

enter a code in order to leave. Residents were not given access to the code because many of them had a tendency to wander. Even so, the occasional resident did manage to escape.

I wasn't concerned that Edie had wandered off, in fact, I had no doubt she'd known exactly what she was doing and where she was going when she'd left. The problem was, she wasn't supposed to leave at all.

I went to the main hall where I could see the nurse's station. If Abby was there, I didn't want to miss a chance to speak to her. She was nowhere to be seen. I turned and strode quickly down the hall toward Edie's room where I stopped in the doorway and stood, quietly watching as she hung her coat and scarf in her wardrobe. She was so tiny she had to stand on her tiptoes to place her hat on the shelf. She closed the wardrobe doors softly, turned and gave a startled cry. Her hands flew to her chest, as though to keep her heart from jumping out. "Mah God, lassie, ye scared me near tae death!" Her voice was thin and breathless.

"I see now why you asked me not to lock your wardrobe this morning."

Edie's face flushed with guilt before she looked at the floor, shoulders slumped in defeat. "You saw me, then."

"You're not supposed to leave."

Her eyes flew to my face and she stood up straighter. "I've every right to go where I please, don't I? Am I to be a prisoner here, then?"

"Oh, Edie, I wish I hadn't seen you, but now that I know…." I closed my eyes and rubbed my fingers across my temples, groaning in frustration. When I opened my eyes, Edie was standing, watching me expectantly. I sighed. "It's complicated. The other residents are locked in for their own safety. You shouldn't even be in this damn place—you and I both know that. But if I know you can leave and I do nothing and something happens to you, I'm at fault."

"And why would anyone know that you know? There's no one here but us, lass."

"*I* would know. And *I* would be the one dealing with a guilty conscience."

"If I promise you won't catch me doing it again, will you not tell anyone?"

I sighed in resignation. "I should report it, but I won't since you're here and you're safe and you've promised." I glanced at the door thoughtfully. "How did you get out anyway?"

She laughed. "Getting out was the easy part. I stood here in my doorway and watched someone punch in the code. And I only went home—to Tom and Anne's, that is. There were some things there I wanted, personal things I had tucked away somewhere safe. They're in the wardrobe now and I'll be needing you to lock it up every day for me."

I felt bad for chastising her. She was right. She was a grown woman, capable of making her own decisions. "I'm sorry," I said as I secured her locker. "I know being in here must be hard on you. I'm working on getting you out, I promise."

Edie patted my arm reassuringly. "Don't you be worrying, lass. It'll all work out in the end."

I left Edie's room and hurried to the nurse's station, hoping to find Abby there. As I walked, I went over my conversation with Edie. She was right. Even I, who had been working in Dementia for less than three months, had quickly become lax. We assumed the residents were either too unaware to know they could enter a code and leave, or unable to remember it long enough to use it. I wondered how many other things I'd become so complacent about, in work, and in life.

I rounded the corner to the nurse's station where Abby sat, recording the events of her day in the documentation binder.

I took a seat beside her, pulled the support worker binder from the shelf and flipped to the charting section. "Do you have time to talk before you leave today?"

Abby glanced first at me, then at the clock on the wall. "I have a few minutes. I'm almost done here."

I nodded, pulled a black pen from one of the many pockets of my blue scrubs and began recording.

We worked in silence for a few minutes before Abby closed the thick, black binder and placed it back on the shelf. She turned her chair toward me and waited expectantly.

I laid my pen down and turned to face her, feeling nervous and unsure of where to begin. What if she didn't believe me? I folded my hands in my lap to keep from fidgeting, cleared my throat and blurted, "You know my resident, Edith MacAdams?"

Abby nodded.

"Have you ever had a conversation with her?"

"Not a long conversation, but I've spoken with her, yes. Why do you ask?"

I steadied myself, looked her straight in the eyes and said, "I think there's been a mistake. I don't think she belongs in here. She doesn't act like she has dementia at all."

Abby was quiet for a moment, brow wrinkled in thought. Finally, she nodded "Okay, I'm listening."

I was so relieved that words poured from my mouth. "She knows the name of every person here. She always knows what day it is and what's happening that day. The only thing she's confused about is why she's here. Oh, and the other residents confuse her, too. She thinks they're all crazy." I gave a short laugh at the thought. "She told me she was on a bunch of meds before she was put in the hospital and she remembers being confused. She also remembers doing the memory tests and knows she didn't do well because she was so out of it at the time."

I paused to take a breath and felt the heat creep up my neck, into my face, when I realized I'd been rambling in my excitement.

Abby rolled her chair away from the desk, stood and stretched. "It's nice to see you so excited about your job, Sarah. It's possible she was misdiagnosed, but I need to get to know Edie better before I can do anything. Unfortunately, it's easier to put someone in here than is to get them out."

I realized then that getting Edie out of Tranquility was going to take time. "Okay, well, thanks for taking time to listen." I went back to my recording as Abby gathered her things and left for the day. I was nearly finished when Tracey showed up.

"What's up, buttercup?" she said with a wink. "How 'bout a coffee after work?"

I didn't hesitate long. "I'd love to. I just need to call

home and make sure it's okay with Gran."

* * *

Tracey and I sat and talked in the coffee shop for two hours. I told her about my discussion with Abby.

"Think she took you seriously?"

"I don't know. I hope so, but she was pretty noncommittal."

Tracey snorted. "She usually is. She likes to use a lot of big words and come off as being smart and important, but she sure doesn't like to get her hands dirty."

"What do you mean?"

"I mean she's really good at disappearing when things get nasty, like that day with the mess in John's room."

I wrinkled my brow in thought. It hadn't occurred to me, but Tracey was right. Abby did seem to have a way of finding excuses to leave when things got tough. "Are you saying I shouldn't count on her to help with Edie?"

"Nope, just saying you might have to become a pain in the ass."

"I don't know if I can do that."

"Oh, I'm sure you can."

We laughed and I changed the subject. "So, tell me about yourself. Do you have family here?"

Tracey looked uncomfortable suddenly. "They live a couple hours from here. My parents got divorced when I was thirteen."

I winced. "That's a tough age."

"Yeah, it sucked. When I was seventeen, my mom decided to marry this asshole she was dating, so as soon as I finished high school I moved out, came here, got a job as a waitress and put myself through college."

"Wow. Good for you."

"Yeah, it was tough. Hardest part was leaving my little brother behind. I know I was just young and stupid, but I only got to see my dad every other weekend, then suddenly, there was this guy who was there every day, living in our house like he was trying to take my dad's place or something. I hated him for it. And I was pissed at my mom for marrying somebody else. I guess I always hoped she'd take my dad back, you know?"

"I know. I guess we all want the fairytale." It struck me suddenly that, even though Tracey and I were different in many ways, we had a lot in common.

Friendship was something I'd been lacking since Kayla was born. The few childhood friends I'd had were in college or starting new careers and I was suddenly immersed in motherhood, working nights and helping with Gran's stroke recovery. My friends and I had little in common anymore and friendships quickly became a luxury I no longer had time for. They were also not something I jumped into easily. It took time for me to build a relationship and trust someone enough to feel ready to confide in them and share my feelings.

Regardless how little of myself I was still willing to share, I left the coffee shop knowing the mutual respect Tracey and I had for one another had begun to blossom into a friendship that day.

Chapter 8
Outbreak

I NOW HAD TRACEY ON BOARD in my quest to get Edie out of Dementia, but there was little she or I could do. Abby was the only one of us with the authority to make it happen. Unfortunately, she had little time to spend getting to know Edie.

December brought the norovirus to Tranquility. This "stomach flu" was highly contagious and could spread through a nursing home like wildfire if not quickly contained. For an elderly person with an already weakened immune system, it was sometimes deadly.

Unfortunately, trying to contain an illness that caused vomiting and diarrhea in a group of people who couldn't remember how to find the bathroom was a nightmare. Many of the residents didn't understand or simply didn't remember instructions. It was left up to the staff to be sure residents washed their hands and stayed in the areas they were confined to. Not an easy feat when dealing with people who wandered.

It started with John. It was nearly impossible to keep him in his room, away from others. We weren't allowed to lock him in and he simply wouldn't stay.

I felt bad for Carol, but it was almost comical watching her and John. She'd put him in his room, close the door and walk away. Seconds later, he was out again, sneaking down the hall into another room. She'd come back to discover him gone and go running down the hall to find him. The cleaning staff followed after the residents, disinfecting everything they touched. This game of cat and mouse went on for three days.

It was all in vain. By the time we realized what John had, others had already begun to complain of headaches and fatigue and a few had low-grade fevers. A mere five days after John fell ill, nearly half the residents in Dementia were sick.

The Board of Health was notified. Notices were posted at all entrances, warning visitors of the outbreak. Visiting was discouraged and volunteers were asked to stay away for the duration of the outbreak. All programs and services were canceled.

The cleaning staff worked nonstop during the outbreak. Every surface, especially doorknobs, handrails, toilet handles and faucets, were wiped down numerous times throughout every shift with a disinfectant solution. The constant cleaning only masked the smell and soon the whole unit reeked of sour bodily fluids and chemicals.

Tina's resident, Mr. Roberts, was co-operative and stayed in his room for much of the duration of his illness. While there, he threw up in his shoes, the drawer of his nightstand, and his garbage pail. He had an unfortunate accident reminiscent of John's mess and used the curtain between the beds to clean himself afterwards.

Poor Rose threw up all over her lunch tray and later, in

a planter near the nurse's station. Luckily, she brought the planter along with her when she wandered back into her room.

Every staff member in Dementia worked nonstop to keep the residents comfortable, the unit clean, and the virus in check. We worked through our breaks to help clean up messes and keep residents busy while they were confined to their rooms. We stayed late and worked on our days off in order to keep up with the extra work. Even Sheila worked longer hours in order to handle the extra showers needed by residents who didn't make it to the bathroom in time.

I tried my best to listen at the bathing room door every time I passed, but I was too busy to do any serious eavesdropping. It was only by coincidence that I caught Sheila in the act. I'd just finished attending to Sam, who was sick to his stomach, but fortunately had no bathroom issues so far. When I left his room, I nearly bumped into Rose. Her bottom lip shook when she saw me and she burst into tears. Even before I smelled it, I knew she'd had an accident.

We went to her room to gather what we needed for a shower and then continued on to the bathing room. When I opened the door, I heard Sheila's voice. "...of your whining. Stop it!" It was doubtful Sheila would hear me over the running water, but I put a finger to my mouth, motioned Rose into the room and quietly closed the door. I crept ahead slowly until I could see Sheila standing with her back to me at the side of the tub. She had the spray nozzle in her hand and was rinsing someone's hair as they whimpered in protest.

"Is it cold?" Sheila said, her voice taunting. "Is that why you're acting like a baby? Put your head back. I said *back*!"

She grabbed onto a handful of hair and yanked.

I stepped out. "Sheila!"

She jumped and let out a shriek as she spun around to face me. A flash of guilt crossed her face before she became defensive. "Do you always sneak up on people?"

"I didn't sneak. I've been here for a few minutes. I guess you didn't hear me come in."

"No, and I also didn't hear you knock."

"Rose had an accident, so we came to use the shower. I didn't think it was necessary to knock."

"Of course it is. What if a resident was standing here naked? If I was allowed to lock the door I would, just to keep people with no respect for privacy from barging in."

Ignoring the dig, I leaned to the side to see who was in the tub. It was Mrs. W.

Sheila took a step toward me, her mouth set in a grim line.

I stood my ground, even though my heart was pounding. "I'm watching you," I said softly.

She raised a brow and smirked. "Watch all you want. I'm not doing anything wrong, and who do you think Abby'll believe anyway?"

I stared hard at her for a few long seconds before I turned to Rose and held out a trembling hand. "C'mon Rose, let's get you cleaned up."

My nerves were still rattled when I left Rose in her room twenty minutes later and went to find Abby. She was in the supply room, loading the cart up with lunch meds and barely looked up when I approached. I glanced around to be sure no one was nearby.

"What is it, Sarah?"

I clasped my hands together tightly in front of me to keep from chewing nervously at a nail. "Uh, I just...."

Abby pulled the cart through the door and locked the door. She turned to me, glancing at her watch. "Make it quick. I have to go."

"I just took Rose to the bathing room for a shower and when I walked in Sheila was..."

She let out an exasperated sigh. "She was what? Spit it out."

"She was yelling at Mrs. W, taunting her, calling her a baby for whining that the water was cold. Then when Mrs. W wouldn't put her head back, she grabbed her hair and pulled."

Abby said nothing for a moment, just stood looking at me thoughtfully.

I looked away and shifted nervously from one foot to the other, waiting. Was she trying to decide whether or not to believe me? Maybe I shouldn't have told her. Maybe I should have waited and talked to Tracey first, or just recorded it in the binder. What if she fired me?

"I'll have a talk with Sheila," Abby said finally. "But honestly, Sarah, you can't come running to me, bothering me with every little incident. We all know Sheila can be a little gruff at times—"

"Oh, no," I said, standing up straight, hands fisted at my sides. "She was not being gruff. I'm not okay with the way she treats residents."

Abby's expression hardened. "You don't have to be okay with it, I do. You're new. You don't know Sheila the way I do, or how things work around here. I suggest you watch your step." She took hold of her cart and walked away.

I went to the staff bathroom, splashed water on my face and took a few deep breaths before I went to Hall B to find Tracey. I needed someone to be on my side.

Not only was Tracey on my side, she was outraged. "Are you kidding me!" she whispered loudly over Mrs. Amaral's head as we got her ready for lunch. "If Abby doesn't take this seriously, she'll be in deep shit if and when something happens. You make sure you record this. In fact, from now on, we both need to record every little thing."

I took her advice and recorded the incident before I left that day.

* * *

Despite our efforts, two residents became dehydrated and were sent to the hospital.

Mrs. W was so sick she couldn't even sit in her wheelchair. Her backside became red and sore, leaving her susceptible to infection. She'd been sick for two days when she stopped eating. On the third day she refused fluids as well and was taken to the hospital to receive them intravenously. She was back three days later, pulling her chair slowly with her feet and yelling at anyone who got in her way.

Mr. Gallo ignored the warnings and continued to visit his wife during the outbreak. He helped her wash her hands often and tried a few times to get her to wear a mask, but gave up when it upset her. Despite all his precautions, she became sick a few days after Rose. The illness struck her fast and hard. She had a fever, chills and vomiting the first day and by the second, was too weak to sit up. I checked on her every hour throughout my shift. Every time I went in, I made sure she drank water.

Mr. Gallo sat with her all day, holding her hand and talking to her in his quiet, reassuring way. He put cold cloths on her forehead and ran ice chips across her dry lips. Before I left for the day, I reiterated to him the importance of getting her to drink fluids. The concern in his eyes brought a lump to my throat and when he bent over her, stroking her hair and whispering in Italian, tears stung my eyes and I had to leave the room. Someday, I wanted someone to look at me that way.

* * *

Mr. Gallo was there again the next morning when I came into the room before breakfast. He looked exhausted. His usually kind, smiling face was troubled and weary. A vase of red roses stood on the table beside the bed.

"You're here early today, Mr. Gallo. And I see you brought flowers."

"Yes, my sister, Gina, she give me ride. Is anniversary today."

"Oh, that's nice. How many years?"

"Fifty."

"Wow, congratulations," I said, drawing the curtain around the bed for privacy. I checked Mrs. Gallo's incontinence product for signs she needed changing. It was bone dry. She whimpered, making me wonder if she may have been in some pain. I pulled her nightgown down, straightened it, and pulled the blankets up to her chest. I looked down at her face. Her pale skin was loose and so dry it flaked. Her chest rose and fell quickly with each shallow breath. I tried to keep the concern from showing when I turned to Mr. Gallo. "How was she after I left yesterday?"

"She vomit all day. Last night nothing coming out. Just…." He waved his hand in front of his mouth as he searched for the right words.

"Dry heaves?"

He nodded.

"Did she drink anything?"

"I give little bit water all day, like you tell me. Later, she vomit every time after the drink. I tell the girl about this. She tell me, just keep giving water, but I gotta go before ten o'clock to get home with the bus, so, what happens at night, I don't know."

I pulled the curtains open and stripped off my gloves. "Try to get her to drink some water, please, Mr. Gallo." I went into the bathroom to dispose of the gloves and scrubbed my hands with soap and hot water. They were red, raw and sore, dried out by frequent washings. It didn't matter. It had to be done.

Ten minutes later I was back in the room with Abby. She checked Mrs. Gallo's temperature, pulse and blood pressure, listened to her breathing, then went to the nurse's station to read the night shift's charts.

I waited impatiently with Mr. Gallo. We tried to get Mrs. Gallo to drink. She was too weak to use a straw, so I lifted her head and shoulders off the bed as he held the glass to her mouth. She barely opened her dry, cracked lips in an effort to drink. The water ran out of her mouth and down her neck. I was afraid she was too weak even to swallow.

Abby wasn't gone long. She strode back into the room with a concerned look on her face and said to Mr. Gallo, "According to the charts, your wife drank only a few sips of water through the night. The nurse on duty was not overly concerned because she had stopped throwing up, had no bouts of diarrhea, and slept nearly the entire night."

She looked at me. "Has she voided yet today?"

"No. Nothing."

Her face darkened. "Nothing last night either."

"What this mean?" Mr. Gallo asked. His head shook back and forth slightly and the hand in his lap trembled visibly. He no longer looked concerned, he looked scared.

"Mr. Gallo, your wife is severely dehydrated. She needs more care than we can give her here. She needs to go to the hospital to be put on IV."

He nodded uncertainly. "I go with my Bella?"

"Of course you can." Abby said. She left the room to go call the hospital.

I helped Mr. Gallo pack a small bag of clothing and toiletries for his wife. His hand shook so hard he nearly dropped her dentures. He took a seat beside his wife and held her hand as I finished the rest of the packing.

Twenty minutes later, Abby and I stood watching the paramedics wheel Mrs. Gallo, wrapped in blankets and strapped to a gurney, out of Dementia. Mr. Gallo shuffled out behind them, looking weary and suddenly much older.

Abby shook her head in disgust and said in a low voice, "She should have been on IV through the night. I don't know what they were thinking."

I went back to work with a heavy heart. A strange,

overwhelming feeling of dread settled over me and followed me through the day.

I went home right after work, straight to the laundry room to throw my scrubs into the washer on the hottest cycle. I jumped in the shower and scrubbed myself thoroughly from head to toe. It had become a routine for me since the outbreak. I could practically feel the germs crawling on my skin by the end of the workday. The last thing I wanted to do was take those germs home to my family.

Gran and I were sitting at the kitchen island before dinner chopping vegetables for the salad while Mom made chicken-fried rice. I jumped when Gran touched my hand.

"You seem preoccupied tonight, Sarah. Is everything okay?"

"One of my residents was sent to the hospital today. I'm just worried about her."

"It's out of your hands now," she said, patting my hand. "There's no point worrying. I'm sure you did the best you could to help her."

Tears of frustration sprang to my eyes. "That's the thing. I know I did the best I could when I was with her, but someone last night dropped the ball. I should have made sure they knew how sick she was."

"Sarah, honey, there's no point beating yourself up over things that have already happened. You could spend your whole life doing that and it won't change a thing."

A tear trickled slowly down my cheek. I wiped it angrily away.

"I can't tell you everything will be okay, but I hope it is. Why don't you go distract yourself with that sweet little bundle of energy of yours? We'll call you when dinner's ready."

Kayla did distract me for a while, but I slept little that night. The feeling of dread still lurked there, clutching at my heart.

* * *

Abby was sitting at the nurse's station when I got to work the next morning. She didn't have to say a word. I knew as soon as I walked through the door.

Mrs. Gallo had died during the night.

My morning routine should have been easier with one less resident to fill my time. Instead, it threw me off. That, and the lack of sleep the night before, left me struggling all day to stay focused on my work.

Breakfast was over, beds made, and residents busy at their various activities. I had no excuses left for putting off what I'd been dreading.

It was strange walking into Mrs. Gallo's room, knowing she wasn't there. The night staff had stripped the bed and disinfected the whole room. The curtains between the beds had been sent to laundry to be cleaned and sanitized. The room looked big, cold and empty and smelled of bleach.

I went into the bathroom to gather up what hadn't gone to the hospital with Mrs. Gallo. A few minutes later, I came out carrying a box of toiletries, to find a well-dressed woman with dark hair standing at the wardrobe. "Oh, hello," I said, placing the box on a nearby chair. I swiped my fingers quickly across the dampness under my eyes.

"Yes, hello. I am Gina, Mr. Gallo's sister." She pulled a suitcase out of the bottom of the wardrobe and tossed it on the bed. "Everything here belong to Isabella, no?" She gestured toward the wardrobe.

"Yes, and this box as well. I packed her things from the bathroom."

"Okay, good. I pack the rest. My brother is not good to be here today." Gina turned her back to me and began removing Mrs. Gallo's clothes from the wardrobe.

I had the feeling I'd been dismissed. "Would you like me to help you with that?"

"No, no. You are busy. I can do."

I left the room without another word, feeling strangely relieved. Gina's dismissive, aloof behavior was so much easier to deal with right now than kindness.

Lunch was the hardest part of the day. Mrs. Gallo's spot at the table was glaringly empty. Edie sat in her usual chair, across from Mr. Gallo's empty seat, eating her lunch in silence. I sat with my back to the table so I wouldn't have to look at the empty chairs.

I went to the nurse's station earlier than usual that afternoon, did my recording, and left a few minutes before the end of my shift. I didn't care. I didn't want to see or talk to anyone. I needed to get out of there.

I called Gran to let her know I'd be late, and then drove to the park down the street. It was an oasis in the middle of the city and a place I went often when I needed to be alone. There were footpaths everywhere leading to secluded little clearings near the water. I stuck to the main walkway. The park was deserted and strangely quiet and the paths too muddy and slippery to attempt. I sat on a bench overlooking the water. It flowed cold and fast over the rocks.

Downstream, where the river narrowed, ice and snowdrifts hugged the shoreline. Big, wet snowflakes fell gently from the sky onto the trees and tall, brown grass, turning the world around me white.

One lonely goose, left behind when the others flew south, swam toward me hoping for an easy meal. He looked cold and hungry and I was sorry I had nothing to feed him. I had heard that Canada geese mated for life and wondered if his mate had died.

I thought of Mr. Gallo, suddenly alone in the world without his mate. Fifty years of loving her. Fifty years of Christmases spent together, reliving traditions and creating new memories. This Christmas he would be without her.

The thought overwhelmed me and I began to cry. I don't know how long I sat there, but when I left the park, the sky had begun to darken and I was a wet, shivering mess.

Later that night, I lay in Kayla's bed and held her close as she drifted off to sleep. I felt sad and, at the same time, incredibly lucky to have someone to love.

CHAPTER 9
MERRY CHRISTMAS

FINALLY, AFTER NEARLY TWO EXHAUSTING weeks, the outbreak was over. Those who had been sick had shown no signs of illness for at least forty-eight hours and no new cases had surfaced in that time. Mrs. Gallo was the sole casualty.

On the twenty-third of December, with the sound of carols drifting through the halls and snow falling gently outside the windows, the staff and residents spent the afternoon bringing Christmas to Dementia.

I sat in a quiet corner of the lounge, sipping a mug of hot chocolate and watching the residents. It was like watching children on Christmas Eve as they prepared for Santa's arrival. They chattered excitedly and sang along to the old carols of their childhood while stringing popcorn and transforming colorful strips of construction paper into chains to hang on the tree.

The room even smelled like Christmas. It was filled with the wonderful aromas of chocolate, cinnamon and pine. It nearly covered the sharp smell of bleach that still lingered in the air and reminded me of death.

The sound of the residents' happy laughter should have

made me forget the calamity of the past few weeks. Instead, it made me painfully aware of who was missing.

Edie finished the string of popcorn she'd been working on. It was so long she had to loop it over her arm three times to carry it to the tree.

I put my mug down and went to help. We worked together silently, draping the delicate garland carefully over the branches, then stood back to have a look.

I felt Edie's comforting hand on my back.

"It wasn't your fault, lass. These things happen sometimes. You shouldn't take it so hard."

My chest tightened and my eyes welled up with emotion. I managed to hold back the tears and gave her hand a squeeze of gratitude.

* * *

The next afternoon, I dropped most of my residents off in the auditorium for the Christmas Eve service, and headed to the nurse's station where I pulled the chart for the woman who would be taking Mrs. Gallo's old bed. She was coming in that day to unpack her things and have a quick tour, but wasn't staying. She would go home to spend Christmas with her family, then come back later in the week.

I looked over her information while I waited. Her name was Georgia Jones, and according to her chart she was ninety-eight years old. I continued skimming the medical charts. She'd been diagnosed with Alzheimer's eight months earlier. The only other medical condition listed was mild hearing loss. There was an additional, barely legible note at the bottom of the page: *Patient occasionally indulges in cigars and whiskey.* I raised an eyebrow and turned the page.

I was preparing to read a surprisingly short list of medications, when I heard a loud voice.

"Lord Jesus in heaven, save us from fools."

I looked up to see a tall woman striding down the hall toward me. She wore a long, flowing, multi-colored kaftan and a deep purple head wrap. Gold hoops dangled from her ears, nearly touching her shoulders and jingling with every step.

A middle-aged man followed behind, struggling to keep up. The woman's coat was draped over his one arm and with the other, he pulled a large wheeled suitcase.

"This is no hospital. Don't you dare be lyin' to your Ma." She paused to wave her cane at the man.

"I'm not lying. People come here to be taken care of when they're sick."

"I am *not* sick. I'm healthy as a horse and you know it. I can take care of myself just fine."

He lowered his voice as they approached the desk. "It doesn't matter. You're not staying; you're coming back home with me for Christmas. We'll talk about this later with the family, okay?"

I smiled at them as I stood up and walked around the desk. I held my hand out to the woman. "You must be Mrs. Jones."

She shook my hand. Her grip was surprisingly firm. "Yes, I am, but I prefer Georgia."

"Nice to meet you, Georgia. I'm Sarah." I marveled at how few wrinkles there were on her smooth, coffee colored skin. This woman could not be nearly a century old.

She turned to the man and said, "Did you hear that?

She's been named after a desert."

He shook his head. "No, it's *Sarah*, not Sahara."

"That's what I just said. Clean your ears out, son."

I chuckled and held out my hand to the man. "I don't think I caught your name."

"Lloyd, her grandson," he said, shaking my hand.

Georgia made a startled sound, put her hand to her chest and looked more closely at Lloyd. "My grandson? Lord have mercy, you've grown up all of a sudden. I was thinking you were your pa." Her face softened, and she reached for his hand. "You look just like him, you know."

"I know, Ma," he said, patting her hand reassuringly. "Only I'm better looking."

Georgia snorted. "I doubt it. Conceit is not attractive, my boy."

I was enjoying their banter, but I needed to get Georgia settled before the end of my shift. I gestured toward her suitcase. "If you'd like to come with me, I'll show you where to put your things, then we can take a quick tour."

Georgia stared at the bag as though seeing it for the first time. She looked at Lloyd in confusion.

Before she could say a word, he put his arm around her shoulder and spoke quietly, but clearly, into her ear. "It's Christmas Eve, Ma. Most of the family will be there when we go home. And look at you, all dressed up, ready for a party. Let's get this done, so we can go home, okay?"

She looked up at him uncertainly before she nodded. "Fine, let's go get it over with."

They followed me down the hall toward Georgia's room. I pointed out the dining room and lounge as we passed by. Georgia had an opinion about everything. The dining room was too crowded with tables. The lounge was dark and drab. The whole place could use a coat of paint and some brighter colors.

When we stopped to look at the lounge, Sam, and Tracey's resident, Mrs. Martin, were the only ones there. The TV was on. I shook my head at the sight of Ricky Ricardo explaining Santa to little Ricky while waving a cigarette in the air between them.

Sam sat on the couch drumming his fingers against his leg and humming along to his music. Mrs. Martin, who had been a librarian once, rearranged the books on the built-in shelves along the back wall.

Lloyd asked, "Is it always so quiet in here? Where is everyone?"

"Oh no, it's rarely this quiet. Most of the residents are at the Christmas Eve service in the auditorium," I explained.

We continued on to Georgia's room. I unlocked the wardrobe so she could unpack and put away her things. Lloyd and I stepped into the hallway outside the door to place a photo of her into the slot below her name. It was an old black and white of a young, beautiful Georgia, standing tall and looking proud and defiant.

Every resident in Dementia had their name and photo on the wall outside their door to help them find their room. We tried to use old photos because many of the residents who had lost their short-term memory wouldn't recognize themselves in a more current photo.

Lloyd spoke to me in a low voice. "I'm glad you were available to do this on such short notice. She's having a good day today."

I smiled at him. "Me too. It's a good time to do it, because of the Christmas Eve service."

"Good, good." He looked at me thoughtfully, and a solemn look came over his face. "This was a really hard decision for my family. We feel she belongs at home with the people who love her. We've been taking turns staying with her when we can, but her children aren't young anymore. My father's the oldest and the only one who stayed in town. The rest moved away when they were young. He's almost eighty and he's been alone since my mother died a few years ago. The cousins are spread across the country now and all busy with their own families and jobs." He looked at his grandmother. "She's a very strong-willed, opinionated woman and she's used to being in charge. She's hard enough to deal with normally, but lately she's been almost impossible to manage." He sighed heavily. "It doesn't matter though, I still hate doing this."

"It's not easy for anyone," I said.

He swung around to face me, his expression fierce and desperate. "No, you don't understand. She's the matriarch of our family. She's the glue that holds us together. Without her, I'm afraid the family will fall apart."

I really did understand, and not just because I saw it every day with each resident's family. I knew as well as anyone what it meant to lose someone and how easy it was to lash out at the nearest person. He was angry at the situation and at the disease and feeling guilty for leaving her. I smiled and put a hand on his arm.

"I'm sorry," he said, rubbing his fingers across his eyes.

"A few weeks ago, she found my dad's car keys and drove to the grocery store. When she tried to park, she hit the gas instead of the brake and drove into the building. She leaves the stove on, the water running, hell, one day she decided the windows needed cleaning. She was halfway up the ladder when my father found her. It's been pure luck so far that no one's been hurt."

I touched his arm reassuringly. "I'll take good care of her."

"I know you will." He smiled apologetically. "But I don't envy you the job."

* * *

I had Christmas morning off for the first time in five years. Tracey had volunteered to work since she had no family in town. I'd tried to convince her to come for turkey dinner after work, but she said she was planning to drive to her mom's to spend a couple days there.

Previous years, I'd come home from nightshift just in time to open gifts. It was nice to wake up to Kayla's excited shrieks when she saw the presents under the tree. I lay in bed listening to her excitement grow as she pulled things from her stocking. It was quiet for a moment, then I heard her little feet pounding as she ran down the hall toward my room.

She burst through the door and launched herself onto the bed. "Mommy, it's Christmas! Santa was here. I can tell, 'cause there's presents under the tree, and all the cookies and milk are gone." She held up a miniature toy horse. It was pink and sparkly with a long silky mane and tail. "And look what he put in my stocking!" Her dark eyes were wide and glistening with excitement as she bounced up and down on her hands and knees beside me. "Please get up now, Mommy. Please, please, please, so we can open presents."

I caught her mid-bounce and pulled her in for a quick hug. "Okay, okay. I'll be right out. Maybe you should go wake up Nana and Gran, too."

She bounced out of my arms and right off the bed. "I will. I'll wake them up right now. Hurry up, Mommy," she yelled, running from the room.

We spent a leisurely morning opening gifts. Kayla had hot chocolate and candy from her stocking for breakfast. Mom, Gran and I indulged in coffee with Irish cream and shared a box of chocolates.

Later, Kayla convinced Gran to play the game of *Trouble* she'd opened that morning. Mom and I worked together in the kitchen as we listened to the laughter and "pop, pop" of the dice bubble from the other room.

I was sitting at the island peeling potatoes. Mom stood at the stove humming "Silent Night" under her breath as she made the stuffing. It occurred to me that she was happy. I put down the peeler and took a sip of coffee as I watched her work. The tiny diamonds in her wedding band sparkled under the bright light above the stove and I realized I'd never seen her without it. My hand went to the pendant my dad had given me. "Would you ever get married again?" I blurted the thought aloud and regretted it instantly.

Mom turned to me with her mouth agape. "Would I…what in the world made you ask that?"

"I don't know. It just occurred to me that I've never seen you take off your wedding ring. Tracey talks about her stepdad and it makes me realize you're still young. I mean, you never know, you could meet someone someday. Like the man at the food court, he seemed nice."

She put her head down, turned her back and busied herself stirring onions. "Andrew is very nice, but I'm afraid no one would ever be able to compare to your father."

I kicked myself for bringing it up when only a moment ago she'd been so happy. "I'm sorry, I didn't mean to make you sad."

She turned to face me again. Butter-laden fried onions threatened to fly off the spoon as she waved it in the air between us. "Nothing could make me sad today, sweetie. Having us all here today, together, makes me happy. You, Gran and Kayla are all I need." She pointed the spoon at me emphatically. "You," she said as a greasy onion flew off and landed on my arm, "on the other hand, should be dating."

Oh, here we go, I thought, popping the onion in my mouth. Luckily, at that moment, Kayla came running into the kitchen to announce that she'd beaten Gran and was looking for her next victim.

CHAPTER 10
THE CALM BEFORE THE STORM

I WENT BACK TO WORK the day after Christmas feeling rested and relaxed. Edie was in her usual spot, in her chair beside the window, when I walked into her room. "Morning, Edie. I wasn't expecting you back until later today."

She snorted. "That woman always finds a reason to cut our visits short. She'll not be happy 'til I'm dead."

I simply nodded and went on with my work. I knew enough to leave Edie alone when she was annoyed.

Most of the residents who had been away overnight were brought back throughout the day. The people who dropped them off looked tired, frustrated, relieved, and guilty for feeling relieved. The residents were tired as well and out of sorts from the change in routine.

Christmas was over and Dementia was back to its usual state of organized chaos.

Georgia returned that afternoon at the end of my shift. I'd already changed my shoes and collected my purse and coat from my locker in the change room. I was sitting behind the desk at the nurse's station, finishing my documentation, when I saw her.

She entered with an entourage. At least fifteen people of

varying ages followed her as she marched with an air of dignity and authority toward the nurse's station.

They stopped in front of the desk and Lloyd stepped out of the crowd of people to stand beside his grandmother. A little girl, about Kayla's age, stepped forward as well and slipped her hand inside Georgia's. The others spoke quietly amongst themselves as they looked around curiously.

Many of the residents were napping, but a few wandered the halls or watched TV in the lounge.

Mrs. W was nearby, shuffling slowly down the hall in her wheelchair. Her head lolled back and forth as a trail of drool ran down her chin onto the towel draped across her chest. Her constant moaning was occasionally interspersed with cries of frustration. Sam had come out of the lounge and was wandering the halls, singing along loudly to his music. Raised voices could be heard plainly coming from the lounge. Lily and Beth were arguing.

I stepped out from behind the desk and smiled. "Welcome back, Georgia." My eyes swept over the group. I met the steady gaze of a pair of masculine hazel eyes and lingered for a moment before I realized I was staring. I looked away, but not before I felt the heat of embarrassment stain my cheeks.

I cleared my throat and looked at Georgia. "I uh, hope you had a nice Christmas."

Georgia nodded, but didn't speak. She crossed her arms over her chest and looked away.

Lloyd looked at her and asked, "Do you remember Sarah, Ma?"

"Of course, I do," she insisted, but there was no

recognition in her eyes when she looked at me.

Lloyd sighed and gave me an apologetic smile. "Christmas was very nice, thank you." He motioned to the people behind him. "Lots of family here to visit, as you can see."

The little girl beside Georgia piped up. "Are you gonna take care of Ma?"

"Well, I think your ma can take care of herself, but I'll be here to help if she needs me to."

"You're pretty," she blurted.

I felt my face redden again. "Thank you."

Lloyd smiled fondly at the girl. "This is my granddaughter, Alisha. She's the older of two great-great grandchildren."

"Wow, that's impressive." I bent down to talk to her. "Nice to meet you, Alisha."

She became shy with the formality and hid her face in Georgia's skirt.

I straightened up and said to Lloyd, "My shift is nearly over, but Connie should be here any minute and she'll help you get your grandmother settled in."

"No problem. I'll show the rest of the family around while we're waiting, if that's okay?"

"Of course, that'll be fine."

They wandered off in the direction of the lounge.

I hoped Lily and Beth weren't still arguing and I hoped Sam had his clothes on.

I went behind the desk and bent down to get my purse and coat. When I straightened up, the owner of the hazel eyes stood on the other side of the desk, watching me intently. He looked a few years older than me, maybe closer to thirty. His dark hair was buzzed close to his head, he had a little cleft in his chin, and, up close, his eyes were more green than hazel.

I realized I was staring again. "Is there something I can do for you?" I instantly regretted the question and felt heat creep into my cheeks once more.

He smiled and a dimple appeared. All thoughts left my head.

I was stirred from my bemused state by the realization that he had spoken. "I'm sorry, what did you say?"

He tilted his head and smirked, clearly amused. The dimple deepened. "I was just introducing myself. I'm Jay. I'm one of Georgia's many great-grandchildren."

"I'm Sarah."

"Ah, yes, Sahara. Heard that story last night. My father likes you. I think it makes it easier for him, knowing you'll be looking after Ma."

"Good. I'm glad."

"Okay, well, I should go catch up with the others. I'm sure I'll see you again."

I nodded, too tongue-tied and flustered to string a proper sentence together. My pulse raced and I realized I hadn't reacted that way to a man since I'd met Kayla's dad.

When Connie walked into the nurse's station a moment later, I was still standing there watching Jay saunter away. We chatted for a few minutes, and I filled her in about Georgia before I left.

I spent the entire drive home thinking about Jay, feeling foolish for acting like a teenage girl, and wondering how long

I'd have to wait before I'd get to see him again.

* * *

I was still thinking of him two days later. I couldn't seem to get his face out of my head. Or his voice, or his smile, or the way he'd smelled, like spicy cologne. I lay on my bed reading after tucking Kayla in for the night, but couldn't concentrate. After reading the same paragraph three times, I gave up and flipped on the TV. That didn't help either. Finally, I called Tracey.

Twenty minutes later, we met at the coffee shop on Main. I stripped off my hat and gloves as I walked to the table where Tracey sat.

"Wow, your cheeks are all rosy. Did you walk here?"

I nodded as I took off my coat and hung it over the back of the chair.

"I could have picked you up, you know."

"It's only a fifteen minute walk. I needed some fresh air to clear my head." I sat down across from her and picked up the cup of decaf-mocha she'd bought for me. "Thanks. I missed you the past few days. How was your trip home?"

She shrugged indifferently. "Okay. Good thing I was only there for a few days. Any longer and I might have killed my stepdad. Why'd you need to clear your head?"

"My new resident, Georgia, came in the day after Christmas with her family."

"Something happen?"

"No, no, nothing bad. She came in with a bunch of people; children, grandchildren, even a great-great granddaughter." I paused as I took a sip of coffee.

"Uh-huh, and?"

"Well, one of her great-grandsons was… nice looking and he stayed behind to talk to me when they went to look around, that's all."

She squinted at me suspiciously. "Hmmm. How nice looking?"

"Very. But, that's just my opinion."

"Describe him to me."

I thought for a moment. "Okay, you know the guy who plays Jackson Avery on *Grey's Anatomy*?"

Tracey's mouth fell open. "Oh my God, are you serious? Did you jump him? I want details."

I laughed. "For one thing, that's how I ended up pregnant the first time. Also, I don't think it's a good idea to get into a relationship with a resident's relative."

"Who said anything about a relationship?"

I rolled my eyes.

"Okay, if it was Sam or Albert, people might have a problem with it."

"Ewww. I hope they would. So would I."

"No, seriously," she said when she'd finished laughing, "there's no rule against it at work, they just frown on it. Do you go home and tell your family about stuff that happens at work?"

I nodded. I often told Mom and Gran stories about funny or interesting things the residents said or did.

"See? They frown on that too, but if nobody knows, nobody cares. If you like him, you should go for it."

* * *

I was unsure of what to expect from my new resident. I was also concerned about Rose's reaction to her new roommate, but they barely acknowledged one another the first few days. Georgia was kept busy with visitors throughout the rest of the week and was rarely in her room. Grandchildren came and went, taking her out for lunch or home for a few hours. Connie told me that Lloyd spent the first few evenings with Georgia. He had supper with her, then sat in her room and watched TV until she fell asleep. The visitors dwindled as her family made their way home after the Christmas holidays.

I walked into Hall B one morning to see Rose, wringing her hands and pacing outside her room in her pajamas. Her short, brown hair was sticking up on one side where she had slept on it. She wasn't wearing her glasses, so I spoke as I approached. She still jumped at the sound of my voice. "What's wrong, Rose?"

"I, I, um ... don't like her… in my room."

"I understand, Rose, but it's her room now too. Tell you what, why don't we go talk to her together?"

Rose shook her head. "N…n…no, no, no."

"It's okay, Rose. I'll be with you. She's a nice lady."

Rose looked at me suspiciously.

"Please, Rose?"

She shrugged her shoulders in resignation. "Okay, okay."

I properly introduced the women and had them engage in a short conversation. Later, when Georgia became annoyed with Rose for following her, I took her aside and explained some of Rose's special needs. After that, they seemed to come to an understanding. It might only last as long as they remembered meeting, but for the moment, it was a problem solved.

By the time we went to the dining room for lunch, Georgia seemed to have taken Rose under her wing. I purposely steered them toward Edie's table. I hoped Georgia, with her ability to carry on a conversation, might provide Edie with some much-needed companionship.

I introduced them, initiated a conversation, and then sat at my regular table with Mrs. Sellers. I fastened an apron around her neck and placed a bowl of soup in front of her. She stared at me vacantly. I picked up her spoon and placed it in her hand. "Eat your soup, Mrs. Sellers."

She stared blankly at the spoon for a moment before dipping it into her soup. I nodded at her encouragingly as I listened to Edie and Georgia complaining about the food at the next table. I smiled proudly. They were talking. To each other.

My pleasure faded when Sheila came in, wheeling Mrs. W quickly through the maze of tables. Cries of surprise and irritation rang out as she barreled through, rolling over feet and clipping people as she went. I flinched, hoping she didn't bump Georgia. She might have been new, but I had a feeling that wouldn't keep her from stating her opinion.

Sheila's shrill voice carried throughout the dining room. "We wouldn't be late for lunch if *someone* had been a little more co-operative with her bath. I don't understand why you fight me every time. You would think you people would be happy to get a bath."

I glanced across the room to where Tracey sat and we exchanged a knowing look.

Edie lowered her head and continued eating, but not

before I'd seen the look of disgust on her face. Beside her, Georgia had put down her spoon and was watching Sheila warily.

Sheila wheeled Mrs. W into her usual empty spot at the table beside Tracey's. Mrs. W slumped uncomfortably in her chair. Sheila continued to rant as she grabbed her beneath the arms and pulled her up straight.

Mrs. W cried out.

"Oh, stop that. I'm not hurting you," Sheila scolded. She picked the apron up off the table and put it around Mrs. W's neck.

I saw her hands tremble slightly and heard the underlying rage in her carefully controlled voice. What had happened in that bathing room to get her this riled up?

"Now, my dear, you're going to sit here and co-operate and eat all your lunch like a good girl, aren't you?" Sheila said, sitting down hard in her chair.

I willed it to break. It didn't.

I took a deep breath to calm myself and looked over at Tracey again. She raised an eyebrow, shrugged a shoulder and shook her head, as if to ask, *What can we do*?

I heard Lily and Beth disagreeing beside me and turned to them. "What's the problem, ladies?"

"That's my cup of tea. Lily took my cup of tea," whined Beth.

"It's okay, Beth. I'll get you another." I went to the kitchen with an empty teacup, filled it and brought it back to the table. I placed it in front of Beth, along with the milk and sugar.

Beth smiled sweetly. "Thank you, dear."

Two of the kitchen staff came around with a cart and cleared away soup bowls. They were doling out plates of tuna patties and green beans when Sheila started again.

"Oh, no, we're not doing this again. Eat your lunch, or you'll go hungry until supper."

Mrs. W grunted stubbornly and tried to push her chair back from the table. Sheila grabbed the chair and yanked it back, causing Mrs. W's head to snap back against the headrest.

I watched Sheila struggle to control her simmering anger. I'd never before seen her act this badly in front of others. Residents were becoming restless and agitated by her loud, angry voice. Even some of the other staff looked troubled.

Mrs. Sellers dropped her napkin. I bent to pick it up and caught a movement in the hallway from the corner of my eye. It was Abby, preparing to hand out lunchtime meds. Sheila couldn't see her from where she sat.

Edie, however, had a perfect view of her. She looked at Abby, then at me, and smiled deviously. "Nasty cow," she said, so quietly I barely heard it.

Georgia looked at her in confusion and asked, "Nasty cow? Who's a nasty cow?" Her voice was not quiet.

Albert was sitting at their table as well. He looked from Georgia to Edie. "Nasty cow. Nasty cow!" He laughed wildly, pounding his fist on the table, then went back to eating as though nothing had been funny at all.

Sheila turned to look at them suspiciously, then whipped around quickly when Mrs. W began to cough and sputter. She swiped a napkin irritably across Mrs. W's chin.

Her back was rigid and her movements stiff.

"Her." Edie nodded toward Sheila.

Georgia made a face and nodded. She took a bite of her tuna patty and stared thoughtfully at Sheila as she chewed.

Again, Mrs. W pushed away from the table and again Sheila yanked her back.

Abby stood in the doorway now, frowning as she watched the power struggle.

Before Abby could say or do anything, Edie's Scottish brogue rang out. "For God's sake, ya nasty bitch. Leave the poor woman be."

The room fell silent.

The loud "bang" of Sheila's fist hitting the table echoed through the room. She stood, marched over to Edie, and put a finger in her face. "You need to learn to mind your own damn business."

Georgia's hand snaked out and wrapped around Sheila's wrist. "You. Are not nice."

Sheila stared at the hand on her arm as though shocked that anyone dared touch her. She looked slowly from her arm to Georgia.

I saw the look of utter fury on Sheila's face and pushed my chair away from the table. Before I could even stand up, Abby was there, pulling Sheila away. As she led her from the room, Georgia called after them, "Lord have mercy on your soul."

* * *

Tracey and I discussed the lunchtime incident after work as we crossed the parking lot to our cars. She insisted Abby would do nothing. "Sheila's been getting away with this for so long, people think it's normal. Like I said before, Abby's scared of her. She won't do anything to cross her."

I held out hope that Sheila had crossed a line Abby wouldn't be able to ignore. No one else would get away with treating a resident that way, not even a visiting relative. Sheila had mistreated Mrs. W and set a bad example for every staff member. Abby simply could not let her get away with it.

* * *

Sheila was back at work the next day. Rumor had it that Abby had simply warned her about her behavior and sent her home early after the incident. She had not been written up or disciplined in any way.

Edie had a bath scheduled that morning and I was concerned about her being alone with Sheila after what had happened the day before. When I voiced my concern to Edie, she shrugged it off and marched bravely down the hall to the bathing room.

She came back to her room half an hour later, as I wheeled Mrs. Sellers out of the bathroom.

"How'd it go?" I asked

"Fine, fine," Edie replied, hanging her housecoat in the wardrobe.

I locked up both wardrobes. "Did she say anything about yesterday?"

"Not a word. She barely spoke to me at all, just did what needed to be done and sent me on my way."

That made me nervous. A quiet Sheila was a dangerous Sheila. Her silence and compliance were out of character. I was afraid it was the calm before the storm.

CHAPTER 11
FORGIVENESS

THE NEXT COUPLE OF WEEKS were relatively uneventful. Abby may not have formally disciplined her, but Sheila must have taken her warning seriously. She remained uncharacteristically quiet, kept her head down, did her work and didn't speak to anyone unless she had to.

Georgia settled in more easily than I had dared to hope. She had visitors often, which helped the transition, but I liked to think Rose and Edie had something to do with it as well.

Rose looked up to Georgia. She often followed her around, doing everything she did. Georgia didn't seem to mind. She was patient and protective of her, treating her as though she were one of her grandchildren. Georgia also provided some much-needed companionship for Edie. They sat together at every meal, played cards and board games and attended activities together, often with Rose trailing along behind. There were days when Georgia didn't remember Edie, or Rose didn't remember Georgia, but they were somehow still drawn together. Edie simply took those days in stride. She had a way of making Georgia feel at ease in her company, whether she remembered her or not.

So it was that Edie, Georgia and Rose became an unlikely trio of mismatched companions. Edie was a natural leader and Georgia commanded attention with her presence alone. Other residents seemed drawn to them and often trailed after the pair and looked to them for help.

One day, I escorted a few of the women to the craft room for Crochet Club. Lily and Beth were already there. Beth was struggling to remember and frustrated nearly to tears. She dropped her crochet needle in her lap and looked around the room. Her gaze rested on Edie and Georgia who chatted and crocheted easily. She got up, moved to the empty chair beside Edie and touched her on the arm. Edie looked over at Beth's pleading face. She held her needle and yarn up and worked slowly, explaining each step. She then had Beth do it with her. Her words of praise had Beth's face lighting up.

The newfound role of leader gave Edie a purpose. It was something for her to look forward to each day. Her depression seemed to lift a little, but she often seemed lonely when Georgia went home with Lloyd on the weekends. She watched Georgia's many visitors come and go with a look of envy on her face and often kept to her room when Georgia was gone.

Tom and Ann were Edie's only visitors. Every Saturday at one o'clock they came to see her. By two o'clock they were gone. They rarely took Edie home, or on outings. I was sure, if it had been up to Tom, Edie would have gone home with them more often, but he seemed to have little say about what went on in his life.

Regardless, Edie looked forward to their visits. She was

sitting on a bench in the main hall one Saturday, waiting for them. Georgia sat beside her, cane resting across her legs, purse and coat laid neatly across the bench beside her, overnight bag at her feet. She was waiting for Lloyd to pick her up and take her home for a visit.

Both women had dressed carefully that morning. We'd spent extra time picking out nice outfits and doing their hair. Georgia wore dark red lipstick. Her favorite gold hoop earrings dangled from her ears. Edie wore a more subdued color on her lips and had even applied a touch of perfume.

I was wheeling Mrs. Sellers out of the dining room when Anne arrived with Tom close behind. It was one o'clock sharp. She marched directly to Edie, looked her up and down, and without even a greeting, said, "My goodness, aren't we all dressed up today?"

Edie simply nodded and stood to greet Tom with a smile. "Hello, dear."

"Hello, Mother," he replied, hugging her. He took her hand and held her at arm's length. "You look very nice today."

"Thank you, lad, that's ni—"

"Why don't you ever tell me I look nice?" Anne interrupted. "You give your mother a compliment, but not your own wife?"

Tom sputtered and stammered, but didn't even have a chance to reply.

Anne looked at Edie. "Where in the world is your wheelchair? I tell you every time I see you, you should be using it. If you fall and end up with a broken hip, it'll be nobody's fault but your own." She turned to Tom. "I told you didn't I? When she came home for Christmas, I said, 'She's going to fall, and when she does, I'm going to tell you I told you so.'"

Edie's expression was tight with anger. A couple of months ago she would have said nothing. She would have swallowed her angry words to avoid an argument. Now, I wasn't so sure.

I was on my way to Mrs. Sellers' room to help her with mouth care and toileting, but there was no way I was going to miss this. I pushed her chair closer to the wall and bent over with the pretense of tucking her lap blanket around her legs. I peeked through my blonde ponytail as it swung across my face.

Anne didn't wait for a response from Tom. She turned to Edie, and, oblivious to her mother-in-law's growing fury, continued on. "We worry about you, Mother. We're not young anymore, you know. We wouldn't be able to look after you if something happened."

Georgia snorted loudly.

Anne glanced at her. She looked thoughtfully at the cane on her lap, then at Edie. "Well, since you won't use the wheelchair we bought you, maybe we should get you a cane or a walker."

"*Ye* booght me?" Edie exclaimed. "Ye booght that wheelchair *wi' mah* money!"

Anne's expression grew dark. It reminded me of Sheila. I shuddered at the thought and it occurred to me Edie might be better off in Dementia than living with Anne.

"Money that we look after for you. Just like we look after everything."

"By yer ain choice!" Edie cried.

"Stop talking that way. You sound like a fool."

"Ah soond loch a Scot," Edie shot back in an even heavier brogue. There was pride and defiance in her voice.

"N-no need to get angry, you two," Tom stammered, looking around uncomfortably.

Edie rounded on him, but reigned in her temper when she saw the desperate look on his face. "No need to get angry, you say? No need, when she criticizes and demeans me with every word out of her mouth? Maybe you're willing to put up with it, but I'm not. Not anymore."

Anne's mouth dropped. "How dare you? How dare you speak that way after all I've done for you? You, you, ungrateful old—"

Georgia's voice rang out, cutting Anne off before she could say something irrevocable. "Oh, Lord Jesus in heaven, silence this woman's tongue."

Anne stared at Georgia speechlessly as the older woman took her cane in hand and came slowly to her feet. She pulled herself up to her full height, looked down at Anne, and said, "Shame on you."

Anne glared at her. She opened her mouth to speak, but Georgia was not finished.

"Shame on you," she said again, waving a finger in Anne's face. "Speaking to her that way. You should be ashamed of yourself."

"I don't—I only—"

"Did your mother not teach you any manners? Did she not teach you to respect your elders? If one of my children spoke to me that way, I would box their ears. Shame on you!"

Anne pressed her lips tightly together. She didn't look as ashamed as she should have after being publicly scolded by a ninety-eight year old woman, but she certainly looked guilty. And she wisely kept her mouth shut.

There was a long, uncomfortable silence.

Georgia stomped back to her seat and sat down with a thud, while Edie, Tom and Anne wandered off toward the lounge.

The show was over. I leaned over Mrs. Sellers' shoulder and said quietly, "I'm going to take you to your room now, Mrs. Sellers." I straightened up. And looked right at him.

Jay strolled into Dementia wearing jeans and a tailored pea coat that showed off his long, lean body and broad shoulders.

My heart stopped for a moment, until I noticed Lloyd behind him and remembered they were there to get Georgia. Jay went straight to Georgia, lifted her carefully from her seat on the bench, and wrapped his arms around her. He kissed her cheek loudly before he let her go and turned to gather her things. Our eyes met. Once again I'd been caught staring.

He smiled and walked toward me.

I wiped my palms on my scrub shirt and cleared my throat as he approached.

"Hi Sarah. We're here to get Ma."

"Great, I, uh…helped her pack her bag this morning. She's really excited to go home."

"We're excited to have her home. We've missed her."

"I'm sure she misses you too. She seems to be settling in well, though."

"You mean she's not cantankerous and bossy?"

"No, not very often. She's become friends with another resident of mine, Edie. And she's taken her roommate, Rose, under her wing. It's funny, I know some days she doesn't remember them, but they always end up together. I don't know if I'd say she's happy, but for the most part she seems content."

Jay looked at Georgia, his expression soft with affection. "I guess that's all we can hope for. Sometimes I think she's even forgotten how to be happy."

Without thinking, I touched his arm in consolation. "I'm sorry. I'm close to my grandmother too and I know how hard it is when they're sick."

Jay smiled, put his hand over mine, which was still resting much too familiarly on his arm, and said, "Thank you."

A shiver went through my body and I felt warm suddenly. I quickly pulled my hand out from beneath his and looked away as I felt the heat creep up my neck. Would I ever be able to look at him or talk to him without blushing and tripping over my words?

"I should go. I, um… I have work to do," I said, taking hold of Mrs. Seller's wheelchair.

"Wait. What time do you finish work?"

"Two-thirty."

"How about meeting me for coffee when you're done?"

I stared at him blankly. Had he just asked me out?

"Sarah?"

"I—I can't, I'm sorry, it's frowned on. I look after your grandmother. It just isn't professional."

"It's only coffee. And who's going to know?"

I shook my head. "I'm sorry, I can't. Please be sure to sign Georgia out before you leave." I hurried away, pushing Mrs. Sellers ahead of me. I already regretted saying no.

I beat myself up for days over the way I'd handled Jay. I lay awake at night thinking about it. What would have been the harm in meeting him for coffee? Coffee could lead to drinks, which could lead to dinner, which, judging by the level of attraction I felt for him, could lead to, well, lots of things.

The whole spiel about it being unprofessional was simply an excuse. I couldn't tell him the truth. I was scared. I'd been hurt before and now I had Kayla to think of. I would never date a man who couldn't accept Kayla if things got serious, so I'd made it a rule to tell every guy I went out with about her by the second date. Third dates did not exist in my world. Who was I kidding? First dates barely existed in my world.

I didn't tell Tracey about Jay asking me out. I knew what she'd say about me turning him down and I didn't want to hear it. I kept the feelings of regret, the fear of always being alone, bottled up inside like I always had. I had every right to be scared, I told myself, when every man I'd ever loved had abandoned me.

* * *

It had been nearly a week since Jay had asked me out for coffee. I hadn't seen him since. Lloyd had been alone when he brought Georgia back to Tranquility that Sunday. I was sure Jay was avoiding me and I didn't blame him in the least.

I'd made it clear that I wasn't interested in going out with him.

I wasn't having a good day at work. Tracey was off sick and her replacement, Maria, didn't know our routine. Mrs. Amaral didn't like Maria, or the change in routine, and became obstinate and uncharacteristically aggressive. I spent a good part of my morning trying to calm her and worked through my break to help Maria catch up.

Sam thought he needed to go to work and I had to convince him numerous times throughout the morning that it was his day off. I couldn't even distract him from it with his music. Lily and Beth bickered like children and mediating quickly became tedious. Albert wandered into John's room looking for his precious Hairball and the two men nearly came to blows.

By the time lunch was over, I was hungry, tired and stressed. I'd just finished helping Rose get cleaned up and changed. She'd had an accident when I was unable to take her to the bathroom right away after lunch. Again, I'd been busy helping Maria, and had fallen behind on my own routine.

I was in the hallway outside Rose's room, crouched in front of the supply cart getting clean towels for her bathroom, deep in thought, immersed in my own misery and longing for the day to finally end.

"Hello, Sarah."

I was so startled by the deep voice above me that I nearly fell over. I put one hand on the floor to catch myself and looked up at Mr. Gallo.

He smiled. "I so sorry. I no wanna scare you."

I stood up and smiled tentatively. "It's okay, I didn't hear you walk up." I gave a short, nervous laugh. I hadn't seen Mr. Gallo since the day Abby had sent his wife to the hospital. He was leaning on a walker, looking much older and frailer than last time I'd seen him.

"I know, it take so long for me to come back. I so sick after Christmas, and the Parkinson's, it gets bad after my Bella.... I live with my sister, Gina, now."

"It's okay, Mr. Gallo. I wasn't expecting you to come see me. I mean... there's no reason—"

"There is much reason. Gina, she tell me you very upset when she come."

I shook my head in denial.

"You no feel bad. Is no your fault. You take good care of my Bella."

All the emotions I'd struggled so hard to contain that day rose to the surface. Tears welled up in my eyes. *Damn it, why does he have to be so nice*? I swiped a tissue from the box on the supply cart and dabbed at my eyes.

"No cry! No, no, no. The tears of a woman, they are no good for my heart." He put a shaking hand over his heart as if to prove my tears were hurting it.

I couldn't help but laugh a little at his theatrics. I wiped away the last of the tears and managed a smile for him. "Thank you. You didn't have to do this, but it means a lot to me."

He stepped around his walker and pulled me in for a hug. I could feel his thin, frail body trembling and nearly started crying again.

Luckily Sam came out of his room at that moment, saw

me and yelled, "What the hell? Get me outta here. I'm late for work."

That put an end to the tears.

CHAPTER 12
INFLUENZA

I HAD LITTLE TIME OVER the next couple of weeks to think about Jay or Mr. Gallo. It seemed as though we'd barely recovered from the norovirus when influenza struck. Most of the staff and residents had been given flu shots in the fall, but some still became ill. They wanted nothing more than to stay in bed and sleep. We didn't have to chase after them and try to keep them in their rooms, as we had last time, and there were fewer accidents involving bodily fluids.

We were kept busy nonetheless. Caring for residents who wanted only to stay in bed meant constant repositioning and checking for signs of bedsores. We encouraged them to get up at least long enough to use the washroom or brush their teeth. They were given sponge baths and spent part of each day in a sitting position to keep their lungs clear of fluid. We constantly pushed fluids to prevent dehydration.

Mrs. Sellers was the first of my residents to get sick. It hit her hard and I took no chances. A few days into the illness, she developed a fever, a deep, thick cough, and a rattle in her chest. She complained of pain in her chest and refused to drink anything. I reported it to Abby and, within an hour, Mrs. Sellers was on her way to the hospital.

Rose, Lily and Beth came down with the flu as well, but were not nearly as ill as Mrs. Sellers. Rose was miserable. She became petulant and sulky and complained constantly. She was so unpleasant that even Georgia avoided her.

Lloyd came to visit that Thursday after dinner as he always did. Connie explained the situation to him and he came back Friday after work to sign Georgia out for the weekend. By the time he dropped her off again on Sunday evening, Rose was feeling better and back to her usual good-natured self.

Lily and Beth were sick enough to want to stay in bed, but not too sick to aggravate each other. For three long days they stayed in their room together. I went in often to check on them, made sure they drank plenty of water, reminded them to use the bathroom, and gave them cool cloths for their foreheads. If they weren't sleeping, they were complaining, and the complaining always led to more arguing.

"Stop coughing."

"I can't stop. You stop listening."

"She talks too much. It keeps me awake."

"No, I don't. She's lying."

"I'll tell Mother and you'll be in trouble."

"Well then, you'll be a tattletale. Nobody likes a tattletale."

It was never ending and it gave me a headache. It also made me happy I only had one daughter.

Mrs. Sellers came back to Tranquility nearly a week after she'd been sent to the hospital. She'd been treated for pneumonia, which we'd caught early. I breathed a sigh of relief. Caring for the others had kept my mind off her most days, but I couldn't help but worry after losing Mrs. Gallo.

I worried about Gran as well. She tired easily and often looked pale and drawn. When I voiced my concern, she insisted she was fine.

"I'm eighty-four years old, Sarah. Of course I get tired."

"Have you called the doctor yet?"

"I'll call first thing tomorrow."

Two days later, I came home from work to find her on the floor beside the couch, struggling to sit up. I ran over and crouched down beside her. "What happened? Did you fall?"

She batted my hand away when I tried to help. She grabbed onto the couch with one hand, pulled herself into a sitting position, and sat for a moment catching her breath. Finally, she looked up at me and said, "I'm fine."

"Okay, good to know."

She turned over onto her knees, put a hand on the couch and pushed herself up off the floor. I helped her get settled on the couch and sat down beside her. "Now tell me what happened."

She waved her hand in annoyance. "It's nothing. I went to sit on the couch, missed and ended up on the floor."

"Were you dizzy or lightheaded before it happened?"

"I was tired, that's all."

"Gran...."

"I cleaned up the damn kitchen, okay? After I swept the floor I felt a little lightheaded, so I came in here to lie down. It's nothing. I'm fine."

"It's not nothing, Gran. You could have hurt yourself and there'd have been no one here to help you. Did you make that doctor's appointment like you said you would?"

"I forgot." She grumbled and complained about the fuss I was making, but called the doctor right away.

I knew then that the fall had scared her. I pulled an ottoman over for her feet and tucked a blanket around her legs. When she was settled in front of the TV with the remote, I went to the kitchen to make tea.

Not wanting to leave Gran alone, I called the mother of one of Kayla's friends, and asked her to bring Kayla home from school. She assured me it was no problem. After I hung up the phone, I fixed the tea and carried it into the living room. I set one on the coffee table in front of Gran and sank into the armchair beside her with a sigh.

A short time later, I heard the front door bang and Kayla's excited voice flooded the house with life. "She's home, Gran. Brace yourself," I warned.

Kayla flew into the living room, her short, dark hair bouncing as she ran over and launched herself into my lap.

"Hey, munchkin. How was school?"

"Really, really good, Mommy. Mrs. Anderson liked my painting so much she hanged it on the wall. She said I'm an artist!" Her brown eyes glistened with excitement.

"Hung it on the wall, and your teacher's right, you're an amazing artist."

Mom had always been a stickler for spelling and grammar. It had driven me crazy when I was a kid, but I found myself doing the same thing to Kayla.

Kayla jumped off my lap and sat on the couch beside Gran, looking up at her with concern. "Are you, okay, Gran? You look sick."

Gran put her arm around Kayla's shoulder and pulled her tight against her side. "I'm fine, sweetheart. Just a little tired, that's all." She leaned over and kissed the top of Kayla's head.

Kayla wiggled out from under her arm and made a beeline for the door. "I'm going to play with my toys," she yelled, running from the room.

Mom came home about an hour later. I left her and Kayla to fuss over Gran and went upstairs to shower and change. After I got dressed, I called Tracey and arranged to meet her for coffee after dinner.

* * *

Tracey burst into the coffee shop with a rush of frosty air, shaking the snow from her long, red hair and lamenting the cold weather.

"You know it's winter, right?" I said.

She made a face as she took off her coat and hung it on the back of the chair. She slid into her seat and wrapped her hands around the hot cup of latte. "Course I know it's winter, smartass. Doesn't mean I have to like it. So what's up?"

"Nothing. I just felt like getting out of the house."

"Uh-uh, not buying it."

I was amazed by how she always seemed to know when there was something on my mind. "I'm worried about Gran. She's been off for a couple months, tired and pale. Then I came home today to find her on the floor beside the couch."

"Oh shit. She okay?"

"I think so. She made a doctor's appointment finally. I've been on her case about it for a while."

"That's all you can do. She's a grown woman."

"I know," I mumbled dejectedly. "I just worry about her since she had the stroke a couple of years ago. I don't think I could handle losing her right now. She was like a parent to me after my dad died." My fingers went to the pendant at my neck.

Tracey glanced at it. "Did you get that from him?"

I nodded and looked away, swallowing the sudden lump in my throat.

"So, have you seen Jay lately?"

My face fell. I must have looked about ready to cry.

"Oh, man." Tracey said. "Sorry. Thought I was doing a good thing changing the subject. Is it really that bad? I mean, you barely know the guy, right?"

"Right. But I didn't tell you, he asked me out for coffee a few weeks ago and I said no."

"Sarah! We talked about this. I told you—"

"I know, I know. I messed up. And I haven't been able to stop thinking about him since."

"Well then, we'll just have to do something about that."

I groaned. "Great. One more thing for me to worry about."

CHAPTER 13
IN LIKE A LION

MARCH ANNOUNCED ITSELF FORCEFULLY WITH a blast of cold and a late winter snowstorm. I was happy for the short drive to work that morning. Nearly half a foot of snow had fallen through the night, and the roads were a slushy, slippery mess.

It was a relatively quiet day in Dementia. After breakfast, Edie and Georgia decided to go to the solarium to watch the birds flit in and out of the feeders in the gently falling snow. Lily, Beth and Rose tagged along behind.

I left Mrs. Sellers watching TV in the lounge with a few other residents and continued to Hall B to start making beds. Edie had made her own bed, as she did every morning. Mrs. Sellers' linens needed changing. I stripped the bed and put the dirty sheets into the linen bag in the hall. Housekeeping would be around shortly with clean linens. I headed down the hall to make the twins' beds.

Sam's deep, raspy voice drifted out of his room. I smiled and hummed along to the upbeat chorus as I straightened sheets and tucked blankets. "Wake Up Little Susie" was a song Gran used to listen to on her old record player. She would often play it when we went to visit and she and I would dance. I remembered laughing and shrieking as she twirled me round and round.

Tracey's voice interrupted my reminiscing. "Hey, you started without me." She went to the opposite side of the bed to help.

"I figured you were off somewhere napping."

She laughed. We worked in companionable silence until we heard Edie's concerned voice calling from the hallway. "Sarah! Sarah, where are you?"

"I'm here." Tracey and I hurried to the hallway to meet her. "What's wrong?" I asked.

Edie put her hand on my arm to steady herself as she bent over, gasping for air. Georgia was right behind her. She was out of breath and looking worried as well. Rose brought up the rear, shuffling along at her own pace and looking confused.

I was scared now and thinking the worst. I didn't see Lily or Beth anywhere. Had something happened to one of them? "Edie, what is wrong?"

She straightened up and took a deep breath. "There's a… man."

I took her hand in mine. "Where? What's he doing?"

"In the…courtyard," she gasped.

Georgia chimed in before I could ask any more questions. "Lord, save us. He's naked."

I sighed. "Oh, not again."

"This should be fun," Tracey said, smirking.

Sam, was my first thought. No, it can't be, he's in his room.

"Who is it, Edie?"

"John."

Tracey and I exchanged a knowing look.

I glanced at Edie. "Will you find Abby for me, please?" I left them behind as I ran toward the solarium. All I could think of was how cold it was outside and how quickly he could get hypothermia.

I saw John through the wall of windows as soon as I entered the solarium. He wandered along the snow-covered garden path, waving his hands wildly and talking to himself. He wasn't completely naked; he was wearing underwear and socks.

"At least he's not walking around in the snow barefoot," I said to Tracey as she ran in behind me.

"True, but his socks have gotta be soaked."

"He looks pretty upset."

"Yeah. He seems to like me. I'll go talk to him. Hold the door for me, okay? I might be in a hurry to get back in." She grinned, opened the door and stepped outside.

I stood in the doorway, holding the door slightly ajar. The snow came down harder now. It danced and swirled around the enclosed courtyard as though searching for a way out. A gust of cold air and snow hit me in the face and I closed the door all but a crack.

Tracey walked slowly toward John, calling his name as she approached. She stopped just beyond arm's reach. He was unresponsive and continued to pace back and forth, muttering to himself. He'd worn a path, about ten feet long, into the snow. The wet socks sagged off his feet. His bare skin was mottled and covered in goose bumps.

"John," Tracey called again. She moved a little closer.

"Aren't you cold?"

Finally he seemed to hear her and looked up. His face went pale. "Mary," he whimpered.

"Hi, John. Why don't you come inside with me and get warm?"

He stared at her for a moment, and then shook his head as though to clear it. "You—you're here. Why did you leave me?"

"I'm here now. It's cold. Come inside with me. Please?"

John's face darkened. He took a step toward her. "Why are you here? Did they send you? You're here to take me back to that place, aren't you?"

Tracey put her hands out in front of her body and backed slowly toward the door. "I'm not taking you anywhere. I just want you to come inside and get warm."

I didn't like the look on John's face. I opened the door a little wider and said in a low voice, "I think you should come in, Trace."

Tracey didn't look at me. She shook her snow-covered head to let me know she'd heard. "Please, John?"

He wavered, nearly taken in by the pleading tone of her voice, then his face changed, his expression hardened. He put his closed fists to his temples, shut his eyes tightly and rocked his head back and forth. When he opened his eyes again, they were hard and empty. His hands dropped to his sides. His voice was flat and emotionless. "You're tricking me."

"No, I'm not. You're cold, John. I'm afraid you're gonna get sick."

"You're always tricking me, trying to make me do what

you want. They said you would." He took a step toward her.

Tracey took a step back.

I opened the door all the way and said her name.

She glanced over her shoulder and took another step back.

"Bitch," John spat, rushing toward her.

She turned and ran the last few steps to the door. I pulled it closed behind her and locked it just as John crashed into it, roaring with fury.

Tracey stood looking out the door with one hand over her chest, breathing heavily. "Well, that didn't work out how I planned."

We looked at each other. "Now what do we do?" I asked.

Abby and Carol rushed into the room as John launched himself at the door a second time. We jumped back, startled by the loud crash. He banged furiously on the glass as he spewed obscenities.

Abby stood beside us, looking out at the deranged, half-naked man. "Any idea what set him off?"

"Not sure," Tracey said. "I went out to try to get him to come in, but it just pissed him off more. He came at me and chased me back inside."

Abby nodded, taking in Tracey's wet clothing and hair. "Did he hurt you?"

"Nope, I'm faster than him."

Abby's mouth twitched as though she wanted to smile. Instead she blew out a long, loud breath. "How are we going to get him in here without someone getting hurt?"

After a short discussion, Abby decided it was too

dangerous to handle on our own and went to call for help. By then, there was a crowd of people in the solarium. Edie, Georgia and Rose had come back and a few others had wandered in to see what all the commotion was about.

John became more and more agitated as people continued to crowd into the room to peer curiously through the windows.

"Edie…" I began. There was no need to say more. Edie rounded up the residents and shooed them out of the room.

I closed the door. From the wall of windows in the solarium, Tracey and I were able to look across the courtyard and into the doors and windows opposite us. I watched as curious residents, and a few of the kitchen and housekeeping staff, crowded around the glass doors that accessed the courtyard from Hall A.

By the time the police and paramedics arrived with Abby, John was in a state of complete rage. He paced away from the door and back again, shouting and waving his hands wildly in the air. We moved to the far side of the room, hoping if we were out of sight, he would calm down and move away from the door. It didn't help.

The police decided the best way to approach him was from behind. The bigger of the two left the room with Abby, who took him to Hall A. The other one stood at the solarium door to keep John's attention.

The two paramedics waited with the gurney in the hallway. Tracey opened the door and stood where she could talk to them and watch the drama unfold at the same time.

I watched the big, burly cop open the door into the courtyard and sneak up quietly behind John. He moved quickly for his size and had wrapped his arms around John's chest and lifted him off his feet before John knew anyone was there.

John fought hard, but couldn't loosen the big man's grip. The other cop opened the door and John was carried, kicking and screaming, inside. It took all four men to get him onto the gurney and strapped down. At the end of it, they were all a little breathless and would no doubt have a few bruises for their efforts.

We stood in the hallway, watching the paramedics wheel John away. They had removed his wet socks and wrapped him in blankets, but his body trembled with cold now that the anger and adrenaline had subsided.

I noticed a look pass between Tracey and one of the paramedics as the two men wheeled the gurney out of Dementia. I turned to her with a raised brow. "What was that about?"

She shrugged nonchalantly as we turned and headed toward Hall B. "His name's Kyle. I slipped him my number. We're gonna go out this weekend."

"Why doesn't that surprise me?"

She grinned mischievously. "He's just my type; big, strong and ruggedly handsome." She turned into the twins' room. "And he has a stethoscope, so maybe we can play doctor," she added, wiggling her eyebrows lecherously.

I rolled my eyes and laughed as we picked up where we'd left off making beds. I was beginning to like Tracey a lot. Her lighthearted nature and dry, sometimes tawdry, sense of humor offset my serious nature perfectly.

Seeing the exchange between Tracey and the paramedic

made me think of Jay. I thought about him a lot and it frustrated me. It shouldn't be so hard to forget someone I barely knew. It was those eyes. And that smile. And the way he'd made me feel when he stood too close and put his hand over mine. I felt warm suddenly.

Tracey looked at me through narrowed eyes. "You thinking about him again?"

"No, just thinking about what to make for dinner tonight."

"Uh-huh, 'cause you always blush when you think about food. You got it bad, girl. We really need to do something about it."

I made a face at her and we moved on to Sam's room. He was stretched out in his recliner wearing his ear buds, eyes closed, head bobbing along to the beat of the music.

"Hi, Sam," I said loudly to let him know we were there.

He opened his eyes, raised his brows and smiled lewdly.

"Watch out," I whispered, "I know that look."

Tracey wiggled her brows. "I might like it."

We laughed quietly as we went to work making Sam's bed.

It occurred to me that I would miss Tracey when I quit work to go to school in the fall and I realized I hadn't told her about it. Not purposely, it simply hadn't come up.

I glanced around. Sam's eyes were now on Tracey's backside, but he was still immersed in his music. "So, I applied to nursing school."

Tracey dropped her side of the blanket. "Are you kidding me?"

I shook my head, puzzled by her reaction.

She laughed, picked up the blanket and continued working. “I’ve been wanting to apply for a couple years, but I keep putting it off. It’s the thought of giving up work and going into debt. I don’t have to tell you how hard it is. You have a kid to take care of and you’re doing it.”

“True, but I can live with my mom until I’m done with school. That’ll help a lot. And I think the longer I put it off, the harder it’ll be. I’m already getting too comfortable here.”

Tracey nodded. Her face was aglow with excitement. “You’re right. I just have to do it. I’m gonna look into it tonight.”

Her enthusiasm was contagious. I hadn’t allowed myself to become too excited about school. I hadn’t even told anyone other than Mom, Gran, and now, Tracey. Now, for the first time, I felt good about my choice and was looking forward to starting a new chapter in my life.

Chapter 14
The Queen's Corset

SCHOOL HAD BEEN ON MY mind a lot since I'd told Tracey about applying a few days earlier. Somehow, talking about it made it seem more real. It also made me realize I might only have a matter of months to get Edie out of Dementia. It had to happen before I left or she could be in there for the rest of her life.

A couple of months had passed since I'd spoken to Abby about it. I'd noticed her watching Edie at times, but she'd said nothing to me about her thoughts on the matter. I needed to bring it up again and find out what she was planning to do.

I went to the nurse's station near the end of my shift that Friday. I'd timed it so I was there before the other support workers showed up to do their documentation, knowing it was the only time I might catch Abby with a few minutes to spare. Sure enough, she was there, sitting at the desk alone, doing her paperwork.

She looked up as I approached.

"Hi, Abby. Do you have a minute?"

She glanced at the clock on the wall and nodded. "Make it quick."

I leaned across the top level of the two-tiered desk. "It's been a couple months since we talked about Edie. I'm just wondering if you've had a chance to talk to her?"

Abby sighed. "You know how hard it's been lately to do anything except what's absolutely necessary. I haven't had a chance to sit down and speak with her in depth, but based on observation alone, I think there's a possibility you could be right. There's also the chance she's very good at hiding her symptoms. It happens a lot in the early stages."

I didn't like the sound of that. I needed more from her. I needed her to commit to something. "So, what's the next step?"

"Well, I still need to talk to her. At that point, if I think there's something to it, I'll need to set up a meeting with Edie, her son and the doctor."

"Her son," I repeated. If Tom were there, Anne would be as well. "Does he have to be there?"

She looked at me curiously. "When a resident is admitted to Dementia, it's usually because they're no longer capable of their own decision making. So, yes, the substitute decision maker would normally be present at a meeting regarding the resident's health or care. But, I'm sure you knew that."

I hesitated, trying to choose my words carefully. "I think her daughter-in-law is a big part of the reason Edie's in here in the first place. If Edie's son goes to the meeting, so will his wife, and she can be a little… intimidating."

"Well, let's worry about that when the time comes. I'll try to find time to speak to Edie next week, so we can get this moving." She picked up her pen and went back to work, dismissing me without words.

It was something. Not exactly what I would call a commitment, but it was a start. If it didn't pan out I'd have to be more persistent. And, if persistence didn't pay off, I might have to take Tracey's advice and become a pain in the ass. I was hoping it wouldn't get to that point.

I headed back to Hall B to do one last check of my residents before doing my documentation and leaving for the day. I peeked into the lounge on my way by. Albert and a few other residents were sitting, watching TV. Mrs. Martin was busy at the bookshelf, humming softly as she rearranged the books. Edie and Georgia sat at the table in the corner playing cards. I heard Georgia ask, "What do I do now?", and marveled at Edie's incredible patience.

I left the lounge and continued down the hall, peeking into each room as I went. Beth was in her room resting. Alone. I frowned and hurried on. It wasn't like the twins to be apart. I did a double take as I walked past Sam's room. He and Lily were half-lying on the bed in a mess of tangled naked limbs, kissing and groping each other frantically.

"Oh, my God!" I covered my eyes with one hand, hoping not to see anything more as I leaned across the threshold and pulled the door shut. I stood in the hallway, flabbergasted and wondered what to do. I'd never encountered this in Palliative Care. I needed to find Tracey.

She was at the nurse's station doing her documentation. I leaned over the top of the desk. "Trace, I need your help."

"Why? What's wrong?"

"Sam and Lily are making out in his room."

She threw her head back and laughed. "Doubt they

need my help, then. 'Cept, at their age it's probably like trying to shove a marshmallow through a donut hole."

I struggled to keep a straight face. Where did she come up with these things? "It's not funny. What am I supposed to do?"

"Nothing," she said, wiping the tears from her eyes.

"Nothing?"

"Seriously. They're two grown adults. If they wanna have sex—"

I groaned and put my face in my hands. "Oh, my God, stop."

"Well, it's true. You gonna go in there and pull them apart?"

"No, but…."

"Me neither. And why should we? It's not like they're doing anything wrong."

I dropped my hands to my sides and sighed. She was right. "Fine. I have to finish my rounds."

"Okay, when you're done, meet me here. I need to tell you about something."

"What?"

"It'll wait. In fact, I don't wanna talk about it here. We'll talk later."

"Aha. Got it." If she didn't want to talk about it here, it was probably about Sheila. It occurred to me as I walked away that I hadn't seen Rose for a while. "Hey, Trace," I called over my shoulder. "Have you seen Rose lately?"

"Nope."

I passed the lounge again on my way back to Hall B and glanced in to be sure she hadn't wandered in since I'd looked in earlier. There were no activities at the moment, so the auditorium and craft room would be locked. The dining hall was also closed up until dinnertime. I checked each room on both sides of Hall B, except Sam's, which I rushed past, trying to block out the sound of grunts and giggles coming from behind the closed door. I didn't see Rose anywhere. That left only the solarium, the relaxation room and Hall A.

I heard John's raised voice as soon as I rounded the corner into Hall A. He'd come back two days after the incident in the courtyard. "Get out, out. Get out, stupid cow."

Oh, this is not good, I thought, increasing my pace to a near run.

"D-Don't say that," Rose stuttered.

His voice went up a notch. "Get out. Out, out, out, get out. Get the hell out!"

I rushed into the room as John pushed Rose. She lost her balance and fell over, barely catching herself on the bed. She began to cry.

John didn't even acknowledge me. He stomped over to the chair in the corner and sat there with his arms crossed, looking out the window while I helped Rose out of the room.

We walked slowly, past the solarium and bathing room, to her room, where I checked her for injuries. When I was sure she was unhurt, I helped her settle in for a nap, then headed to the nurse's station. I still had to do my daily recording and now had to fill out an incident report as well.

Tracey was still there. "Find Rose?"

"She was in John's room."

"Uh-oh."

"She's okay. He was upset that she was in there, so he pushed her. She landed on the bed, thank God, but now I have to fill out a report."

"You're gonna have to talk to Abby about John before poor Rose ends up hurt."

"I know. I'd report it to her now, but I think she's gone. I'll have to talk to her Monday. Honestly, I was surprised he was allowed back last time."

"Not me. You know as well as I do why people like John end up in nursing homes. Our beds are cheaper than psychiatric beds. Bottom line. He'll be here 'til he hurts someone so bad that they have no choice."

I nodded my agreement, but didn't have time to get into a discussion about the problems within our health care system. I looked at the clock. "It's after two-thirty, you weren't waiting for me, were you?"

She rolled her eyes. "No, I love it here so much that I don't wanna leave. Of course I was waiting for you. It's Friday."

"Uh-huh," I said, opening the binder. I pulled a pen from my shirt pocket and began recording. "And what's so special about Friday?"

"Um, it's *Friday*. Friday's always special."

"Not if you have to work Saturday."

"Oh, c'mon. We'll go to *The Queen's*. It'll be packed with single men playing darts and drinking pints."

"Exactly. It'll be packed and they'll have a band playing. It'll be crowded and noisy and full of drunk, obnoxious men."

Tracey rolled her eyes. "Exactly why we should go.

Please? I haven't been out for ages. I have to work tomorrow too. We'll go early, have dinner, leave early. Please, please, please?"

I looked up from the chart, into her pleading face. "Oh, my God, you sound just like Kayla." I sighed. "Fine, but I have to check with my mom first and make sure she doesn't mind watching Kayla." Who was I kidding? Mom would be pushing me out the door.

Tracey squealed in excitement and gave me a quick hug before she stood up and put on her coat. "Text me later," she called as she rushed out the door.

What, I wondered as I went back to my documenting, *have I gotten myself into*?

I was putting my coat on a few minutes later when Jay walked in. It was the first time I'd seen him since he'd asked me out for coffee a month earlier. I froze in the middle of buttoning my coat, hoping he wouldn't notice me.

He did, of course, and turned in my direction. My thumb went to my mouth and I caught myself biting at a hangnail. I pulled my hand away quickly and looked around for my purse. It was on the chair beside me. I picked it up and held it in front of me as he approached.

"Hi, Sarah."

I cleared my throat nervously. "Hi."

"How've you been?"

"Good, thanks." I slid my purse strap over my shoulder and pulled my gloves out of my coat pocket. I put them on as I spoke, looking down at them instead of at Jay. "I believe Georgia's in the lounge playing cards with Edie. I'm just leaving."

"Thanks. I finished work early, so I'm signing her out and taking her to my Dad's for the weekend. I'll let the afternoon shift know."

"Okay. Uh, I have to go. Have a good weekend." I stepped out from behind the desk, brushed past him and rushed to the door, where I entered the code with trembling fingers. I looked back as the door closed behind me. He was gone.

Seeing Jay had confirmed my suspicions that I'd blown it that day when he'd asked me out for coffee. He'd been little more than polite just now. And if he hadn't been completely put off by my cold shoulder that day, the blast of icy formality today should have convinced him of my indifference.

I kicked myself all the way home, going over our conversations in my mind. I imagined how different things could have been if only I'd responded differently. I was attracted to him. He'd obviously been interested in me. So what was my problem?

You're scared, that's your problem. Of course I'm scared. It's not just me who could get hurt. I have Kayla to think about. Reasoning with myself only left me questioning my own sanity. It didn't help me feel any better about the situation.

I wasn't at all in the mood to go out that night and thought seriously about cancelling. I couldn't do it. Tracey had been so excited and I couldn't bear the thought of disappointing her. I would suck it up and go to the pub just long enough to make her happy.

Gran met me at the door when I walked into the house.

She had an excited smile on her face and an envelope in her hand. She held it out. "This came for you today. It's from the university."

I took it from her and turned it over in my hands.

"Oh for heaven's sake, Sarah. Open it!"

I ripped it open. A smile spread slowly across my face as I read it. I looked up at Gran. "I got in."

"Oh!" she cried in excitement, reaching out and pulling me in for a hug. "I knew you would. I'm so proud of you."

Mom was just as excited as Gran when she came home from work and heard the news. "It couldn't have worked out better that you're going out. You can celebrate with your new friend tonight and tomorrow night the four of us will go out somewhere special."

Suddenly, I was excited about going out with Tracey.

Kayla was excited as well. I so seldom dressed up that watching me get ready was a novelty for her. She sat on the bathroom counter and looked on in quiet fascination as I styled my hair and put makeup on. Kayla was always talking; in fact, she rarely stopped, so her silence was a little unnerving.

I swept a light coat of peachy gloss across my lips and turned to face her. "How do I look?"

She threw her arms around me. "You're beautiful, Mommy!" she cried.

I lifted her off the counter and carried her into my bedroom, where I tossed her playfully onto the bed and tickled her until she laughed uncontrollably. I stopped before it turned into hysterics, and blew a big, wet raspberry on her belly.

When Kayla's laughter subsided, she looked up at me and covered her mouth with her hand. Her eyes twinkled mischievously.

I tapped her forehead with my finger. "What's going on in that cute little head of yours?"

She giggled. "Your lipstick's all gone."

I touched my lips and laughed. "You're right. It's all over your belly." I pulled a tissue from the box on the nightstand and handed it to her. "Here, clean your belly while I put more lipstick on."

I pulled my gloss out of my pocket and reapplied, then wandered over to the closet. "Now, I need you to help me pick out something to wear."

We settled on a pair of black, skinny jeans, black boots with heels, and a bright turquoise, silky top that ended at the top of my thighs and hugged my curves a little too tightly for my comfort. Kayla's first choice had been a deep red, sheer blouse and mine, a plain, brown sweater, so we'd compromised.

* * *

The pub was busy, but not as crowded and noisy as it would be later in the evening. *The Queen's Corset* had been around as long as I could remember. It was clean and well kept, worn enough to be comfortable and small enough to be cozy. The menu was standard pub fare—hearty, stick-to-your-ribs type food.

I arrived early enough to get a booth and was sipping a margarita when Tracey sauntered into the pub fifteen minutes late with an excited smile on her face. The smile widened when she saw me and she practically skipped over to the booth, peeling her faded black leather jacket off as she went. The leopard print dress she wore hugged her body, showing off every curve. Long legs were encased in silky, black tights and huge gold hoop earrings brushed her shoulders with each step. She slid into the seat across from me and rubbed her hands together in anticipation. "Oh, man, do I need a beer. I've been so looking forward to this all day."

The waitress came over and I waited until Tracey had ordered her beer before I said, "Okay, tell me what happened today."

Tracey looked at me blankly for a second. "Oh, right. Dammit, I didn't wanna talk about work tonight."

"Then you should have waited for me after work instead of taking off so fast."

"Hey, it takes a while to get myself looking this good. I needed every spare minute."

I doubted it. She was just as gorgeous without all the makeup and sexy clothes. "So, what happened?"

"I sent Mrs. Martin in for her bath today and when I picked her up, she told me Sheila slapped her."

My mouth fell open. "Seriously? Did you find any marks?"

Tracey's face darkened. "No. When I asked her where, she pointed to the top of her head."

"Well, apparently Sheila's smarter than I gave her credit for. It's the only place you can hit someone and not leave a mark. Did you record it?"

The waitress came over with a tray full of drinks and placed a mug of frosty beer in front of Tracey. "Of course,"

Tracey said when she was gone. "Okay, enough about work. Let's talk about something else, something happy."

"I got accepted."

"Accepted for what?"

"I got a letter today. From the university."

Her eyes widened as my words finally sank in. "You—oh, my God!" She squealed in excitement. "I'm so happy for you. Dinner's on me tonight."

We chatted over crispy, beer-battered fish and chips, purposely talking about everything except Tranquility. We sat back as the waitress cleared away our dishes, holding our stomachs and laughing when she offered dessert.

"Another bite and I'll probably explode," Tracey groaned, "but I'll have another Guinness."

The waitress looked at me.

"Just water, please." I watched Tracey finish off the last of the dark beer in her glass. "I don't know how you drink that stuff on a full stomach."

She wiped her mouth with the back of her hand and belched. "S'cuse me," she said, giggling. "I make room for it."

I shook my head at her and laughed. She was incorrigible. Her bubbly, open personality attracted attention and made her approachable. Her wavy red hair, ivory skin and curvy figure made her sexy. Men had been shooting looks in her direction since we'd come in. She seemed oblivious to it, which only added to her charm.

"Oh, shit," she said.

So much for charm, I mused. "What's wrong?" I followed her gaze to the door.

Jay stood there, looking around the crowded room, but hadn't yet spotted us at our booth in the corner.

I leaned across the table. "What is he doing here?"

"I uh…might have invited him."

I shook my head in disbelief. "Pardon? When did this happen?"

My reaction was clearly not what she'd hoped for. She managed to look slightly remorseful. "This afternoon. I saw him when I was leaving work. We talked and…it just kind of happened. You know me, I always say too much. Before I knew it, I invited him."

"How did you know who he was? Have you ever even seen him before?"

"Duh. How could I *not* know? Look at him."

I glanced at Jay. He unbuttoned his coat as he scanned the room. She had a point.

"Anyway," she continued, "remember last Sunday when you were off? He came in with Lloyd when he brought Georgia back and I met them outside her room."

I tore my eyes away from him and leaned across the table. "Well, you could have at least told me."

"Sorry. I meant to. I kind of forgot. Besides, we said we had to do something, remember?"

He'd spotted us and was walking toward the booth. "No, *we* didn't. *You* did," I said quickly.

Tracey looked up and smiled innocently at Jay as he drew near. He avoided eye contact and played nervously with the keys in his hand. It was the first time I'd ever seen him look uneasy. I'd found his confidence attractive, but this nervous, awkward side of him was endearing.

He approached the table hesitantly.

Tracey smiled brightly. "Hey, Jay. You're just in time. Sarah got accepted to nursing school. You can help us celebrate. Have a seat." She gestured toward the length of empty bench beside me.

I gave her a look, but moved over to make room. When Jay didn't sit, I looked up at him questioningly.

He gave me a meaningful look and said quietly, "Are you sure? I don't want to intrude."

He looked so serious and sounded genuinely concerned. I felt a strange pressure in my chest. I'd practically eaten him up with my eyes the first time we'd met. He'd felt the attraction and acted on it, only to be met with cold rejection. The fact that he was there, trying again, said a lot.

I smiled and patted the seat beside me. "I'm sure."

Chapter 15
When Disaster Strikes

I WENT TO WORK THE NEXT morning feeling tired, but happy. I'd stayed out later than planned. A band had come on shortly after Jay joined us and the noise level had gone up a few notches. They played upbeat, toe-tapping, pub-appropriate music from bands like *The Fables* and *Great Big Sea*. One of Tracey's many admirers had finally found the nerve to ask her to dance.

Jay and I left her tearing up the small dance floor and went to a quiet café down the street where we talked over coffee until the waiter began putting chairs up on the tables around us.

I could still feel the warmth of his lips where they'd brushed my cheek before I got in my car to go home, and was distracted all morning thinking about that kiss. I forgot to unlock Edie's wardrobe and she had to come out into the hall in her nightgown to find me. I put Mrs. Sellers' sweater on backwards and had to dress the poor woman's top half twice. The whole morning was filled with one little blunder after another.

I blamed it on lack of sleep, but Edie wasn't fooled. "What's the young man's name?" she asked as we went into the dining room for lunch.

"I have no time for men, Edie."

She snorted in disbelief and went to take her seat.

Tracey was worse off than I was. She said she'd taken a cab home at midnight, but the three or four beers she'd consumed had left her a little groggy. For once I was glad I was working on a Saturday. At least the workload was a little lighter with a few of the residents out with their families.

Despite feeling tired and a little out of sorts, I was happier than I'd been in a long time. It wasn't only because of Jay. Being out with Tracey had also made me realize how right my mom was. I needed to get out more. And I needed a friend like Tracey to remind me that I was still young.

Life was good. I had a friend for the first time in a long time. The prospect of a romantic relationship was on the horizon. All my plans for school and the future were falling into place.

* * *

I was helping people with toileting and mouth care shortly after lunch. I sent Albert into the bathroom and stood outside reminding him of what to do. "Rinse your mouth, Albert. That's good. You can put your toothbrush away now...in the toothbrush holder on the counter in front of you. Now, do you need to use the toilet? No, Albert, I don't need to see it. Turn around, please."

Emily, the nurse on duty that day, poked her head around the corner. "Sarah, your mom called. She said it was important and to call her back on her cell as soon as you can."

I instructed Albert to wash his hands and hurried to the

nurse's station. I tried not to think of what could be wrong.

The last time my mom had called me at work was a year ago, when Kayla had fallen and split her lip open. *She must be out*, I thought, *otherwise she would have had me call the home phone*. I picked up the phone and punched in the number.

"Mom, what's wrong?" I asked as soon as she answered.

"Sarah," she sobbed. "I'm at the hospital. Gran's had another stroke—a bad one."

"Oh, my God. Where's Kayla?"

"I left her next door with Mrs. Curtis. Is that okay?"

"It's fine, Mom. I just have to let the nurse know I'm leaving. I'll be there as soon as I can."

I found Emily in the supply room stocking her cart, quickly explained what had happened, then hurried to the change room to get my things. I saw Tracey on my way there and told her as well.

Her face fell. "Shit. I hope she's okay. Call me if you need anything."

I waved my thanks and continued into the change room. The lock slipped through my fingers and clattered loudly to the floor when I opened my locker and I realized my hands were shaking. Resting my head against my locker, I took a deep breath. *Gran's okay. Mom needs you. Calm down.* I took another deep, steadying breath, grabbed what I needed, and left the room.

Edie was in the main hall, sitting in a quiet corner reading, when I rushed through with my coat and purse. She glanced at her watch then back at me in surprise. I gave her a quick wave. I could tell by the look on her face that she knew something was wrong, but I didn't stop. I knew Tracey would fill her in for me.

I nearly ran to the car, slipping and sliding on the snow-covered pavement. Panic set in again as I imagined all the things that might have happened. My fingers fumbled to insert the key in the ignition and I swore under my breath in frustration. Finally, I started the car and drove too quickly out of the parking lot, fishtailing as the old tires spun on ice.

Somehow, after a close call with a red light, I made it to the hospital and found Mom sitting in the ER waiting area. It was packed, but Gran would have been rushed through right away. Mom started crying when she saw me. I sat down on the hard plastic chair beside her, put my arm around her shoulders and pulled her close.

I looked around the room. It was as cold and impersonal as the nurse who sat at the triage desk assessing people with brisk efficiency. The walls were the same dingy white as the dirty snow banks that lined the streets. One of the fluorescent ceiling lights buzzed and flickered annoyingly overhead.

Beside us, a young couple fussed over their baby. She was wrapped in a pink blanket and cradled in her father's arms. I could hear the wheeze of her tiny lungs as she struggled to breathe.

The man sitting across from us had a blood-soaked bandage wrapped around his right index finger. His hand rested carefully on his lap atop a bloody towel. His weathered face was lined with dirt. Bits of sawdust stuck to his hair and his plaid, flannel shirt.

I'd been here with Gran after her last stroke. The people

were different, but the faces always had the same look of weary resignation.

Mom sat up and fished a tissue from her purse. She wiped the tears from her blotchy face and blew her nose. I slouched in my chair and rested my head on her shoulder.

I was startled awake by loud voices and a sudden gust of cold air. I lifted my head and rubbed the stiffness from my neck as I watched paramedics rush by with a man on a gurney. They wheeled him straight past triage, through the sliding doors, into the ER.

The man with the bloody finger sighed and shifted uncomfortably in his seat. Judging from the glum look on his face, he knew he'd been bumped further down the waiting list. The couple with the baby was gone. I assumed they'd been called in while I was dozing.

The doors opened. "Brenda Scott?"

Mom stood, gathered her purse and coat with trembling hands, and we followed the nurse as she led us through a maze of corridors and sliding doors and left us in a small waiting room. I sat in a big, comfortable armchair facing the TV and looked around the room. We were the only ones there. Mom sat across from me on a loveseat. She played nervously with her wedding ring, turning it round and round on her finger.

Dr. Chang, the neurologist, came in a few minutes later to talk to us about Gran's condition. She'd suffered a massive stroke caused by a blood clot in the brain. They'd done a CT scan, an EKG and administered a clot-dissolving medication. Gran was breathing on her own, but had not woken since having the stroke.

Mom sat unmoving while Dr. Chang spoke, her back rigid, hands clasped tightly in her lap, but the moment he walked out the door, her face crumpled and she collapsed into herself, sobbing. I sat beside her, put my arm around her shoulders and pulled her close. Tears eluded me. A ball of painful emotion burned in my chest, it pushed into my throat, choking me, but there was no release. I'd spent the past ten years holding back tears, pushing emotions deep inside so I could be the strong one. Now, more than ever, Mom needed me to be strong.

We were taken to her room in ICU an hour later. Mom went straight to Gran's side, took her hand and began sobbing softly. I stood behind her. There was nothing I could say that would console her, so I rubbed her back gently.

Gran looked weak and helpless and so much older. After the last stroke, she'd been awake by the time we saw her, and had even managed a lopsided smile. Within days, she'd been up walking with assistance and talking, though her speech had been slurred. I didn't need a doctor to tell me this time was different.

I gave Mom's shoulder a squeeze and walked around to the other side of the bed. I pushed a stray wisp of hair back from Gran's forehead. "When did it happen?"

Mom grabbed a tissue from a box on the table beside the bed. She wiped her eyes and took a long, shuddering breath. "I don't know. You know she likes to sleep late sometimes, so I didn't think anything of it when she didn't come down for breakfast. I tried to wake her about an hour later, but she—Oh, God, Sarah, I should have known something was wrong. I should have checked on her sooner." She pressed her hand to her mouth and began to cry again.

I reached across Gran and took Mom's hand. "You couldn't have known. She's strong. She got through it last time, she can again." I wished I felt as confident as I sounded.

I left a few minutes later to go home. Mrs. Curtis, a sweet lady who'd lived across the street since I was a little girl, had been watching Kayla for hours and I was sure her ears needed a break. She loved Kayla and said she enjoyed the company, but there's only so much constant chatter a person can take.

I filled Mrs. Curtis in on Gran's condition and thanked her for helping out. Kayla and I crossed the street hand in hand. I was trying to find a way to tell her about Gran when she asked, "Did you see Gran, Mommy?"

"I did."

"Did you talk to her?"

"No, munchkin. She was sleeping. She needs to rest so her body can heal."

"Nana was crying when she took me to Mrs. Curtis's house. It scared me," Kayla said as I unlocked the door and we went inside.

I picked her up. She wrapped her tiny arms around my neck and buried her face against me. "It scared me too," I said, giving her a big squeeze before I put her down. "Nana's upset, but she'll be fine, and the doctors and nurses are taking good care of Gran."

I left Kayla in the living room watching TV, and went upstairs to have a quick shower. When I came back down, she was kneeling at the coffee table, coloring, with a look of intense concentration on her face.

I walked over and crouched down beside her to look at the picture. The top half of the paper was blue with a bright yellow happy face sun and one white cloud. The bottom half was green with a white sidewalk through the middle where two people walked hand in hand. I pointed at the smaller figure with short, dark hair. "Is this you?"

She nodded and bit her lip as she continued to color the grass green with slow, deliberate strokes.

I pointed to the taller figure with dark hair and bright red lips and fingernails. "And this must be Gran."

Kayla finished coloring, put the crayon down and studied the picture in silence.

"It's a nice picture. Is it for Gran?"

She nodded again.

"Are you worried about her?"

She looked up at me. Her eyes shone with tears and her bottom lip trembled when she spoke. "I heard Mrs. Curtis talking on the phone. She said it wasn't good that Gran had two strokes and she might not sur-sur-"

"Survive?"

"She might not survive another one. That's what she said. What did she mean, Mommy?"

I moved to the couch, sat down and patted the seat beside me. Kayla climbed up, wiggled her bum back into the seat and looked at me expectantly.

"She means it's going to be harder for Gran to get better this time because her body's still weak from the last stroke." I placed a finger under her chin and smiled. "You know what Gran would tell us right now if she were here?"

"To keep our chins up?"

"Right. And not to worry, because worrying won't change a thing." I smiled reassuringly and pulled Kayla in for a hug. "The doctors and nurses are doing everything they can to help Gran get better, so I don't want you worrying, okay?" It was too bad I couldn't take my own advice.

I called into work and told them I wouldn't be in for the next couple of days. Mom and I took turns staying with Gran at the hospital and being home with Kayla.

Mrs. Curtis and Mrs. Faulkner, a good friend of Mom's, came over with enough food to last the rest of the week. It was a gesture I was thankful for simply because it meant one less thing to worry about.

I took Kayla to school Monday morning and did some laundry and cleaning before I went to the hospital. After Mom left to get some lunch and have a break, I looked at Gran's chart. *Patient unresponsive and unable to swallow.* Has shown no signs of recovery. I stared at her over the top of the clipboard. She was hooked up to a heart monitor and an IV for fluids and was receiving nutrition from a feeding tube.

"Damn it, Gran," I said, slamming the clipboard back into place at the end of the bed. "You can't leave us. We need you. *I* need you."

I turned her on her side and checked her skin carefully for any signs of redness. The nurse who came in while I was doing this gave me a strange look, but I knew they were often so busy that basic care was overlooked. My concern was for Gran, not for what the staff thought.

Dr. Chang came in and spoke to me briefly about

Gran's condition. He was concerned with her lack of progress. "Because she had the stroke while she was sleeping, there was no way to know how long it had been since it happened. There's only a small window of time when the clot-dissolving drugs are most effective. I'm afraid we may have missed it."

After Dr. Chang left, I sat in the chair beside Gran's bed and took her hand in mine. It was wrinkled and splotched with unsightly, brown age spots, the skin so paper-thin it was almost translucent. It seemed as though she'd aged overnight. I stroked her hand lightly with my thumb, letting her to know I was there with her.

It shouldn't be this hard, I thought. In palliative care, I'd held hands and spoken endless words of comfort, listened to deathbed confessions and offered up words of forgiveness that weren't mine to give. I watched people lying helpless in their own waste, a single tube to their stomach the only thing keeping them alive, prolonging their misery. I listened to their moans of pain as they struggled to breathe, as they waited to die.

This was different. This was my grandmother struggling to breathe. Waiting to die.

My head dropped forward and I rested my cheek against her hand. "Please don't leave me, Gran," I whispered as tears slid down my face.

* * *

I went back to work on Tuesday. Kayla was in school and Mom had taken a leave of absence from work. There was no need for both of us to be at the hospital all day. I would relieve Mom for a couple hours in the evenings, after I'd spent some time with Kayla.

The hardest part of going back to work was answering all the questions. They were well intentioned, but all I wanted to do was put my head down, do my work and not think about Gran for a while.

The expressions of sympathy were even worse. They brought all the emotions I'd worked so hard to push down deep, rising back to the surface. By mid-morning, one concerned look from Tracey was all it took to send me running to the bathroom. The pitying smiles tapered off as the day went on and I managed to get my emotions under control.

I went out for coffee with Tracey Wednesday after work. I only had an hour until I had to pick Kayla up from school, but I knew Tracey was worried about me and I needed to talk to someone.

"Hey," Tracey said when I sat down. "Feels like spring today."

It *was* almost spring, I realized. I glanced out the window. In typical Canadian fashion, the weather had gone from winter to spring-like in a day. It was a beautiful sunny day, warm enough for a light jacket. The dirty, grey snow banks were finally melting away. I hadn't even noticed until now.

"You doing okay?" Tracey asked.

"Yeah, I'm hanging in there. I'm tired. I'm worried about Gran… and Mom too."

"She's taking it hard?"

"Really hard. She barely eats. I know she doesn't sleep

much. She'd be there twenty-four-seven if she could."

"She'll be okay. She's lucky she has you to help her through it."

"I know, but she doesn't deal well with illness or death. She's never gotten over my dad. She still wears her wedding ring and it's been ten years."

"Wow, she's never dated anyone since?"

"No, she says no one could ever measure up to him."

"She doesn't have to marry them. She's young enough. I'm sure she still has needs. She could just—"

I cut her off quickly. "Please don't go there. She's my mom, remember?"

She shrugged. "Just sayin'. Hey, you talk to Jay this week?"

"No, I've barely had time to think about him. Why?"

"I find that hard to believe. He was asking about you when he brought Georgia back on Sunday. Probably thought you'd be working and he'd get to see you."

"I really have had too much on my mind to think about him. And I don't have his number anyway."

"S'ok, I talked to him Sunday and told him what happened. Anyway, he has your number, probably just doesn't wanna bother you right now."

"He doesn't have my number. I never gave it to him."

"Yeah, he does. I texted it to him."

"You texted it to him? So, you two text each other now?"

"Don't worry," Tracey said with a wink. "He's nice-looking, but not my type—too skinny. Paramedics are more my type. For now."

Chapter 16
No Proof, No Justice

IT WAS FRIDAY. SOMEHOW, I'D made it through the week.

I went into the dining room at lunchtime, pushing Mrs. W in her wheelchair ahead of me. Rose had gotten in the habit lately of sitting at Edie's table, so I'd started bringing Mrs. W to my table when I could get to her before Sheila did.

Tracey had warned me not to do it. "You're just asking for trouble," she'd said. But we weren't assigned certain residents in the dining room, we helped out wherever needed. Also, I think some twisted part of me was looking for trouble with Sheila. I wanted her to get angry enough to do something stupid.

It was a challenge feeding Mrs. W and keeping the others focused on their meals, and that was exactly what I needed to keep my mind off Gran.

Sheila still sat at her old table, but without Mrs. W to vent her frustrations on, she was much quieter. The first day I'd wheeled Mrs. W to my table, Sheila had glared at me. Now, she simply ignored me as she did Edie.

This was not for lack of trying on Edie's part. She'd

been doing her best to get on Sheila's bad side since the day she and Georgia had called Sheila out for her treatment of Mrs. W. I'd finally caught on to what she was doing and asked her about it one day.

"Well, my dear, I've an idea that if I annoy her enough, she'll eventually do something wrong." She leaned in close and whispered, "I've been acting forgetful around her too, so she thinks I've got the disease like the rest of 'em."

Even though I'd been doing the same thing, her confession concerned me and I'd told her so. "Oh, Edie, you're playing with fire. What if it works and she loses it when no one's around to help you?"

"Pfft, she doesn't scare me. I've lived with Anne, don't forget."

But all Edie's attempts at being annoying seemed to fall on deaf ears. Whatever Abby had said to Sheila that day must have worked enough for her to keep her mouth shut so long. Despite her silence, I could still see the anger and frustration simmering beneath her deceivingly composed exterior and had to wonder who she was taking her frustrations out on.

I got Mrs. W settled at the table, picked up her apron and placed it around her neck. When I lifted her hair to do up the snap, a strange red mark caught my eye. I pulled the apron back and looked more closely. There were faint red marks, like fingerprints, on either side of the base of her neck near the tops of her shoulders.

My eyes went automatically to Sheila. She was watching me. She looked away quickly and proceeded to cut Mr. Roberts' lasagna into pieces, even though he was capable of using a knife and fork. I fastened Mrs. W's apron and sat down to feed her. I didn't look at Sheila again, but I felt her eyes on me throughout lunch. I was sure the strange little marks were bruises left by fingers digging in to the flesh. And, even though I couldn't prove it, I strongly suspected those fingers belonged to Sheila.

I helped my residents get settled after lunch and went to find Abby. She was in the main hall near the nurse's station, giving Mrs. Amaral her insulin injection. I waited until she'd disposed of the needle and stripped off her gloves before I approached. "Abby, if you have a minute, I'd like you to look at some marks I found on Mrs. W's neck."

"What kind of marks?"

"I'm not sure. They looked strange to me and I thought you should see them." I wanted to see her reaction without my own suspicions influencing what she thought.

We walked into Mrs. W's room a few minutes later. Carol hadn't put her in bed for her nap yet. She was sitting in her wheelchair, looking out the window into the courtyard where chickadees flitted in and out of one of the many bird feeders strategically placed outside the windows.

I said her name, speaking softly to avoid startling her, and crouched down so we were eye level. "The nurse is here. She wants to take a look at some marks on your neck, okay?"

She grunted.

I stood, walked to the back of her chair and lifted the hair off her neck.

Abby leaned in for a closer look. When she straightened and looked at me her expression was hard. "When did you find these marks?"

"Today, just before lunch, when I lifted her hair to do

up her apron."

"And what was your first thought?"

"That they were bruises."

"Caused by?"

I hesitated. "Fingers. They look to me like bruises left by fingers."

Carol walked in and stopped short when she saw us. "What's going on?" she asked.

Abby motioned her over and showed her the marks. Carol peered at them. She put her fingers out and touched the bruises gently. "These weren't here yesterday. I would've noticed them when I brushed her hair."

"What about this morning?" Abby asked.

Carol shook her head. "She had a bath this morning. Sheila—" She stopped and a look of realization spread slowly over her face.

The three of us stood looking at one another in uncertain silence. I watched the expression on Carol's face change from outrage, to disbelief, to guilt, and knew she was already doubting her instincts and feeling bad for blaming Sheila.

It was time to say what everyone else was afraid to. "Abby, Sheila is—"

Abby put her hand up to stop me. "No, we're not naming any names or placing any blame. There's no proof of anything." She lowered her voice and gestured toward Mrs. W. "You've seen how aggravated people get when she screams and kicks and chases after them with her chair. It could have been anyone."

"But—"

"Sarah! I don't want to hear another word. Do you understand?"

It wasn't easy, but I shut my mouth. I knew how things worked and I needed to keep my job until school started.

"I'll take care of documenting this," Abby said before she left the room.

I let out the breath I'd been holding, unclenched my fists and looked at Carol accusingly. "You were thinking it too."

She shrugged. "She's right. There's no proof. What do you expect her to do?"

I was still seething with anger when I went to the nurse's station to do my paperwork. I purposely went early to avoid seeing anyone. Despite Abby insisting she would document the incident, I included it in my notes.

Before I left I did my rounds, going into Edie's room last. Mrs. Sellers was in bed, napping. Edie sat in her chair by the window, knitting.

"Off for the day are you?" she asked in a low voice.

I nodded hesitantly.

She dropped her knitting to her lap and looked at me more closely. "What's troubling you, lass?"

"Nothing for you to worry about, Edie. Just...work stuff." I crossed the room and leaned a hip against her bed.

"Is it the Dragon?"

"I can't talk about it here." I quickly changed the subject. "Did Abby talk to you this week?"

"About what, dear?"

"About setting up a meeting to discuss your situation. She told me she would talk to you this week."

"She didn't. But don't you worry yourself about it. It'll work itself out in time."

"But, Edie, you—"

"No, Sarah." She reached for my hand. "You've enough of your own troubles right now. You need to take care of your family and stop worrying about me. Besides, I've things to do before I leave this place."

I wasn't sure what Edie had meant by "things to do" and she'd refused to go into it further when I asked. I mulled it over on my way across the parking lot. I pulled my keys out of my coat pocket and was about to unlock my car, when I felt a hand on my shoulder.

I swallowed a startled cry, swung around quickly, and then let out a sigh of relief when I saw Jay.

"Sorry. I called you as I was walking over, but I guess you didn't hear me."

"No, I didn't. I was thinking about something. Are you here to see Georgia?"

"Actually, I had the day off today so I decided I'd pick her up early and take her to my Dad's for the weekend. I was hoping I'd catch you before you left. Tracey told me what happened to your grandmother. How're you doing?"

I shrugged. "I'm okay. It's been hard."

"Any change?"

"No, not really. It's a waiting game now."

"I'm sorry to hear that. Listen, I know you're busy dealing with everything right now. I just wanted to tell you, I had a good time last Friday. Maybe, when things settle down, call me and we can have dinner?"

I smiled. "I'd like that."

"Good. I'll text you my number. Tracey gave me yours. I hope you don't mind. I didn't want to text you until I was sure you were okay with it."

I thought of my conversation with Tracey and laughed. "No, it's fine. She told me she gave it to you."

I went home, had a quick shower and put on jeans and a t-shirt. I still had some time to kill before I went to get Kayla from school, so I phoned Tracey. I told her about Jay and laughed as she gloated good naturedly about how right she'd been. The conversation took on a more serious tone when I told her about the marks I'd found on Mrs. W.

"So, Abby's just gonna to do nothing?" she said. "It's ridiculous how they all protect each other. Why? Because she's been working there for thirty years?"

"Abby says there's no proof. And she's right. Mrs. W won't remember what happened, and even if she did, she can't put two words together well enough to tell anyone."

Tracey's voice rose in anger. "She should have been fired after what happened in the dining room that day. Even the other residents knew it was wrong. And she's alone with them every day in that room. Who the hell knows what she's doing in there?"

"I agree. Completely. I just don't know what to do about it. If we go over Abby's head, it's our word against theirs and, let's face it, we haven't been here long enough for our word to carry much weight. We could lose our jobs."

I hung up the phone, grabbed a jacket, and walked the few blocks to the school feeling a little lighter. I'm not sure why. Nothing had changed. Gran was still sick, and even after talking to Tracey, I still had no idea what to do about

Sheila. But I had Tracey on my side, a date with Jay to look forward to, and the warm sunshine on my face.

A few brave crocuses poked through the soil in the garden in front of the school. Another sure sign of spring. The bell rang and a swarm of small bodies came flooding out of the doors. I spotted Kayla right away in the bright pink jacket my mother had insisted on buying. Kayla's face lit up when she saw me. She sprinted toward me yelling "Mommy" and flew into my arms. Despite my problems, life was pretty damn good.

Chapter 17
In a Fit of Rage

SATURDAY MORNING AFTER BREAKFAST, I helped Lily and Beth prepare for an outing. It was their sixtieth birthdays and their aunt Helen was coming to take them out for the day. It was a rare event. Helen was well into her eighties and not in the best of health. She and her daughter, Cheryl, lived in a small town about an hour away and weren't often able to visit.

The twins were in their room, putting on makeup and doing their hair. They were excited at the prospect of going out. I listened to them chatter and bicker excitedly as I packed a small bag with some of the things they would need.

"Why does Cheryl have to come?" Beth asked. "She's always mean to us."

"Only to you. She likes me."

"No, Aunt Helen likes me better."

"Does not. I want the red lipstick, Beth. We can't both wear the same color."

They argued over the lipstick until Beth gave in and agreed to use a different shade. I imagined she had spent her whole life giving in to Lily.

"Okay, ladies," I said, opening the wardrobe, "time to

put on your coats and boots."

Beth looked at me blankly. "Why, where are we going?"

"It's your birthdays. Your Aunt Helen and your cousin, Cheryl, are coming to take you out."

They clapped their hands in excitement as though hearing it for the first time.

Ten minutes later, we walked into the main hall. Helen and Cheryl were at the nurse's station, signing the twins out.

"There they are," I said.

"Who?" Beth asked.

Lily sighed impatiently. "Aunt Helen and Cheryl," she said as they turned to greet us.

Beth looked from her aunt to her cousin in confusion. "But you're so old!" she blurted.

Helen laughed as she stepped forward for a hug. "Oh dear, Beth, you are so much like your mother. I've been old for many years. Have I really changed so much?"

I punched in the code and said goodbye as I held the door open for them. Sam, who'd been lurking near the aquarium, darted in behind the women and tried to sneak out with them.

"Sam," I said, taking him by the arm and guiding him back inside. "Just the guy I was looking for. I have a job for you."

I took him to the lounge, opened a cupboard in the entertainment center and pulled out a plastic bin filled with hundreds of buttons. I placed the bin on the table and began sorting the buttons into piles. "I need these sorted, Sam. See, there's a pile for brown, one for white, this one's for black...."

Sam sat down and started sorting. A few other residents wandered over to see what we were doing. I explained to them what to do, then stood back and watched as a few of them sat down to help Sam.

Satisfied I'd successfully distracted him from attempting to leave the unit, I went to Hall B to make beds. Tracey was off that day and Maria preferred to make her residents' beds on her own. I started at the far end of the hall with Mrs. Sellers' bed and worked my way toward the main hall.

I was working on Lily's bed when I heard Rose in the hallway. She stuttered more than usual and her voice was shrill with anxiety. "G-g-go away."

I was on my way to the door before I even heard John's voice.

"Stupid, ugly girl. You look like a pig." He made snorting noises as he followed Rose down the hall.

Rose began to cry. She covered her ears with her hands and tried to move away from him. He stayed right behind her, laughing and making pig noises over her shoulder.

I hurried down the hall to fall into step beside her, wrapped my arm around her shoulders, and pulled her protectively against my side. She stopped and hid her face in my shoulder.

John stopped a few feet away and looked at me uncertainly. I pointed toward Hall A. "Your room is that way, John. Why don't you go find it?"

"My room?" He looked around, taking in his surroundings as though he'd never seen them before. He squinted at me suspiciously. "What are you—?"

"John! I've been looking for you," Maria said, coming

out of the room behind us. He looked around in surprise. Before he could say a word, she took him by the arm and led him away. "Come into the solarium with me. Let's see if the cardinals are there."

He followed willingly, easily distracted by the mention of birds.

I sighed in relief. The look on his face before Maria had stepped in had made me a little uneasy. I pulled Rose in for a proper hug and rubbed her back comfortingly. "It's okay, Rose. He's gone."

I led her to her room where I helped her wash her face and blow her nose. I wiped the tears and snot off my shirt where she'd cried all over it and washed my hands. Before I left the room, I got her settled into her armchair and turned on her little TV.

I went to the twins' room to finish making their beds. When I went back to Rose's room a few minutes later, she was asleep in her chair. I turned the TV down and moved about the room quietly, tidying and making Rose's bed. Weekends were hard for her now that she'd become so attached to Georgia. She didn't know what to do with herself when Georgia was gone, and was more anxious and easily agitated.

Rose had come along late in her parents' lives. When her father had died, her mother had put Rose into Tranquility. A short time later, she'd passed away as well. Georgia had become like a surrogate parent to Rose. When she was gone, I spent a lot of time distracting Rose and finding things to keep her busy. Unfortunately, John also spent more time terrorizing her without Georgia around to act as her protector.

I left Rose and moved on to Sam's room. As soon as I walked in, I knew one of the men had relieved himself somewhere other than in the toilet. The smell of urine was strong. It hadn't smelled earlier when I'd come in to wake them, so it had likely happened right after breakfast.

I followed the smell to the wastebasket in the corner and sighed in relief. It could have been much worse. I pulled on a pair of gloves and exchanged the urine-soaked garbage bag with a clean one.

I was making Sam's bed when I heard a scream. *Rose.* I dropped the blanket and raced out of the room. Maria came out of a room across the hall and we ran to Rose's room together.

Rose lay on the floor in an awkward position, holding her left arm close to her body and moaning in pain. John paced in front of her, waving his hands and muttering under his breath. I tried to go to her, but he roared in anger when I moved toward them. Tracey, the one person who could occasionally calm him, wasn't there.

"John?" I said. No response. I repeated his name more loudly, trying to get his attention. Again, no response, but he was clearly becoming more agitated by the sound of my voice.

I glanced at Maria and whispered, "How did he get back here so fast?"

"I don't know. I left him in the solarium watching the birds. He seemed fine."

I shook my head in disgust. "He can't bloody well remember where his own room is half the time, but he has no trouble finding Rose's."

"Amazing how their minds work sometimes isn't it? I'm going into the bathroom to ring the call bell. Need to get some help in here." Maria moved away slowly, keeping a wary eye on John.

Rose's moaning had turned to painful sobs. Judging by the awkward angle of her arm and the way she cradled it, I guessed it was broken. I moved to the wall and edged my way slowly toward her.

John stopped pacing and moved directly in front of me. His fists were balled at his sides and his expression was hard. "Stay away."

"John, I'm going to see Rose. She's hurt. I need to help her."

"Mind your own damn business," he growled. He began to pace again slowly, keeping his eyes on me the whole time. His body was taut as though ready to pounce.

A shiver of fear went through me. I saw Maria out of the corner of my eye and was relieved when she was standing beside me again.

"Done," she said. "Let's hope someone notices it."

Rose struggled to sit up, but couldn't push herself off the floor with one arm. The injured arm was left dangling and hit the floor as she slumped back down. She screamed in pain.

John marched over to where she lay, looked down at her and yelled, "Shut-up!"

Rose curled into a ball, cradling her arm against her trembling body, and began to sob softly.

John seemed to lose interest in her and went back to

pacing. His mutterings were interspersed with loud outbursts and wild arm gestures.

I tried again to sneak past while he was distracted, but he put himself between me and Rose. I cupped my hand over my mouth and spoke so only Maria could hear. "Do you think you can distract him, so I can go to Rose?"

"Don't you think we should wait for help?"

"No one else here is going near him. We'll have to wait for the police like last time."

Maria looked skeptical.

"Look, if I don't go to her, he might hurt her again."

She sighed in resignation. "Fine. What do you want me to do?"

I refrained from rolling my eyes. *Think of something*, I thought. "I don't know, put something between you and him and say something to get his attention. Just don't let him get between you and the door."

Maria went to the side of Rose's bed closest to the door, putting the bed between herself and John. She said John's name three times loudly before he finally looked at her. "Why don't you come to the lounge with me, John? I'll get you something to drink and you can watch TV."

He laughed hysterically. "Something to drink? I'd love a Scotch, but the bitch won't let me!" He bellowed the last word and pounded his fist against his chest as he swung around to face Maria. He leapt at the bed.

Maria shrieked and jumped back, nearly tripping over her feet in her haste. She backed right out the door as John proceeded to rip apart the bed I had just made so carefully.

I ran behind John to where Rose lay, took her right

hand in mine and whispered, "It's okay, Rose. I'm here."

Maria stood outside the room, calling down the hall for help.

John was in a complete rage now. He tore Rose's sheets off the bed and threw her pillow and blankets across the room. "Get me a Goddamn drink. I want a drink!" He pulled the mattress off the bed, heaved it onto the floor, and kicked it. It slid wildly across the floor, stopping at Rose's feet.

I worked quickly, keeping an eye on John while I checked Rose's head, face and joints for any signs of injury. I was careful not to touch the arm, but could see it was bent at an unnatural angle. It was definitely broken.

John became quiet suddenly. I glanced up to see him looking around the room. His gaze settled on the chair in the corner and he strode across the room toward it.

Oh, shit, I thought. I scrambled across the floor, grabbed the end of Rose's mattress and pulled it toward me. The sound of voices in the hall registered vaguely in my mind as I leaned back and pulled the mattress over Rose and me. "Look out!" I yelled, peering out from under the edge of the mattress.

The chair hit the wall beside the door, broke and crashed to the floor just as Carol and Emily appeared with Maria. They threw their arms over their heads, jumped back and crouched down against the wall in the hallway.

Emily peeked through her fingers at me and Rose huddled under the mattress. "Stay there, Sarah," she said, coming slowly to her feet. "I'm going to get help." She disappeared down the hall.

John seemed to have gotten the worst of the rage out of his system with that last violent outburst. He went back to pacing and mumbling under his breath.

Carol stood in the doorway, taking in the scene inside the room. Maria hung back in the hallway. Neither of the women made any move to step inside the room. I didn't blame them, but John no longer concerned me now that he'd calmed down. My concern at the moment was for Rose, who was still whimpering in pain.

Watching John from the corner of my eye, I crept to Georgia's bed and grabbed her pillow and a blanket. I hurried back to Rose, whispering words of comfort as I tucked the pillow under her head and covered her with the blanket.

Maria quietly filled Carol in on what had happened. A few curious residents milled around in the hallway outside the door. Carol gathered them up and sent them down the hall toward the lounge.

I sat down beside Rose, took her hand in mine, and waited.

Police and paramedics arrived within minutes of each other. John became violent again when he saw the police. It took two burly cops and a paramedic to bring him under control enough to strap him to a gurney. Two paramedics left with John. He cursed and struggled all the way out the door. Kyle, the paramedic Tracey was now seeing, and his partner, checked Rose over carefully and prepared to take her to the hospital for x-rays and treatment. It broke my heart to see her taken away, frightened and crying, but Kyle was surprisingly gentle with her.

I spoke to the police, answered their questions and filled them in on the details of the incident. After they left, I went to the nurse's station to fill out an incident report. As I pulled out the binder and sat down at the desk, I caught myself thinking that I had a good story to tell Mom and Gran that night. *But Gran's not there.* The thought hit me like a punch to the gut, knocking the wind right out of me. I let my head drop into my hands as I struggled to breathe.

"Sarah? What's wrong, lass?"

I took a deep, unsteady breath and looked up to see Edie peering over the top of the desk with a concerned look on her face. "Nothing. Just a bit of a headache."

"More than a bit, I'd say. You're as white as a ghost. Do you want me to get the nurse?"

"No, Edie. Thanks for your concern, but I'm fine."

"You're not fine," she said, pointing a chastising finger in my direction. "You're tryin' to do too much. You need to take some time for yourself now and then."

I thought of Kayla, Mom and Gran. They all needed me in different ways. By the end of the day, the only time I had for myself was for sleeping. I managed a weak smile. "I'll try."

CHAPTER 18
FIRST DATE

I PICKED KAYLA UP FROM her friend Amelia's house on my way home from work. Mom had dropped her off there a few hours earlier, and then had gone to spend some time with Gran at the hospital.

I put a movie on for Kayla to watch while I showered and changed. She was still immersed in it when I came out of my bedroom, so I wandered into the kitchen to make myself a cup of tea.

I plugged in the kettle and checked my phone for messages. There were a few texts from Tracey describing the various forms of torture she was certain would be less painful than the boredom of spending a cold, rainy Saturday in March at home, alone. *Wish u had day off so we cud b bored 2gether*, was the last message she'd sent. I would call her before I went to the hospital to relieve Mom. But first, I would take Edie's advice.

I called Jay. He sounded out of breath when he answered and I could hear voices and the clang of metal in the background. "Did I get you at a bad time?" I asked.

"No, I'm just finishing up at the gym. I'm heading into the showers. Can I call you back in twenty?"

It felt like the longest twenty minutes of my life.

I took my tea into the living room and snuggled on the couch with Kayla. We watched as Marty the zebra was shot from a cannon. He flew through the air gracefully and then hit the side of a cliff. Kayla burst into giggles. She'd watched it countless times since getting it for Christmas the year before and still laughed uncontrollably at the animals' antics.

My phone vibrated inside my sweater pocket. I kissed Kayla's head, lifted her off my lap and set her on the couch before I went into the kitchen to answer it.

"Hi, Sarah. Sorry about that," Jay said.

"No, no, it's fine." I felt nervous suddenly. "I, uh, was calling to see if you were still interested in dinner."

He chuckled softly. "Of course I am. Are you busy tonight?"

I started to object to the short notice and caught myself. I'd already messed up with him once and gotten a second chance. I would make tonight work.

We made plans for seven. That would give me time to go to the hospital for a couple of hours before dinner. I felt a twinge of guilt when I sent Mom a text asking if she minded watching Kayla. I was sure she'd be tired from her day at the hospital, but I also knew Kayla would be a welcome distraction from her worries.

I blow-dried my hair and put on makeup while Kayla finished watching the movie. She came running into the bedroom as I was putting on a pair of silver hoop earrings. "Mommy, why do you look so pretty? Are you going out?"

"I am. Nana's coming home soon to look after you. I'm going to the hospital to see Gran, then out for dinner with a friend."

"With Tracey?"

"No, with Jay, the guy I had coffee with." I put on lipstick, checked my teeth in the mirror and put the tube in my purse. I smiled when I thought of how often I'd watched Gran do the exact same thing.

"Is he hansome, Mommy?"

"Yes, very handsome, and nice and charming. And he smiles a lot and has big dimples."

"As big as mine?"

I gave her a wide-eyed look of wonder. "Maybe even bigger." I picked up my purse and took Kayla's hand as we left the bedroom. "I think we have time for a card game before Nana gets home."

"Go Fish!" Kayla yelled, charging into the living room to find a deck of cards.

I breathed a sigh of relief, glad for once that she had such a short attention span. The tough questions had been avoided for the time being.

* * *

Before I went to the hospital, I called Tracey and filled her in about the incident with John and Rose.

She was outraged. "Damn it, why don't they listen to us? I told Abby John was dangerous. She knew he was harassing Rose. They never do anything about it until it's too late."

"I know, Trace. It's the same with Sheila. The nurses know what she's like, but they won't do anything about it until she hurts someone so badly they have no choice."

Tracey sighed in exasperation and changed the subject.

"I need to get out of this apartment. I was so bored today I actually cleaned. Wanna go out tonight?"

I felt a twinge of guilt. "I can't, sorry."

"Oh, c'mon, don't give me that crap about having to work tomorrow. I have to—"

"Tracey, I have a date tonight."

"Oh. Oh! Good. With Jay?"

"Yeah, we're going out for dinner."

"Don't forget to stop at the drugstore."

I laughed. "My God, Trace, it's our first real date."

"So? I want all the juicy details tomorrow."

"There won't be any juicy details."

I could practically hear her pouting through the phone when she said, "You're no fun. And what am I supposed to do tonight?"

"I don't know. Call Kyle."

"Yeah, I guess. He was my second choice anyway."

"Poor guy," I said. "I'm sure you'll make it up to him. In fact, maybe *you* should make a trip to the drugstore."

"Pffft, I don't think so. He moves slower than a herd of turtles stampeding through peanut butter."

I was still laughing when I hung up the phone a few minutes later.

* * *

It had been a week since Gran's stroke and there was still no change. She drifted in and out of consciousness, never speaking and barely moving. Her breathing was labored and because she was immobile, she was at risk for pneumonia. The head of her bed was kept in a raised position to help keep her lungs clear.

I stood at the side of the bed stroking her hair lightly as I told her about my day. She moaned and turned her head to the side. A trail of drool ran from her mouth, down her chin and I wiped it gently away with a tissue. Fishing an ice chip from the cup on the nightstand, I ran it across her lips. She turned her head toward it eagerly, like a baby rooting instinctively at the breast. I left it a second longer, letting her savor this one last pleasure. She sighed when I took it away.

Her breath hitched, becoming shallow and uneven. She moaned and I reached out to smooth her wrinkled brow with a cool hand. Despite the drugs, I knew she was in some pain. I wished I could make it stop, but in that way I was as helpless as she was.

I checked her for signs of skin breakdown and did her exercises. It was important, since Gran couldn't move herself, to keep her muscles active in order to prevent muscle atrophy. When I'd finished the exercises, I repositioned her and placed pillows strategically to protect pressure points like elbows and heels. I still had an hour before I went to meet Jay, so I sat down and read out loud from a book Mom had left. I often spoke to Gran, or read to her when I visited, hoping the sound of my voice would be comforting to her. This time was for my benefit as well. It kept my mind off my date with Jay.

I wasn't overly nervous about the date itself. We'd hit it off well that night at *The Queen's* and conversation had come easily. I was nervous because I'd decided to tell Jay about Kayla tonight. Technically, it was only our first date, but somehow this was different than other first dates. I felt I needed to tell him.

* * *

I met Jay in the parking lot of the restaurant at seven sharp and we walked in together. He'd suggested the place, a cozy little bistro off the main street. The bar area and lobby were scattered with people waiting for tables. Luckily, Jay had thought to call ahead and make a reservation and we were seated quickly.

I'd never been there. I rarely went out for dinner and when I did I usually went to *The Queen's*. The bistro was higher end than the pub. The atmosphere was intimate and romantic, with private booths, dim lighting and jazz playing softly in the background.

I ordered a steak, medium-rare. Jay gave me a curious look and ordered the same. We talked over glasses of red wine while we waited for our food. We discussed my plans for school. He talked about his four years of university. He'd graduated with a degree in business and now worked for a medical company doing sales and marketing.

I watched Jay talk as I ate, so fascinated with his full, supple lips that I barely tasted the food. Just as I was wondering if his lips were as soft as they looked, he said my name. My eyes flew to his. "Pardon?"

His eyes sparkled with humor as he picked up his napkin and dabbed at his mouth. "I was asking if I had food on my face."

"Uh, no." I glanced at his mouth, saw the teasing curve of his lips and felt the heat of a blush climb my neck. When I looked up, his smile faded and heat flashed in his eyes. *Breathe, Sarah*, I thought to myself as I laid my fork carefully on the side of my plate. "That was delicious."

Jay looked at my plate and smiled. Only a dollop of mashed potatoes and a few vegetables remained. "I'm glad you actually eat when you go on a date."

I gave him a perplexed look. "Why wouldn't I?"

"Some women don't, especially on the first date. It drives me crazy. Of course, most women wouldn't order a steak either."

"Why not? I love steak."

"Exactly!" A confused look came over his face. "But when my sister goes on a date, she orders a salad, eats half of it, goes home and orders pizza. I don't get it."

After dinner we ordered coffee and the conversation turned to family. It was the opening I needed. "Your niece is adorable. How old is she?"

It was clear from the tenderness in his voice that he was fond of his nieces. "Alisha? Yeah, she's pretty special. They both are. She's six. Her little sister, Amanda, is four."

"My daughter, Kayla, is six too."

Jay barely skipped a beat. "And adorable too, I bet, if she looks anything like her mom."

"Actually, she has her dad's smile and my Mom's eyes. She really doesn't look anything like me."

"You're still adorable. Especially when you blush."

I felt my face get hotter and put my hands over my cheeks. "Stop," I said with a short, flustered laugh.

He smiled apologetically and said "Sorry" but he was enjoying my discomfort too much for his remorse to be genuine.

"Seriously, are you not surprised by what I just told you?"

"What, that you have a daughter? Should I be?"

I frowned, a little perplexed by his reaction. "Most guys would be halfway out the door by now."

"I'm not most guys."

* * *

The next day at work, I told Tracey about the date as we made beds. "He's right," I said as I pulled my side of the sheet tight and tucked the corner under. "He's *not* like most guys. He's too good to be true, which makes me think there has to be something wrong with him."

"Sure, like he probably smokes crack. Or maybe he has a tail. You should check it out on the next date, just so you know how you feel about it before things get serious."

I stopped working and stared at her.

She shrugged her shoulders and raised a brow. "What? Okay, so he probably doesn't have a tail, but he's not perfect—nobody is. Stop waiting for something to go wrong and enjoy the moment."

I left Tracey to finish the last beds on her own and headed to the main hall to wait for Rose. She was on her way back to Tranquility. They'd put a cast on her arm and kept her overnight for observation. The halls were quiet. Most of the other residents were in the auditorium attending the morning church service.

I thought about what Tracey had said. She was right. Since Dad's death, I'd been living my life as though something bad waited around every corner. I was twenty-five years old. I should be enjoying my life and looking forward to the future.

Rose was brought back to Dementia in a wheelchair.

Her legs were carefully wrapped in a blanket. Her arm was in a cast and supported across her chest by a sling. She was smiling.

It was Kyle who wheeled her in. He nodded at me as he parked the chair near the nurse's station. He put his hand on Rose's shoulder, bent over and said, "I'll be right back, Rose."

Rose looked up at him and smiled brightly. He left her and walked toward me.

I stepped out from behind the desk, closing the half door behind me. "How is she?"

"Good. Nurse said it was a clean break. Should heal up fine."

"Why do you look worried then?"

"The guy who hurt her, is he here?"

"No. I don't think he'll be coming back."

Kyle's expression darkened. "I hope not." He went back to Rose, crouched down in front of her and unwrapped the blanket from around her legs. He lifted one foot, flipped the footrest up and placed her foot gently on the floor, then repeated this with her other foot. He handled her like a piece of delicate china.

Rose stared at the top of his head and smiled dreamily. She reached out with her good hand and stroked his short brown hair.

Kyle looked up and smiled tenderly. "Let's get you out of this chair." He stood and lifted her easily to her feet in one motion.

Rose was a little unsteady after being off her feet so long. She clung to Kyle's arm with her one good hand and gazed up at him. He was so tall that she looked like a child standing next to him.

"It looks like they took good care of you, Rose," I said.

She nodded distractedly, still smiling up at Kyle.

"Would you like to come with me?" I continued. "We'll go to your room. You can freshen up, put on some clean clothes…Rose?" She wasn't paying attention to me at all. I blinked a few times and smiled wryly at Kyle.

He let go of Rose slowly and held her hand as he explained, "Rose, you're home now. You need to go with…"

"Sarah," I said.

"You need to go with Sarah now."

Rose looked at me as though she'd never seen me before. She hid her face in Kyle's arm and whispered, "D-don't want to."

"She'll take good care of you. I promise."

Rose shook her head forcefully. "You take care of me."

"I can't. I have to go back to work."

I tried again. "It's almost lunchtime, Rose. I'll help you pick out something nice to wear. We'll do your hair and find a pretty color of lipstick." She peeked at me and I knew I finally had her interest. I held my hand out to her and smiled.

She hesitated and looked up at Kyle.

He nodded his head encouragingly. "Go with Sarah, Rose. I'll visit you soon, I promise." He put his hand on her back and guided her toward me.

I took her good arm and patted it reassuringly as I looked up at Kyle and said, "I'll let you out."

He folded the blanket and placed it on the seat of the

wheelchair before following me to the door. Rose shuffled along after him, nearly crashing into his back when he stopped. I punched in the code.

Kyle turned to Rose. He bent down, kissed her cheek and muttered, “Bye, Rose.” As he straightened, he glanced at me self-consciously, cheeks flushed as though embarrassed by his show of affection.

I smiled at him and held the door open as he pushed the empty wheelchair through. I gazed thoughtfully at the door for a moment after I let it close. I had a feeling there was more to Kyle than there appeared.

Rose made an impatient sound and I led her toward her room. “You liked that guy, didn’t you, Rose?”

She nodded enthusiastically. The silly smile was back. “He liked me too.”

She didn’t remember Kyle an hour later when I took her to the dining room for lunch, but for a short time he had made her feel special. I would have to talk to Tracey about him. I had a feeling he could be a keeper.

Chapter 19
March Break

IT WAS MARCH BREAK. I'D requested my two days off that week be consecutive and booked an extra day as well, which meant I had three days in a row to spend with Kayla.

It rained Monday, so Kayla and I spent the day inside by the fireplace playing games and watching movies. I lost three games of rummy before I finally gave up and suggested we bake cookies. "We'll make peanut butter. They're Nana's favorite. She'll be so happy when she comes home from work and smells them."

"Can we take some to Gran at the hospital, Mommy?"

I hesitated, choosing my words carefully. "Gran can't eat cookies right now, munchkin. It's nice of you to think of her though."

Kayla looked thoughtful. Her normally animated expression was sombre. "I miss Gran. Why can't I go see her?" Her brown eyes filled with tears.

I pulled her in for a hug. "I know you miss her, sweetie, but no one under sixteen is allowed in that part of the hospital. As soon as she's well enough to go to a regular room, I'll take you to see her. Sound good?"

Kayla wiped her eyes on my shirt and swiped her hand

across her nose. "Sounds good. Can we make cookies now?"

"As soon as you wash your snotty hands. Gross!" I swatted her bum playfully as she ran off to the bathroom giggling. As quickly as that, she was back to her normal, exuberant self.

We baked the cookies, then moved on to making spaghetti for dinner. Kayla chopped mushrooms while I made meatballs. Mom came home to the smell of fresh-baked cookies, frying meatballs and the God-awful sound of Kayla and me loudly singing "On Top of Spaghetti".

After dinner I left Kayla with Mom and went to the hospital to spend some time with Gran. I was beginning to dread the nightly trips through the cold, depressing hallways. I hated seeing Gran so frail and helpless. I was watching her slowly die, just as I'd watched my dad die. It wasn't how I wanted to remember her. But I did it, and would continue to do it, for her and for Mom.

I left the hospital when visiting hours ended at eight. I turned my phone on as soon as I left the ICU and checked my messages. Jay had sent me a message an hour earlier. I texted him before I left the parking lot and we agreed to meet for coffee.

I darted into the coffee shop, shaking the rain off my head. It was a miserable, cold rain that was supposed to turn to snow sometime through the night.

Jay was sitting at a small table near the window. He stood to greet me and brushed a kiss across my cheek. He'd already bought me a decaf. "Thanks," I said, shrugging out of my coat. Jay took it and hung it on the back of the chair. I sat down, took a sip of coffee, closed my eyes and sighed.

"Long day?"

I opened my eyes and looked at him. His eyes were distractingly green today. "Actually, today was the first of three days off. Kayla's on March break this week, so I booked some time to spend with her." I thought of her non-stop chatter and boundless energy and laughed. "She has a lot of energy. Spending the day with her might be more tiring than working."

Jay laughed too and I caught myself staring at his dimple. "My nieces are the same way. They don't stop until they go to sleep." He became serious suddenly and reached across the table for my hand. "How's your grandmother doing? Any change?"

"No, no change. It's been a week and a half. I'm starting to think there won't be a recovery." His hand tightened around mine. I looked down at my coffee and blinked the tears away. The sudden show of emotion made me feel uncomfortably vulnerable. I pulled my hand free, plucked a napkin from the dispenser and dabbed at the corners of my eyes. I kept the napkin balled tightly in my fist and rested both hands on my lap.

Jay looked disconcerted. "Sorry, I didn't mean to upset you."

I snorted in derision at my own lack of control. "It doesn't take much lately. There's just…a lot going on right now." I smiled a little too brightly and changed the subject. "What about you? Anything new?"

"Actually, my company is sending me to New York for a few days for a training seminar. That's why I wanted to see you tonight. I leave tomorrow."

"Nice. Have you ever been?"

"No. It'll be my first time. I'm hoping I have time to do some sightseeing."

I felt a pang of jealousy. The one thing I'd always wanted to do was travel. When I was young, Dad and I had spent hours looking at maps and travel magazines. After he died, I threw them all away, and with the state my life was in now, travelling was the last thing on my mind. "I'd like to go to New York someday. I've never travelled anywhere unless you count Niagara Falls."

I must have sounded wistful, because Jay wrapped his arm around my shoulder, kissed the top of my head and said, "You will. Someday, you'll go."

Jay walked me to my car about an hour later. The rain had turned to wet snow that melted as soon as it touched the ground. I dug my keys out of my pocket and turned to him. "Well, have a good trip. Call me when you get back, maybe we can have dinner again."

His mouth curved teasingly. "Maybe." His arm went around my waist. "Are we considering this a second date?"

"We—we can."

He pulled me closer. "Good. That means I get to kiss you."

* * *

The next morning, I took Kayla to the library. We watched a magic show together before I left her in a room full of boisterous five- to seven-year-olds for an hour of crafts. I wandered upstairs to the peace and quiet of the reading area, picked out a book and sat in a comfy armchair near the window to wait. My eyes skimmed the same paragraph three times before I gave up and gazed out the window. The weather had changed overnight. It was snowing again. Big, wet flakes stuck to everything, covering the city in a blanket of white.

I'd gone to bed the night before, and woken up that morning, thinking about Jay and the kiss. It had been brief and innocent. Why then, could I not stop thinking about the softness of his lips or the way his hand had curved possessively around my neck?

I sighed in resignation, got up and put the book back where I'd found it. I wandered around and looked at the artwork. Paintings and sculptures from various local artists filled the many rooms and hallways of the sprawling building. The library itself, with its clean, simple lines, walls of glass, and exposed steel beams, was a work of contemporary, structural art.

I went down the floating staircase with its glass rail panels to the main floor and sat on a bench outside the craft room to wait for Kayla. My phone vibrated. I dug around in my purse until I found it. It was a text from Tracey. *Day off. Meet 4 lunch?*

Kayla and I left the library and went to a diner near the hospital. Tracey came in shortly after and I introduced her to Kayla. They hit it off right away, bantering back and forth and teasing each other throughout the meal. Tracey was her usual fun loving, witty self, though I suspected she turned it down a notch when Mom joined us.

Mom excused herself soon after she finished eating. She gave Kayla a hug and kiss, and told her how much she looked forward to having her all to herself at the end of the week.

Kayla glowed. Their affection for one another was obvious.

Mom turned to Tracey and said, “It was very nice meeting you, finally. I’ve heard so much about you the past few months. Sarah needs a friend like you to get her out of the house more often.”

I rolled my eyes. “Mom, really?”

After she left, Tracey said, “I like your mom. You’re a lot like her, aren’t you?”

Before I could answer, Kayla said, “I’m not.” She bounced in her seat as she ate a bowl of ice cream. “I jus look like Nana, but my pers-pers—”

“Personality,” I finished for her. “And it’s rude to interrupt.”

“Sorry. My persnality is like my dad. He’s dead and so’s my grampa. I have pictures of them. You should come to my house and see them.”

“I should. But not right now.”

Kayla’s face fell. “Why not?”

“’Cause I’m taking you and your mom bowling.”

Kayla’s eyes went wide. She looked at me and I nodded in affirmation. She dropped her spoon and clapped her hands. Melted ice cream flew out of her mouth as she exclaimed, “I knewed I would love you, soon as I saw you.”

Tracey let Kayla give her a sloppy ice cream kiss. She looked at me, stuck her bottom lip out, and mouthed, “Oh, my God.” She was hooked.

By the time we finished bowling, Kayla and Tracey were fast friends. We walked out of the bowling alley into the parking lot. Most of the snow had already melted away in the afternoon sun. Kayla skipped along between Tracey and me with her hands in ours. Every few steps, we lifted her off the ground and swung her through the air. Each time, she squealed and laughed in delight, begging breathlessly for more.

When we got to the car, Kayla threw her arms around Tracey's waist. "You should come to our house for dinner." She turned to me excitedly. "Can she, Mommy?"

Tracey began to protest, but I cut her off saying, "Of course she can. We're making homemade pizza."

"I dunno...."

"You're coming," I insisted.

"Pleeeeease?" Kayla begged. She looked up at Tracey, bottom lip out, eyes wide and pleading. It was a hard face to say no to.

"Okay, okay, I'll come, but I'm gonna help make pizza."

* * *

My phone buzzed as we sat down to eat. It was Mom. I knew something was wrong as soon as I heard her voice.

"They think Gran's had another stroke."

"I'll be there as soon as I can."

"But, what about Kayla?"

"Mom, don't worry. I'll figure it out. I'll see you soon."

"Was that Nana, Mommy? Is she comin' home for pizza?"

"No, sweetie, Gran's—" I swallowed hard and looked away, blinking back tears. I pulled Kayla against me and stroked the top of her head. "Gran's having some trouble and I need to go to the hospital. I'll call Mrs. Curtis and see if she minds watching you."

"I can stay with Kayla," Tracey said.

Kayla pulled away and bounced in her chair. "Yes, please, Mommy. It's boring at Mrs. Curtis's house. Please, Mommy, please?"

"Are you sure?" I asked Tracey.

"Absolutely. We're gonna look at photos. Kayla can tell me all about her dad and her grandpa. And then, maybe we'll watch a movie."

Kayla bobbed her head enthusiastically. "Please, Mommy, I'll be so good, I promise."

"Okay, but if I'm not home by nine, I want you to get ready for bed. Deal?"

"Deal! Thank you, Mommy." She jumped down off her chair and came around the table to give me a quick hug before she ran into the living room, yelling, "I'm getting the pictures."

I managed a trembling smile for Tracey. "Thanks."

She put her hand on my arm comfortingly. "It's no problem, really. This is way better than going home to an empty apartment. Go—be with your mom. I'll stay as long as you need me to."

I nodded as I walked away, unable to speak past the tightness in my throat, and grabbed my purse and coat on the way out the door. The drive to the hospital was excruciating. My fingers drummed impatiently on the steering wheel at every light. I swore under my breath at every slow driver. The parking lot was packed and I drove up and down every row before finally finding a spot at the very back.

There was a line at the parking booth. I shoved my hands in my pockets and tried not to look annoyed while two elderly women inserted four dollars worth of quarters into the machine, bickering the whole time. They were a quarter short. They dug through their purses, each blaming the other for not counting the money correctly. I reached into my coat pocket, pulled out a quarter and held it under their noses. They thanked me profusely, while I gritted my teeth waiting for them to finish. When they left, I pushed a five-dollar bill into the slot, grabbed my change and practically ran into the hospital.

I panicked a little when I walked into Gran's room in the ICU and found it empty. Was I too late? I found Mom sitting in the waiting room down the hall. Her face looked weary and drawn with worry.

"They took her for tests," she said in a flat voice.

I fell into the seat beside her, still trying to catch my breath, and took her hand. "What happened to make them think she had another stroke?"

"I'm not sure. She was having trouble breathing. The alarm on the machine went off. The nurse came in and said that the heart monitor showed abnormal readings and her oxygen level was low."

Mom's hand trembled in mine. She took a deep, quavering breath before she continued. "She stopped breathing. Alarms went off, people came running in…I didn't know what was happening. I heard someone say something about another stroke and intubating her. They made me leave. I felt so helpless." She began to cry.

I put my arm around her, pulled her close and comforted her as she cried into my shoulder. It was all I could do.

CHAPTER 20
THEORIES AND ASSUMPTIONS

I LEFT THE HOSPITAL SHORTLY after nine, knowing Tracey had to work early the next morning. We still hadn't heard anything regarding Gran's condition, so before I left, I went to the nurse's station. All they were able to tell me was that she'd been stabilized and was still upstairs awaiting more tests. There was nothing we could do but wait. I tried to convince Mom to come home and get some sleep, but she insisted on staying until Gran was brought back to her room so she could see her.

Kayla was ready for bed, but still up, cuddled on the couch with Tracey, watching a movie when I got home. Thankfully, she was too tired out from her busy day to ask questions and went right to bed after Tracey left.

I went to bed shortly after Kayla, but lay awake, tossing and turning, too upset to sleep. I was still awake when I heard Mom come home shortly after midnight. I finally fell into a fitful sleep and woke early Wednesday morning feeling as though I'd barely slept. I lay in bed for a while, hoping to drift off again, but the thoughts had already begun to turn in my head.

I shuffled out of my bedroom in my housecoat and

slippers, and headed downstairs to the kitchen to put on a pot of coffee. Halfway down the steps, the smell of freshly brewed coffee hit me.

Mom was sitting on a stool at the island, slouched over, staring into the mug she held tightly between her hands. She looked up when I came in and rubbed her red-rimmed eyes. I doubted she'd slept any better than I had.

I pulled a mug off the shelf above the coffeemaker and filled it. "Did you sleep at all?"

"A little."

"Did you get to see Gran?" I leaned back against the counter and took a sip of strong, black coffee.

Her eyes filled at the mention of her mother. "I did." A tear spilled over and she swiped it away in frustration. "She looked so helpless. She's not even breathing on her own now. I hate this. I hate seeing her this way." She pushed her mug away, laid her head on her arms on the counter, and began to sob.

"Mommy, why's Nana crying?" Kayla stood in the doorway, looking tousled and sleepy. Her tiny face was crumpled with worry.

Mom sat up, startled by the sound of Kayla's voice. She swiped a tissue from the box beside her and hurriedly mopped up the tears.

I held out my hand to Kayla. She walked hesitantly toward me and put her hand in mine. I crouched down in front of her. "Gran had another stroke last night, sweetie. She's very sick now and that makes Nana sad."

"Is Gran gonna die?"

Mom made a choking sound and covered her face.

I cupped Kayla's chin in my hand and managed a shaky smile. "We don't know, Kayla. We have to go to the hospital today and talk to the doctor." I gave her a hug and sent her upstairs to get dressed.

* * *

I left Kayla with Mrs. Curtis an hour later, promising her I'd be back soon. Mom was at the hospital when I got there, sitting in her usual spot beside Gran's bed, staring blankly at the magazine on her lap. She jumped a little when I put my hand on her shoulder.

"Sorry, I didn't mean to startle you." I went to the other side of the bed and picked up Gran's hand. It felt cold and lifeless. She was perfectly still and unresponsive when I gently squeezed her hand. There were tubes and machines everywhere. The room was deathly quiet save the soft "whoosh, whoosh" of the ventilator.

It reminded me of Palliative Care, where it was so quiet it was eerie. The walls there were too white and sterile. The residents were mainly bedridden or confined to wheelchairs, so the halls were empty and every sound seemed to echo. The staff spoke in low tones and walked quietly as to not disturb those who were sleeping or in pain. Even the visitors were somber and quiet. It was a place devoid of joy. A place where people went to die.

Working there hadn't been without its rewards. I'd taken pride in knowing I was helping people live their final days with as much comfort and dignity as possible. For some, I was the only person they'd seen all day other than the nurses who often came and went like ghosts with barely a word spoken. But I'd become too attached to the residents and watching them die had brought back too many memories of my dad's death. I'd left work every day feeling torn up inside and emotionally exhausted.

It was exactly how Mom looked now. "Did you see the doctor this morning?" I asked.

"I did. He said the tests showed she had another stroke. She's still on the ventilator." She waved her hand toward the machine. "He said the stroke weakened the muscles used for breathing. He's so vague. He won't say how long he thinks she'll need the machine, or when she might wake up. It's so frustrating."

I just nodded and listened. Mom was either in denial, or didn't understand how bad the situation was. I knew from my experience in Palliative that Gran was unlikely to recover. She'd had two strokes within two weeks, remained unresponsive, and was now unable to breathe on her own. Unless a miracle happened, or Gran gave in and let go, Mom would have some tough choices to make in the weeks ahead.

* * *

I went back to work on Thursday. I'd contacted Amelia's mom the night before. She worked part-time, but had taken the week off to be home with Amelia. When I explained the situation to her, she insisted my mom drop Kayla off in the morning to spend the day.

It was hard to get back into the swing of the work routine after having three days off. I'd missed my residents, though, and their antics helped distract me from worrying about Gran.

Rose had lost much of her independence because of the cast on her arm. She couldn't dress herself or cut her own food. She even needed my help to use the toilet because she was unable to pull her pants up or down. It was time consuming for me and frustrating for Rose. She was sullen and sulky during our morning routine.

I found Mrs. W shuffling about the main hall before breakfast and took her into the dining room. I assumed the dirty looks Sheila sent my way were because I'd taken Mrs. W to my table, but I soon felt the cold, condemning stares of other co-workers. Someone must have told Sheila, and everyone else, about my accusations. I tried not to care, but I couldn't help but feel like I was back in grade school where tattletales were either picked on or shunned.

Rose struggled until Edie stepped in to help. Georgia followed suit. They fawned over her as though she were an injured child. They pushed her chair in for her, unfolded her napkin and fixed her tea the way she liked. Rose thrived on the attention and by the time breakfast was over, her mood had greatly improved.

Later, when I gathered my residents and directed them to the dining room for lunch, I looked for Mrs. W in her usual spot in the main hall. She wasn't there, or in the lounge. I walked into the dining room with a sinking feeling in my stomach. Sure enough, she was across the room with Sheila.

Sheila sat back in her chair with her arms folded across her chest and stared at me. I wanted so badly to slap the smug smirk off her face. I kept my face carefully composed, turned my back on her, and sat between Beth and Mrs. Sellers.

The mellow sounds of Frank Sinatra wafted from the overhead speakers. The soft background music seemed to relax the residents. It was played at every meal, but I'd become so used to it, I barely noticed anymore.

Sam hummed along while he chewed. He'd been in a good mood all morning, humming and whistling everywhere he went. I watched him reach across to Lily's plate and snatch a French fry. I waited for Lily to scold him, but she was distracted with trying to keep her burger together while she took a bite. Sam had eaten all of his fries, but had barely touched the chicken burger and coleslaw. He took another fry and dipped it in the dollop of ketchup on Lily's plate before popping it in his mouth.

I reminded Mrs. Sellers to eat and turned her plate so she could reach the fries. Beth tried to get up from the table. I turned to her and put my hand on her arm. "Where are you going, Beth?"

"I have to go see Mother. She needs me."

"She's fine, Aunt Helen's looking after her. Do you want ketchup with your fries?"

Beth settled back into her chair and nodded. I placed the ketchup bottle, upside down, into her hands. "Here, squeeze some onto your plate beside the fries."

I watched Sam out of the corner of my eye. He continued to steal Lily's fries. Finally, she put her burger down and looked at him. She smiled through a mouthful of food, picked up half her fries and put them on his plate. Sam leaned over and gave her a big, loud kiss on the cheek. Lily blushed and giggled.

I shook my head in disbelief and smiled fondly at Sam. If it had been anyone but him, including Beth, they'd have been thoroughly chastised. I had no doubt he'd been charming the ladies since long before I was born and they still loved him.

Mrs. Sellers coughed. I placed her water beside her hand and instructed her to drink. I heard a familiar nasal whine behind me.

"No, don't spit your food out. Eat nicely, hon." Sheila's voice was syrupy sweet.

It made me shudder and I resisted the urge to turn and look.

"Oh dear, are we not hungry today?"

Another loud voice filled the room. "Who in the good Lord's name is she talking to?"

I glanced back at Georgia.

She watched Sheila with a scowl on her face. "She's a full-grown woman, you know, not a child."

Sheila didn't respond.

Georgia went back to eating, but continued to mumble to herself. "Lord Almighty, people have no respect. That's no way to speak to a grown woman."

Edie patted Georgia's hand and murmured her agreement.

I turned back to the table with a satisfied smile, and met Carol's stare. She was sitting at the next table over with her new resident, a quiet, timid man who'd taken John's place. She looked away as soon as our eyes met, but not before I saw the flash of guilt that crossed her face.

I went to the staff room after lunch to take my break. I filled my water bottle from the cooler, took my yogurt out of the fridge and sat down at the table with a magazine. I was lounging in my chair, flipping through the magazine, thoroughly enjoying my strawberry yogurt, when the door opened a few minutes later.

Sheila walked in.

I sat up in my chair and put my yogurt on the table. I'd lost my appetite. I picked up the magazine. It shook visibly in my hands. I quickly dropped it onto my lap, stared at it blankly and willed myself to breathe.

Sheila sauntered to the fridge, took out a cola, cracked it open and leaned a hip casually against the counter. She didn't even look at me when she spoke, but stared at the can in her hand, "I heard you accused me of leaving those marks on Mrs. W's neck."

I looked up quickly. "I never said—"

She slammed the can onto the counter, crossed the room, slapped her hands down on the table and leaned across in front of me until her face was inches from mine. "Carol told me exactly what you said. You think you can come in here and tell us how things should be? I've been here thirty years. *Thirty years*! Since the place opened. No one tells me how to do my job, especially some twenty-something kid who's been here for what—six months?"

She laughed, straightened up and paced in front of me. "You have no idea. None. You know who did that to Mrs. W? John. I saw him the day before, getting angry at her because she went after him with her chair."

I shifted in my seat. John wouldn't have gone near Mrs. W. He was afraid of her because she fought back. He had only ever picked on residents he knew he could easily bully. *Just like Sheila,* I thought. I kept my mouth shut. Arguing with her was useless, and I'd only end up saying something that would get me in trouble.

For some reason my silence seemed to anger her more. She bent over in front of me again and put her finger in my face. "You need to learn to mind your own damn business. I could get you fired like *that*," she said, snapping her fingers. "Believe me, you don't wanna mess—"

The door opened behind Sheila and she straightened up quickly. It was Abby. She looked from me to Sheila, then went to the water cooler and poured herself a drink.

Sheila gave me one last look before she ambled across the room and flopped down on the couch. She picked up a magazine from the pile on the coffee table and flipped through it as though nothing had happened.

I took a deep breath to steady myself, placed my magazine on the table and went to the sink to wash my spoon. No one said a word, but I could feel their eyes on my back as I dried the spoon and put it away. I went back to the table and picked up the half empty yogurt container.

Abby stood silently by the water cooler. I looked directly into her eyes. She stared at me impassively for a moment before she looked away.

I tossed my yogurt container in the recycle bin without a word, yanked the door open and hurried down the hall to the staff bathroom. I closed the door, locked it, turned and stared at my pale face in the mirror as I took a deep shaky breath. "Now what?" I asked my reflection.

I did my paperwork early that afternoon and left work at two-thirty sharp. I wasn't in the mood to see or speak to anyone.

My phone went off as I crossed the parking lot. I pulled

it out of my coat pocket. Tracey had sent me a text asking where I was.

In the parking lot, I answered.

Wait 4 me

I threw my purse inside the car, leaned against it, and played with my keys impatiently while I waited. I barely noticed the warmth of the March sun on my face or the robin singing in a nearby tree. The scene with Sheila played over again in my mind as I thought of all the things I wished I had said.

The sound of approaching footsteps broke through my thoughts and I looked up to see Tracey hurrying toward me.

"Hey," she said breathlessly. "Why'd you leave so fast? I wanted to talk to you."

"I needed to get out of there."

"Uh-oh, what happened?"

"You mean besides the fact that you're the only who would talk to me all day?" I took a deep breath. "Look, I don't want to talk about this here."

"Okay, so let's go have coffee."

"I can't. I have to pick Kayla up from her friend's place. She's been there all day."

"Okay, then I'll meet you at your place and we'll talk there." I hesitated, but Tracey wouldn't take no for an answer. "Go, get Kayla," she said, "I'll be at your place in thirty."

Half an hour later, I had Kayla settled in front of the TV, watching a movie and eating a snack of apple slices, crackers and cheese. She'd talked excitedly all the way home about her day with Amelia. I was glad she'd had fun, but her constant chatter had made my head hurt.

I threw in a load of laundry and headed to the kitchen, where I put on a pot of coffee and started unloading the dishwasher. Mom must have turned it on before she'd left that morning. I wondered how she was doing. I understood why she felt she should be at the hospital with Gran as much as possible, but I could see it was taking a toll on her. A knock at the door interrupted my thoughts and I went to answer it.

Tracey didn't wait for me to open the door. She let herself in. "Hello?" she called as I came around the corner.

Kayla came flying out of the living room and pushed past me in the narrow hallway. She threw her arms around Tracey's waist and gazed up at her. "Tracey! I didn't know you were coming over. Come watch the movie with me."

"Not right now, kiddo. I came over to talk to your mom."

Kayla pushed her bottom lip out and hung her head dejectedly.

"Kayla, stop sulking," I said a little too sternly. The pounding in my head was making me irritable.

"Tell you what, when I'm done talking to your mom, I'll come see you," Tracey promised, tousling Kayla's hair playfully.

Kayla went begrudgingly back to the living room to watch her movie. Tracey and I went to the kitchen. She pulled up a stool and waited quietly while I poured us both a cup of coffee. I dragged a stool around to the other side of the island so I could sit facing her.

She didn't say a word until I'd sat down and taken a sip

of coffee. "So, what happened?"

I sighed and massaged my temples in an attempt to ease the throbbing pain. "Sheila got me alone in the staff room."

"Oh, shit," Tracey blurted. She clamped her hand over her mouth and peered into the living room. "What'd she say?" she continued more quietly.

I told her what Sheila had said and about Abby walking in.

"Wow, I heard she was a bully, but this is way more than that. She threatened you, Sarah. You should go talk to the administrator."

I shook my head emphatically. "You know exactly how that'll go. I'll go in there with my theories and assumptions, because right now that's all they are and they'll ask if I have any proof, which I don't. They'll talk to Sheila, who'll deny everything, then Abby, who'll back Sheila up. Sheila will find a way to twist it around and say I have a vendetta against her and I'll end up jobless and looking like a fool."

I took a deep breath and sat back, waiting for Tracey to shoot down everything I'd said and tell me how it was really going to work.

"You're right."

My shoulders sagged and I let out a defeated sigh. "Are you kidding me? You pick now to agree with me? What happened to the Tracey who believes there's always a bright side? A solution to every problem?"

"There's a solution. We just haven't found it yet. And you're right, there's no proof."

"So," I said slowly, "maybe that's the solution."

"What is?"

"We get proof."

Chapter 21
Realization Dawns

MOM OFFERED TO STAY HOME with Kayla Friday while I worked. She didn't say it, but I knew she needed a break from the hospital. I hoped being with Kayla would take her mind off Gran for a while.

Edie was scheduled to have a bath at seven-thirty that morning—right after Mrs. W. I went into her room shortly after six-thirty to unlock her wardrobe and help her gather her things.

She put her hand on my arm as we packed her clothes and toiletries into a small mesh bag. "I'm sorry to bring it up when I'm sure you'd rather be forgetting your troubles, but I've been worried about you. How're you holding up, lassie?"

"I'm doing okay, Edie. Thanks for asking, but please don't worry about me."

"Och, well, I've few enough people in my life to worry about. I need something to keep my mind occupied."

It warmed my heart knowing Edie was concerned about me and I left the room feeling a little lighter. "Don't do anything to anger the Dragon today," I warned on my way out.

Later, when Tracey and I went in to make Mrs. Sellers'

bed, I was surprised to find Edie in her room. She looked forward to Pet Therapy on Friday mornings. "Edie, I thought you'd be in the auditorium with the pets this morning."

"I was hoping to talk to you for a moment if you've the time." She looked pointedly at Tracey.

Tracey could take a hint. "I'll be next door making beds. Come get me when you're done."

"Come on, then," Edie said, when Tracey was gone. "I'll not be holding you up. We can talk while we work." She went to Mrs. Sellers' bed and began straightening the bottom sheet. She spoke quietly and kept an eye on the door as we worked. "I went down to the bathing room early this morning to wait on the bench in the hall. I could hear her in there, badgering and bullying poor Mrs. W the whole time. She was ordering her about, calling her nasty names an' saying things she must have known would set her off. The whole time she was banging things about." Edie's brogue became more pronounced as she spoke and by the time she'd finished, her face was tight with anger.

"What kind of names," I asked.

"She called her a dirty Polack."

My jaw dropped. I was speechless. The way Sheila spoke to the residents was condescending and disrespectful, in my opinion. Racial slurs, however, were another thing altogether. And, after seeing Mrs. W's reaction to the holocaust documentary that day in the lounge, I could only imagine how she must have reacted to the name-calling.

"You remember, lass, when I told you I was planning to act differently around Sheila to give her the idea I have the disease?"

I nodded.

"Well, it's been working. And since I called her out in the dining room, I can tell she has it in for me. She's careful, mind you, but it's little things she says and does that give it away."

I hadn't seen Sheila speak to Edie at all since the confrontation between them in the dining room, so I was unsure of what she meant. "Like what?"

"The way she looks at me for one. Her eyes are hard and full of hate like her heart. She makes fun of my accent and tries to make it seem like a joke, but I know she's trying to get a rise out of me. She's a bitter, miserable woman. I believe the only joy she finds in life is in terrorizing helpless, old people."

We pulled the last blanket up, folded the top down and tucked it under the pillow. Edie smoothed the wrinkles out as she rounded the bed and came to stand beside me. "That's not all. This morning when she put me in the bath it was barely lukewarm. When I complained about it, she said it was because the hot water was running out. Now, I know that's a load of malarkey."

"Yes, it is. You were the second bath this morning, so there's no way the hot water was low."

"Exactly. I know you told me not to anger the Dragon, but I just couldn't help myself."

"Oh, Edie, what did you do?"

"No, no, it's fine, lass. I know how far to push and when to stop. I made an awful fuss about the water, though, and I could see the rage boiling up in her. She scrubbed my back so hard she likely took a layer of skin off. Then she threw the cloth into the water and told me to wash my 'fish'." She wrinkled her nose in distaste when she said the word.

I'd heard Sheila and Carol refer to the women's privates that way. They didn't seem to think there was anything wrong with it, but I found it offensive and apparently many of the residents did as well.

"She drained the water and left me sitting in the tub while she washed my hair. The water she used to rinse my hair was downright cold. By the time she took me out of the tub, I was shivering and covered in goose bumps. I used to enjoy a nice soak in the tub, but that was not a pleasant experience."

I gave Edie a quick reassuring hug. "Be careful with Sheila, and be patient. Tracey and I are working on a plan."

We walked to the door together. I stopped Edie before we stepped into the hall. "I haven't forgotten about you, Edie. I don't know if we can depend on Abby for help, but I'll find a way to get you out of here."

"I know you will, lass. But as I said before, don't be worrying yourself over me. These things have a way of working themselves out."

When I went to gather the residents for lunch, I found Mrs. Sellers in her room, crying and pulling at her mouth frantically.

I bent down in front of her, concerned she'd somehow hurt herself. "What's wrong, Mrs. Sellers?" She mumbled something inaudible. I pulled her hands gently away from her mouth. "It's okay, I'm going to help you. Tell me what's wrong."

"No teef, no teef." She pulled her hands free, opened her toothless mouth wide and pointed inside.

No teeth. It finally occurred to me why she was so upset; the poor woman was distraught over the fact she had no teeth in her mouth.

I went to the bathroom, assuming her teeth would be there. They weren't. I checked all the cabinets and drawers, the toilet and the wastebasket.

Tracey popped her head in while I was searching the room. She looked at Mrs. Sellers, who was still crying, and asked, "You okay?"

"I will be, as soon as I find her teeth."

"Oh, that sucks. I'll make sure all your residents get to the dining room."

"Thanks, Trace," I said, opening the nightstand drawer for a second look.

"No prob. I had a resident once who flushed her teeth down the toilet."

I shot her a reproving look. "You're not helping."

She smiled wickedly and flounced away calling, "Check under the pillow, maybe she left them for the tooth fairy."

I continued to search the room for a few minutes after she left. They were nowhere to be found. I stood in the middle of the room, watching helplessly as Mrs. Sellers continued to bemoan the loss of her teeth.

"Where could they be?" I wondered aloud, surveying the room "Where haven't I looked?" My eyes drifted to the bed. They settled on the pillow. I marched over and lifted it up. Nothing.

I went to Mrs. Sellers and crouched in front of her. "Do

you know where your teeth are?" I asked, pointing at her mouth. She burst into tears.

I sighed in frustration and hung my head. *Think like a resident*, I told myself. *Aside from the toilet, where could they be?* Albert's name popped into my head. I looked up and patted Mrs. Sellers' hand. "I'll be right back."

I hurried down the hall to Albert's room and opened the nightstand drawer. He'd filled it with treasures again since I'd cleaned it out last. The teeth were nestled between the red scarf Georgia had lost the week before and a neatly stacked pile of cookies. I stared at the teeth balefully, put on a glove and picked them up. *I need to check Albert's drawers more regularly.* I laughed at the thought and hurried back to Mrs. Sellers' room.

I went into Edie's room that afternoon during my rounds. Mrs. Sellers was asleep in her bed. She would sleep until Connie came on shift and got her up again. Edie was in her chair by the window with her tartan blanket on her lap, knitting.

Earlier, when I'd come in to help Mrs. Sellers prepare for her nap, I'd opened Edie's wardrobe so she could get her knitting bag. I went to the wardrobe now, closed the door and took out my key, intending to lock it.

"Leave it, please, lass. I'll want to put this away when I'm finished. I'll have Connie lock it up later."

* * *

I headed straight to the hospital after work to spend some time with Gran. From there, I'd go home to be with Kayla while Mom went to sit with Gran for the evening.

I went through the usual routine with Gran. I checked

her for skin tears and bedsores and performed her exercises. When I finished, I shifted her to her side and placed pillows under her arm and between her knees. She moaned when I turned her. I stroked her hair and spoke quietly to her, but there was no response. I sighed and sat down to read to her.

An hour later, I came home and Mom left to go to the hospital. I put the bean burritos she had prepared for dinner in the oven, made myself tea and flopped down on the couch to watch Kayla play the Wii.

Later, after Kayla went to bed, I tidied the kitchen and swept the floor. I was exhausted. I went into the living room and lay on the couch with a book.

The sound of the door opening woke me. "What time is it?" I asked when Mom came into the room.

She sank into the recliner with a tired sigh. "A little after nine."

"I meant to read for a bit before bed, but I guess I dozed off."

Mom stared blankly into the flames dancing in the gas fireplace. Her face was lined with fatigue, her eyes bright with the sheen of unshed tears. "She's not coming back to us is she?"

My heart ached for her. I understood how hard it must have been for her to come to that realization. It was something she hadn't been able to do with my dad. She'd been in denial until the end. "No, Mom," I said gently. "She's not."

* * *

The next morning dawned clear and unseasonably cold for mid-March. I wiped the salt and slush from my boots as I entered Tranquility.

Tracey called out to me as I opened the doors leading into Long-Term. "Hey, Sar, wait up."

I stopped and held the door open.

"Wow, you look like hell," she said when she caught up.

"Gee, thanks."

"Sorry, didn't mean it like that. You just look exhausted."

"Yeah, I know. I didn't sleep well last night." I waved at Marg when she looked up from her desk at reception.

Tracey smiled brightly and waved. "Hiya, Marg."

Marg didn't even smile. She gave a slight nod of recognition, put her head down and went back to work.

Tracey was impervious. "Hey, did you hear what happened here yesterday?"

"No, what?"

"You know my friend, Meghan?"

I stared at her blankly.

"I worked with her in Long-Term. Anyway, she texted me last night on her break and said she heard a resident got out of Dementia yesterday afternoon. Apparently, the police picked her up at her son's place a couple hours later."

I stopped walking and gave Tracey an astonished look. "Did she say who it was?"

"Nope. But I think I know."

"Edie," I said flatly.

"That was my first thought."

"Damn it! She told me she wouldn't do that again."

Tracey's mouth fell open. "You mean it's happened before?"

I cringed. "She got out once, a few months ago. I caught her sneaking back in and she told me I wouldn't *catch* her doing it again."

Tracey laughed. "Is that how she said it, that you wouldn't catch her doing it?" She shook her head incredulously. "She's one smart lady."

"Smarter than me, apparently. I promised her I wouldn't tell anyone because she'd promised not to do it again." I sighed as Tracey punched in the code and we went through the doors into Dementia. "At least someone else caught her this time and I don't have to be the one to rat her out."

When I marched into Edie's room fifteen minutes later she was sitting in her chair, wringing her hands. She jumped up when she saw me and immediately began defending herself. "I'm sorry, lassie, but I had tae do it. There was something important I needed tae take care of."

I shook my head at her accusingly. "You told me you wouldn't leave again."

"Well, technically—"

"How you said it doesn't matter, Edie. You led me to believe something that wasn't true."

She hung her head in shame. "You're right. It was wrong of me and for that, I apologize. But, I won't apologize for coming and going as I please, when I've every right to."

I couldn't disagree with her, so I left it alone.

* * *

I was in the lounge after lunch, helping some of the residents settle in to watch a Saturday afternoon movie. Tina and Tracey were helping a few residents prepare for their naps. Carol had the day off and because Abby and Sheila rarely worked on the weekends, it had been a relatively stress-free day for me.

Maria wheeled Mrs. W in and left her beside Mr. Roberts while she unlocked the cabinet that held the DVDs. Mrs. W had been in a confrontational mood all day and I questioned the prudence of leaving her in a room full of residents, but she seemed calm enough for now.

I surveyed the room. Edie was in the corner with her knitting. Tom and Anne had cancelled their Saturday visit because Anne was feeling "under the weather." Edie hadn't appeared troubled by the news. Georgia sat beside Edie, overnight bag on the floor and coat draped over the back of her chair. She was waiting for Lloyd to pick her up and take her home for the night.

I noticed Mrs. Sellers' blanket was slipping off her lap and made my way across the room to her. I passed Mrs. Amaral and smiled at her. She grabbed my hand tightly and tugged. I bent over to see what she wanted. She put her hand on my face, pulled me in close and gave me a big, loud kiss on the cheek. I kissed her cheek in return and smiled warmly.

"Obrigada," she repeated over and over, patting my cheek affectionately.

"You're welcome, Mrs. Amaral." I pulled slowly out of her grasp and made my way to Mrs. Sellers. I bent down to retrieve her blanket and tucked it around her legs, glancing up when I heard Sam teasing the twins.

"Ladies, keep your hands to yourselves." He sat in the middle of the couch with Lily on one side and Beth on the other. They covered their mouths with their hands and giggled flirtatiously.

Rose was in an armchair next to Georgia with her injured arm propped on a pillow in her lap. She frowned as she watched Sam and the twins. It was obvious she had a crush on Sam and I wondered if she was sometimes jealous of the attention he paid the twins.

I went over and crouched down so I was eye level with her. "Rose?"

She pulled her eyes away from the trio on the couch and looked at me vacantly.

"Do you like James Dean?"

She wrinkled her brow in thought before she smiled brightly and nodded. "He's handsome."

"Yes, he is. Maria's turning the movie on now and he's in it." I patted her good hand and stood up in time to see Mrs. W preparing to ram her chair into Mr. Roberts' legs. I rushed over and grabbed the handles of her chair. She yelled and swung her arm back wildly in my direction. I jumped back, but not quickly enough. Her hand connected with my mouth and pushed my lip into my teeth. The pain brought tears to my eyes. I choked down an angry word and put my hand to my mouth. I could taste the blood.

"Here now!" Edie called, rising from her chair.

Georgia got up as well. "Good Lord, did that woman just hit that poor girl?"

Maria rushed toward me in concern. "Are you okay?"

I didn't have time to answer. Mrs. W was aiming once

more for Mr. Roberts. I reached for the chair again, but not in time. He bellowed angrily and came to his feet as the chair bumped the side of his leg. Maria jumped between the angry residents. She took Mr. Roberts by the hand and spoke to him soothingly as she led him to a chair across the room.

Georgia shook her head and clucked her tongue in disapproval as she sat back down. Sam had a hand on each of the twins' knees and was humming obliviously.

Edie pulled a tissue from the box on the coffee table and handed it to me. I held it gently to my bloody lip. "You should have the nurse look at that, lass, in case you need stitches."

I doubted it was that bad, but I thanked her and wheeled Mrs. W through the main hall to the nurse's station. Emily was there. "Uh-oh, what happened to you?"

Mrs. W shifted restlessly in her chair and moaned loudly. I made a motion toward her. "She took a swing and I wasn't fast enough," I managed to mutter over my puffy lip.

Emily came around the desk. She pulled a glove out of her pocket, put it on, pulled my lip down gently and checked inside. "The inside of your lip is a little shredded, but you don't need any stitches. It might hurt to eat for a few days and it's swelling up fast. You should go put some ice on it."

Maria came out of the lounge as Emily stripped off the glove. She winced when she saw my lip. "Is it bad?"

Emily answered for me. "She won't need stitches." She looked at Mrs. W, whose moaning had turned into wailing. "I think you should take Mrs. W to her room and get her calmed down."

Maria wheeled Mrs. W away and I headed to the staff room for ice. When I came back out, Emily was gone. I sat down at the nurse's station to fill out an incident report. I held the bag of ice, wrapped in paper towel, gently against my mouth with one hand and wrote with the other.

A few minutes later I heard the bang of the door and a familiar voice. I looked up to see Lloyd and Jay walking through the main hall toward me. My stomach fluttered.

They were laughing as they approached the desk.

All traces of humor left Jay's face when he noticed the ice. "What happened?"

I flinched in pain as I pulled the ice away from my mouth enough to talk. "Accident. Got in the way of someone's hand."

Lloyd looked around the hall. "It wasn't my grandmother, was it?"

"No—"

He put up his hand to stop me. "Don't try to talk. Is she in her room?"

I shook my head no.

"In the lounge?"

I nodded and gave him a look of gratitude.

"Thanks, Sarah." He turned to Jay. "I'll go get Ma and meet you back here."

Jay pointed to his mouth. "Can I see it?"

"Really? It's nasty."

"Really. I want to see how bad it is."

I pulled the bag of ice from my face reluctantly. The paper towel was soaked with blood.

Jay didn't react to the sight of my bloody, swollen lip,

other than to look at me sympathetically. "It looks painful. Has it stopped bleeding?"

"Think so. Nurse looked at it. Don't need stitches." I wanted to ask him about his trip, but it hurt to talk.

Lloyd came out of the lounge with Georgia. He put her bag down on a nearby bench and held out her coat. "Here, Ma, put your coat on. It's cold outside today."

"Looks like we're leaving," Jay said. "Can I call you later?"

I nodded my head and tried to smile. It ended up being more of a grimace and I made a sound of pain and frustration.

Jay winced. "Keep putting ice on it. The swelling will go down. I guess there'll be no kissing on our next date." He winked at me and sauntered away.

I watched him sweep Georgia into a hug and plant a big, wet kiss on her cheek. I imagined those lean, muscular arms around me and realized I was staring. I cleared my throat, picked up the bag of half-melted ice and headed to the staff room for more.

I went back into the lounge before doing my rounds. Edie made me sit beside her so she could take a good look at my mouth. She shook her head in disgust over the incident. I reassured her my lip would be back to normal in a few days.

"It's not right," she insisted.

I patted her hand reassuringly. "She didn't mean to hurt me, Edie. She can't help it."

I left the lounge and headed to the change room to get my things. Tracey was sitting on the bench between the lockers changing out of her work shoes. She looked up when she heard the door open. “Hey, Sar—Oh, my God! What the hell happened to your face?”

I waved a hand in the air. It didn’t hurt too badly as long as I didn’t talk too much, or open my mouth too wide. “Looks worse than it is. Mrs. W was mad. I got in her way.”

Tracey waited for me while I changed my shoes and gathered my things and we made our way to the parking lot together.

“Jay’s back,” I said. “Came in with his dad to get Georgia.”

“So, he saw you with your face all bloody and swollen?”

I nodded. “Said he’d call me later.”

“Wow, he saw your face like that and he’s still gonna call you? He’s a keeper.”

“So’s Kyle.”

Tracey stopped walking and looked at me suspiciously. “What do you mean?”

“He brought Rose back from the hospital. She had a huge crush on him and he was treating her like a queen.”

Tracey’s expression softened. “Yeah, he’s pretty sweet.”

We pushed the main door open and pulled our coats closed tight against the bitter wind. A few snowflakes danced in the air before melting when they hit the pavement. Spring was only a few days away, but it certainly didn’t feel like it.

“So, what are you gonna do if Jay wants to go out? You can’t eat or drink coffee. You can’t go back to his place and make out. What’s left?”

I laughed, then swore at the pain. She was right.

* * *

Jay took me out anyway. We went to a movie. It was a mediocre comedy, but it still made me laugh enough to cause some pain. I'd applied ice off and on throughout the afternoon. The swelling had gone down a lot, but my lip was still a bloody, bruised mess. People stared at it while we stood in line to buy tickets. Some even shot dirty looks at Jay, as though he'd been responsible. It made me uncomfortable and I was glad for the dark cover of the theater.

After the movie, Jay took me to fast food drive-through for fries and milkshakes. "It was the only thing I could think of that you might be able to eat," he said sheepishly.

"Are you kidding? I love fast food. Especially fries. This is perfect."

We drove to the park and sat in the car overlooking the river. I polished off my fries in no time. I was so hungry even the sting of the salt on my lip didn't slow me down. The milkshake was so thick it hurt to suck it through the straw. Jay had been thoughtful enough to ask for a plastic spoon, so I removed the lid and dug in that way.

We ate in comfortable silence, watching the reflection of the moon sparkle on the gently flowing water.

Jay finished his fries. He put the empty carton into the paper bag with mine, crumpled it shut and tossed it into the backseat. I glanced around at his immaculately clean car and raised a brow.

He smiled jauntily. "I'll clean it up later. How's your mouth? Still sore?"

"Not nearly as bad as earlier. I think the ice helped a lot." I thought of Kayla's reaction and laughed. "It upset Kayla a little when she first saw it, then she turned into a little mother. She wanted to look at it, asked if I needed to get stitches like she did when she cut her lip open. She even made me lay down while she went to the kitchen and got me a bag of ice."

"I'm impressed. Maybe she'll be a nurse someday too."

"Maybe. She told me she didn't think going out tonight was a good idea. Apparently, I should be in bed resting."

"Hmm, she sounds like a character. I'd like to meet her sometime."

He said it so casually, like it was no big deal, but I was at a loss for words. I'd never brought anyone I dated home to meet Kayla and never would unless I thought it would be long-term. Even introducing her to Tracey had been a big step for me. I put my shake into the cup holder between the seats, folded my arms across my chest and stared out the window. The silence stretched on and a feeling of tension filled the air.

Jay shifted in his seat uneasily. "You got quiet all of a sudden. What's wrong?"

I glanced at his puzzled expression and realized he had no clue what I was thinking. I folded my hands in my lap and stared at them.

"Sarah?"

"I just…I wouldn't…." I sighed and blurted it out. "I've never brought a guy home."

"Oh. What about Kayla's dad?"

"No, I mean to meet Kayla. She's never met anyone I dated."

"Oh. Oh! I get it. I didn't mean…."

"I know. It's fine."

I asked Jay to take me home shortly after the awkward conversation. My mouth was throbbing and I had to work the next morning, but the sudden strained silence was good enough reason to end the date. The drive home was no less awkward. He asked about Gran and I filled him in about the stroke. We talked a little about the seminar in New York and about Georgia. The short exchanges were interspersed with long, uncomfortable silences.

After what seemed like an eternity, we pulled up in front of my house. Jay turned to me as if to say something. I quickly thanked him for the evening and got out of the car before he could speak. I hurried into the house without looking back, closed the door and waited until I heard his car pull away. I let out a huge sigh and banged my head gently against the door. "Stupid, stupid, stupid." I was messing up a good thing because I was afraid to get too close. I was afraid of my heart getting broken again, only this time, I had Kayla's heart to think of as well.

CHAPTER 22
ETHAN

JAY WASN'T WITH LLOYD WHEN he brought Georgia back to Tranquility Sunday afternoon. I was both relieved and disappointed. I told myself it was for the best. There was enough going on in my life without adding to it.

I went straight home after work to shower and change before picking Kayla up from Amelia's birthday party. Mom had dropped her off there before she went to the hospital. After my shower, I wandered aimlessly into the kitchen, still in my housecoat with my hair wrapped in a towel.

My purse was slung over the back of one of the chairs. It buzzed insistently. I pulled my phone out and checked my messages. Tracey had texted me three times while I was in the shower. She wanted to meet later for coffee. I swallowed the lump of regret in my throat. I'd hoped it was Jay. I poured myself a coffee and sat down to send her a reply confirming I would meet her at *Tim's* after I went to see Gran.

* * *

"Wow, your lip looks better already," Tracey said when I walked into the coffee shop. "Think you can handle drinking something hot?"

"No, I'll stick to an iced cappuccino."

We ordered our drinks and looked around the crowded room for a couple empty seats. "Wanna drive to the park and walk around? It's a nice night," Tracey said.

"Sure, why not?"

We strolled in companionable silence along the path that followed the river, until we spotted a bench and sat down. The river was narrow there and the water was high from the melting snow. It flowed quickly, carrying bits of debris and ice downstream.

"So," Tracey said, "what's up with you today? You seem really down in the dumps."

I shrugged. "I'm just feeling overwhelmed lately, between worrying about Gran and Mom and trying to figure out what to do about Edie and Sheila. It's a lot to handle all at once, you know?"

"No way. There's more to it than that. All that crap's been going on for weeks, but something's different today. Did something happen last night with Jay?"

Damn it, why won't she leave it alone? I sat in rigid silence, staring off into the darkness beyond the river.

"Sarah, will you talk to me already? I'm trying to help you here."

My shoulders slumped and I hung my head in misery. "I was talking about Kayla last night and Jay said he'd like to meet her. It kind of freaked me out, I guess."

"Did you argue?"

"No, not really. I told him I'd never brought a guy home to meet Kayla. He said he didn't mean it that way. And then it got awkward, so I asked him to take me home."

"Hmm, and you haven't heard from him today?"

"No."

"Text him when you get home. Tell him you want to meet up tomorrow to talk about last night."

"I'm not doing that. I messed up, Trace. He probably doesn't want to talk to me."

"Sarah, he thinks you're pissed. That's why you haven't heard from him. He thinks *he* messed up."

I shook my head slowly. "I don't know...."

"What are you so afraid of?"

I stared at her in exasperation. "Why do you keep digging? Can you not just leave this alone?"

"No, I can't. You keep everything bottled up inside. You try to be everything to everybody. You're Kayla's mom *and* her dad. You're an emotional crutch for your mom, a nurse to your grandmother and you care more about your residents than some of their own families do. What about you? Who's there for you?"

I was taken aback by Tracey's words. I'd never seen this deep, serious side of her before. And she knew me so much better than I'd thought. Once again, I'd underestimated her. I had a feeling a lot of people did.

"So, what are you so afraid of?" she repeated.

"It's a long story."

"I have all night."

I sighed. "Fine, but don't say I didn't warn you," I said, settling back into my seat. "So, when I was in college, taking the support worker course, I met a guy named Ethan at a party. He was the complete opposite of me; laid back, easy going, didn't plan anything, didn't think about tomorrow."

Tracey smirked. "So, the male version of me, huh? No wonder we hit it off."

"Actually, he was a lot like you in some ways. But, he wasn't nearly as responsible."

"Hey, don't call me that."

I smirked. "Sorry. I meant he didn't have a job or an apartment, just slept on friends' couches and picked up gigs at bars with his band whenever he could. Sometimes, I didn't see him or hear from him for weeks, but I was so busy with school and working part-time that it worked." I took a sip of my half-melted ice cap.

"I'm having trouble picturing you with a guy like that."

"I know. In hindsight, it probably wouldn't have worked." I pictured his face, and smiled fondly. "He had dark, curly hair and big, dark eyes. He was outgoing, charming, charismatic...."

"In other words, Kayla takes after him?" Tracey asked.

"She is a lot like him."

"Did you love him?"

"I did. He made me feel happy and alive for the first time since my dad died."

I looked away and blinked back the tears. I'd never spoken to anyone about my dad's death. Tracey laid her hand on my shoulder comfortingly. I looked at her and smiled dejectedly. "That's a story for another time."

"Gotcha. So, how long did you know Ethan before you found out you were preggers?"

"About three months. God, I was terrified. And, if it terrified me, imagine how he must have felt. He was so far from ready to be a father. Now, I wouldn't go back and change it even if I could. I can't imagine Kayla not being part of my life. But, at the time, I didn't know what to do. I couldn't even bring myself to tell Ethan right away. I think I put it off because I knew I'd lose him." I swiped a tear from my cheek and swirled the last bit of my drink around in my cup.

"What'd he do when you told him?" Tracey asked.

"He told me he wanted no part of raising a baby and that if I was smart, I'd take care of it and get on with my life. I told him I'd already considered my options and decided to keep the baby. I couldn't help it. I already loved her. He left town the next day. It broke my heart. I cried every day for weeks."

Tracey looked heartbroken for me. "Wow, I can't even imagine what you went through. I don't know how you did it."

"I don't either, but somehow I got through it and managed to finish school. Once the shock wore off, Mom was really excited about Kayla. It was the first time since my dad died that I felt like she stepped up and acted like a parent. Good thing, because Ethan wouldn't have been any help, even if he'd stuck around. He could barely support himself let alone a baby."

"You ever hear from him again?"

"I did, actually. When Kayla was about a month old, I called his friend, Ryan, and asked him to let Ethan know he had a daughter. I didn't expect to hear back from him, but a couple months later he sent me a letter and some money. It was the only letter I ever got, but he sent money every couple of months. It wasn't much, but I'm sure it was all he could afford. I sent pictures of Kayla when I had a return address, but I never knew if he got them."

"I'm sure he did." Tracey said. "At least some of them."

"It doesn't really matter anymore." I sat quietly for a moment, staring into the water, deep in thought.

"Sarah?"

"Huh?"

"What happened to Ethan?"

"Oh. Right. Kayla was barely a year old when Ryan phoned me. He never called, so I knew something had to be wrong. Ethan had just bought a motorcycle. Ryan said he'd only been out on it a few times when the accident happened. He was killed instantly."

"Wow, that's harsh."

"It was. Part of me still loved him, but I think I was more upset for Kayla, knowing she'd never have the chance to know her dad."

* * *

I lay awake that night thinking about my talk with Tracey, and realized how right she was. All these years, I'd kept all those emotions inside while I tried to stay strong for everyone else. It had felt good to finally talk to someone.

I didn't call or text Jay. I wanted time to think about what to say. And, despite what Tracey had said, I was still a little annoyed he hadn't contacted me, so I had no qualms about making him wait.

* * *

I went to work the next morning feeling better than I had in weeks. Unfortunately, it didn't last long.

It started before breakfast. The twins bickered like crazy the whole time I was in their room. I left them arguing over lipstick and moved on to the men's room where I put clothes out for Sam and Albert. From there, I went to collect Georgia from her bath. She was in a foul mood. "That woman has no respect for her elders. She scrubbed my back so hard it hurt. And the water was cold."

She complained all the way to the lounge, and although I was interested in hearing what she had to say about Sheila, I was beginning to get a headache. I left her with Edie, hoping the company might cheer her up.

Meanwhile, Sam decided to wander barefoot and in his pajamas into the muddy courtyard. It wasn't hard to spot him. A few residents had noticed him out there and gathered at the windows to watch.

"It's out," Albert said as I walked by.

"Pardon me, Albert?" I asked, pausing behind him.

He gestured at Sam and repeated, "It's out."

I peered over his shoulder.

"His wanker's out."

I made a disgusted sound and turned away. It certainly was out. He stood in front of the window, facing us, peeing in the bush. "Why do boys do that?" I asked no one in particular.

"'Cause we can," Albert replied matter-of-factly.

I got Sam inside and cleaned up in time for breakfast. "Here's your seat, Sam." I gestured to the empty chair beside

Lily and continued on to mine. Sam slapped my backside as I walked past. I stopped and turned around. "Sam, that's not appropriate."

He smiled impertinently, winked and took his seat.

I sighed heavily and continued to my chair. I'd heard Tracey laugh when Sam smacked me. I glanced across the room to where she sat. She had a huge grin on her face. I scowled at her and took my seat.

Mrs. Sellers was already there. I'd left her in the lounge before I went looking for Sam. Tracey had likely wheeled her in for me. I fixed her tea for her and placed it where she could reach.

Lily and Beth were still bickering.

"That's my tea. Why do you always take my tea?"

"I like the way you fix it."

"Fix your own damn tea."

"I'm telling Mother you said a bad word."

Mrs. W coughed.

"Well, if you'd swallow your food, this wouldn't happen."

I rubbed my throbbing temples. Sheila's whiny, patronizing voice grated on my nerves more than usual that morning.

An old country song drifted in from the lounge and Sam started humming. Beside him, Lily began dropping spoons full of oatmeal into her tea. Beth watched her in fascination. She took a spoonful of her own oatmeal and held it over her cup.

I took the spoon gently from Beth's hand. "Lily, Beth, that's oatmeal. You eat it. You don't put it in your tea."

Sam's humming turned into whistling and food flew out of his mouth into Lily's bowl.

Lily looked at him in disgust. "Stop that."

Sam stopped whistling and looked hurt. He stared into his oatmeal dejectedly.

Mrs. W coughed harder and Sheila's voice went up an octave. "Okay, that's it. You're done."

The dining room fell silent for a moment before Albert's voice rang out in a mock falsetto. "You're done. Snookered."

Beth tried to leave the table and I put a hand on her arm to stop her. "It's okay, Beth. Here, drink your tea."

I turned my head to look at Sheila. Her recent silence had been a welcome change, but apparently she was in a bad mood this morning as well. She'd stood up and was hovering over Mrs. W while she ranted. "You're spitting food all over me with your coughing. Why can't you just eat it?"

I'd had enough. The anger had been simmering inside me since the day Sheila had cornered me in the staff room. "Maybe she would if you'd be a little more patient with her."

Sheila swung around and glared at me. "Oh, I see how it is," she said to the room. "Sarah thinks she's an expert now since she started feeding her. I have thirty years experience doing this. I don't need you to tell me how to do my job." She took hold of Mrs. W's chair and wheeled her toward the door.

"Maybe not," Edie said loudly. "But someone ought to tell you how *not* to do it."

Sheila stopped in the doorway, back rigid, face tight with fury, but didn't speak or turn around. After a brief pause, she marched out of the room with Mrs. W.

"Good," Edie said. "Maybe now we can eat in peace." There were a few titters of nervous laughter around the room.

"Amen to that," Georgia said.

I caught Edie's eye and gave her a look that said, *Don't anger the Dragon*. She shrugged as though to say, Too late.

I thought nothing more of the incident until Abby came looking for me. She'd barely spoken to me since the day I'd shown her the marks on Mrs. W's neck and when she did acknowledge me, she was cold and abrupt.

It was late morning. I was in the staff room eating my lunch when Abby walked in. She marched right over to the table and sat down opposite me.

"I need to speak to you."

I put down my sandwich. "Okay."

"You take a lot of liberties around here with protocol. I've been lenient because you were new to Dementia, but you've been overstepping yourself lately. The other staff's behavior is for me to deal with, not you." She leaned in close. "Sheila has been a loyal, hard-working employee at Tranquility for many years. She may not do or say things in a way you agree with, but you need to remember that things were a lot different thirty years ago. Her way isn't your way, but that doesn't make it wrong. Unless you can prove a staff member is abusing someone, don't ever make an accusation that could cost someone their job. Understood?"

The anger had been simmering in my belly since the moment she began speaking. I pushed it down and fought to keep the emotion from my face. "Understood."

"Good, then I assume there will be no more problems

in the future. If there are, I'll be required to give you a written warning."

She stood and turned as though to leave, stopped and looked at me thoughtfully. "Also, about your resident, Edie—I know you believe she doesn't belong here, but I spoke with her the other day and she was extremely confused. It was obvious to me that she's cognitively impaired and I have to wonder if your judgment has been clouded by your attachment to her. I won't be pursuing this matter any further and I'll expect you not to as well. Anything outside of what you are required to do for the residents falls under my authority. Once you bring an issue of this nature to my attention, it's no longer your concern." She looked at me expectantly.

"Also understood," I said.

By the time Abby left the room I was shaking. I threw the rest of my lunch away and spent the last fifteen minutes of my break trying to calm down. I went back to work feeling utterly defeated. I'd lost hope of ever bringing Sheila to justice. Without Abby's help, I had no idea how to get Edie out of Dementia. Gran was dying. My mother was an emotional wreck and I'd likely ruined any chance I may have had with Jay.

* * *

Tracey caught up to me at the nurse's station right before the end of our shift. We sat side by side, documenting our day.

She looked around to be sure we were alone and said in a hushed voice, "I can't believe you did that."

"What?"

"Calling Sheila out in front of everyone."

I laughed humorlessly. "I can't believe it either. I just couldn't take anymore. I don't understand how people can think it's okay for her to treat the residents that way."

"I know. I feel the same way, but I need my job. She's gotten people fired before, you know."

"I believe it. She must have snitched on me right away. Abby found me in the staff room on my lunch break and reamed me out."

"Oh, shit."

"No kidding. I'll fill you in later, but basically she told me to mind my own business, and if it happens again she'll write me up."

Tracey shook her head in disgust. "Sheila has way more influence around here than she should."

"I agree. Oh, and Abby also told me she doesn't believe what I told her about Edie. She said she won't be pursuing it and neither should I."

"Wow, sounds like she's just being vindictive now."

I put my head in my hands dejectedly. "Yeah. I really messed up."

"No, you didn't. It takes guts to stand up to Sheila. More guts than I have. We'll figure this out, somehow."

I wasn't so sure I believed that, but I was grateful for the encouraging words.

* * *

Before heading home for the day, I went looking for Edie. I wanted to talk to her about what Abby had said.

She was in her room, sitting in her chair by the window, reading. She snapped her book shut when I walked in. "Well, lass, what did you get yourself into today?"

"I couldn't help it, Edie. I had to say something."

"I'm not saying you were wrong, but I'm worried you'll get yourself into trouble."

I shook my head. "It's me who should be worrying about you. Abby told me she spoke to you."

"That she did."

"And why would she think you were confused?"

Edie didn't respond. She crossed and uncrossed her legs and looked everywhere but at me.

"What are you doing, Edie? I'm trying to help you get out of here and you're pretending to have dementia? I understand why with Sheila, but with Abby?"

Edie looked at me and sighed in resignation. "I can't leave yet, lass. I need to help you first."

"Help me—Oh, Edie, no." I hung my head in my hands and shook it back and forth. "I never should have told you about Sheila."

"It wouldn't matter if you'd told me or not. I can see for myself what the woman is about and I wouldn't be standing for it either way."

"Please, let me deal with this and don't get involved."

"Well, now, I'm thinking it's a wee bit late for that."

"Edie …."

"I told you before that I wouldn't do anything stupid."

"Right. And then you made Abby believe you have dementia. What if that was your only chance to get out of here?"

She smiled at me gently. "You're worrying too much, lass. When the time is right, it'll happen."

* * *

When I got home from the hospital later that night, I decided to at least try to rectify the one thing I still had some control over. I texted Jay, left the phone in my bedroom and went to read Kayla her bedtime story.

She was half asleep by the time I closed the book. I pulled the blankets up and tucked them around her snugly. "I have tomorrow off. You know what that means."

She gazed up at me sleepily. "You're gonna take me to school?"

"I sure am."

"That's good. Why are you sad, Mommy?"

The question took me by surprise. I hesitated. "I'm always a little sad when I come home from the hospital, sweetie. I feel bad for Gran and I miss having her here with us."

"Me too."

Bending down, I kissed her cheek tenderly. "Goodnight, munchkin. Sweet dreams."

Her eyes fluttered shut and I watched her drift off to sleep. I loved her so much it hurt. She was the one thing in my life I knew was right.

In the kitchen, I emptied the dishwasher and cleaned up the mess left by Kayla's bedtime snack. I made myself an herbal tea, grabbed a couple cookies from the jar and went to my room.

I checked my phone for messages, got into my pajamas and curled up in the armchair with a book. By nine-thirty, I could barely keep my eyes open enough to read. I stood up, stretched, yawned, and headed to the bathroom to brush my teeth.

I'd just climbed into bed and turned off the light when I heard my phone vibrating on the nightstand. I fumbled in the dark for it.

"I didn't wake you did I?" Jay asked when I answered.

"No, I was just heading to bed."

"I'm sorry. I know you have to be up early in the morning. I can call you tomorrow."

"No, it's okay," I said, sitting up and turning on the lamp. "I have tomorrow off."

"Oh, that's good."

There was a moment of awkward silence before we began to speak at the same time.

"I want to—"

"Listen, I'm sorry—"

"Go ahead," I said.

"I want to apologize for Saturday. I knew you were upset when I took you home. I shouldn't have let the night end that way."

"No, I overreacted. I read too much into it when you said you'd like to meet Kayla. I guess I'm overprotective."

"You should be. I feel the same way about my nieces. I would never expect to be allowed into Kayla's life unless you thought the time was right."

I smiled, relieved he understood. "Thanks, I needed to hear something positive today."

"Rough day?"

"Yeah, you could say that."

"Well, maybe tomorrow will be better if you have a dinner date to look forward to."

I chuckled softly. "I'm sure it will." It was already better.

I hung up and drifted off to sleep with a lighter heart.

CHAPTER 23
TOUGH DECISIONS

I DROPPED KAYLA OFF AT SCHOOL Tuesday morning and then headed to the hospital.

Dr. Chang came in on his morning rounds and spoke to me as he examined Gran. "How are you doing? I haven't seen you in a while."

"I'm doing okay, thanks. I'm usually here later in the day."

"I know. I see Brenda when she's here early. She's taking it hard, isn't she?"

"She is. She doesn't deal well with this sort of thing."

"She's stronger than you think. She'll get through it."

He finished with his exam and came around the bed to stand next to me. He put his hand on my shoulder and looked straight at me. "Your mom's going to need you to help her through this. She has some tough decisions coming up. Your grandmother's getting weaker every day. The feeding tube and fluids are only prolonging the inevitable at this point."

I swallowed the lump in my throat. I'd known for a while it was coming, but hearing Dr. Chang say it made it much more real. "I know. I mean, I figured. I worked in palliative care, so I'm familiar with the signs."

"You're a nurse?"

"A support worker, but I'm going to nursing school this fall."

"Good for you. If you've worked in palliative care, you know how it works. It's been a week since we intubated. Every day the risk of infection increases. If she's going to remain on the ventilator indefinitely, we need to do a tracheotomy. If not, we need to take her off support and let her go when she's ready."

"Have you spoken to my mother about this?"

"I did. She said she needs time to think about it."

"She knows Gran's ready," I said. "It kills her to see her this way, but she can't bring herself to let her go either."

Before he left the room, Dr Chang asked, "What does your mother do?"

"She's a receptionist at a dental office, but she's off on a leave of absence right now."

"I, ah, was under the impression she's a widow, but I noticed she wears a wedding band...."

I was beginning to get the idea that Dr. Chang's interest in my mother was not entirely professional. "She took my dad's death really hard. She's just never taken it off."

After he left the room, I leaned over Gran and whispered, "I think Mom may just have an admirer. All that nagging I put up with about getting out more—maybe she needs to take her own advice, huh?"

* * *

I went home at noon to have lunch with Mom before she left to see Gran. She had tuna melts in the oven and was tossing a small salad. I set plates and forks out on the island and poured two glasses of ice water. "I spoke to Dr. Chang this morning," I said.

Her shoulders sagged. "What did he say?"

"The same thing he said to you, Mom. You need to decide soon."

She turned and looked at me in desperation. "I can't right now. I need more time."

"Just do what you think is best for Gran."

"I don't know." She began to cry. "I don't know what's best. I can't—" She covered her mouth with a trembling hand. "I don't know if I can do that. How do I choose to let her die?"

"We talked about this with Gran after the first stroke, Mom," I reminded her gently. "She told us she never wanted to be kept alive by a machine if there was no chance she'd recover. You're not choosing to let her die, you're choosing to take her off the ventilator so she *can* die if she's ready."

"But *I'm* not ready. I'm not ready to let her go."

"Then maybe the best thing right now is to let them do the tracheotomy. If anything, it'll give you time to decide without feeling pressured."

She drew in a deep shaky breath. "I'll think about it."

"We'll talk about it again when you're ready. You'll get through it, Mom. We'll get through it together."

She nodded and managed a teary smile.

We sat down to eat. I stared at my mother thoughtfully. She was still an attractive woman. Her body was trim and fit. Her dark, glossy hair showed only a hint of gray. The fine wrinkles around her eyes and mouth added character to her face.

She looked up and caught me staring. "What?" she asked, picking up her napkin and wiping her mouth. "Do I have food on my face?"

"No."

"Then why are you looking at me like that?"

"I just realized how beautiful you are. I mean…I always knew you were, but I guess I don't always see you that way because you're my mom."

She looked surprised at the compliment. "Thank you, that's sweet. I have to admit I haven't felt beautiful in a long time. I guess I kind of gave up on myself after your dad…. I just didn't care anymore. And now, with everything that's going on with Gran…well, sometimes I can barely find the energy to comb my hair."

I waited until she took a sip of water and said, "You could do worse than Dr. Chang."

She choked and grabbed her napkin to keep from spewing water everywhere. When she'd finished coughing she gave me an annoyed look. "I have no idea what you're talking about."

"Oh, so you're not interested? Because, I got the impression this morning that he is."

"Oh, please, he's not interested in me."

"Okay, I'm just saying. He's a doctor and he's not bad looking for an old guy. It wouldn't be such a bad thing."

Mom just rolled her eyes and took a bite of her tuna melt, but there was a gleam in her eye that hadn't been there earlier.

* * *

It was a cool day, but I decided to take advantage of the sunshine by taking Kayla and Amelia to the park after school. They played tag on the jungle gym, then giggled and shrieked while I pushed them on the swings. We left the park, breathless and rosy-cheeked, an hour later.

We dropped Amelia off at her house on the way home. Kayla walked beside me, holding my hand. She was quiet now that we were alone and the usual bounce was missing from her step.

I gave her hand a squeeze. "You're awfully quiet all of a sudden. Are you feeling okay?"

"I'm fine, Mommy. I was just thinking about Gran."

"I think about her a lot too. Do you want to tell me what you were thinking?"

"Before, when I asked you if Gran was gonna die, you said you didn't know."

"That's right, I didn't know. I still don't."

"I think if Gran was gonna be okay, like last time, you and Nana wouldn't be so sad."

I stopped and crouched down next to her. "No one can know for sure when Gran might die, not even the doctor. But, yes, she's very sick and the thought of her dying makes us all sad."

"What'll happen to Gran if she dies, Mommy?"

"Well…she'll go to a nice place where she won't be sick or in pain anymore, just like Grandpa and your daddy."

"Does that mean we won't get to see her anymore?"

I nodded and put my arm around her. "It does, sweetie."

Her eyes welled up with tears. Her bottom lip quivered.

"I don't want Gran to die, Mommy. I'd miss her too much."

I hugged her to me tightly as I fought back tears. "We all will, munchkin. You just have to remember how lucky you are that she's been a part of your life." I pulled away and looked at her. "No matter what happens," I said, putting my hand over her heart, "she'll always be in here."

* * *

Mom came home from the hospital early to spend the evening with Kayla. I kissed them goodbye and hurried to my car. I was running a few minutes behind for my date with Jay and I hated being late. I'd suggested *The Queen's*, knowing it wouldn't be too busy on a weeknight. It was also casual and not nearly as intimate as the restaurant Jay had taken me to last time. My lip was still bruised and a little sore and with Saturday night still hanging over my head, intimate was the last thing I wanted.

Jay was already there, sitting in a booth. I slid onto the bench across from him. The conversation was casual until the waitress brought our drinks and finished taking our order. As soon as she walked away Jay said, "Can we talk about Saturday night now? Let's just get it out of the way so we're not feeling awkward all evening."

I was a little surprised by his directness, but he was right. We wouldn't be able to relax and enjoy one another's company with tension hanging in the air between us. I nodded. "Okay, go ahead."

"When I told you I'd like to meet your daughter, I said it casually without thinking of it from your perspective and what a big deal that would be for you. And for her."

"I know. I realized that later, after I'd had some time to

think about it. Like I said, I overreacted."

"No, you didn't. I think about my sister and her kids. What if she was in your position? I wouldn't want her bringing every guy she dated into their lives."

"When I started dating again after Kayla was born, I made it a rule to tell my dates about her by the end of the second date. I've never had a third date. As soon as they hear about her they run the other way."

"Well, technically, you told me about Kayla on our first date. Tonight's our fourth and I'm not running anywhere."

I looked into his eyes and felt my heart skip a beat. "No, I don't think you're the running type. If and when the time is right, you'll meet her."

"I know that. And I know you're just doing your job as a mom and protecting her, and I respect that. It's just…I like you a lot and I don't want this to stand in the way of us getting to know each other." He looked vulnerable suddenly.

I smiled at him reassuringly. "I like you too. But I'm warning you; this is all new to me. I'm probably going to mess up along the way."

"I doubt it. I won't let you."

Jay was right. Talking about it cleared the air and conversation flowed the rest of the evening. The date ended at my car with a kiss so deep and intense it left my heart pounding. I drove home with the smell of his cologne still in my nostrils, my lips still tingling, wishing the night had never ended.

* * *

Mom was watching TV in the living room when I got home. I went in to say goodnight. She patted the seat next to hers on the couch. "Come sit. We need to talk."

I sat obediently beside her and waited.

She took a deep breath. "I thought about what we talked about this morning. I'm going to tell Dr. Chang to go ahead with the tracheotomy. You're right, it'll give me time to think."

That she had made a decision at all was enough for the moment. I'd told her to decide what was best for Gran, but she had to be able to live with that decision.

"Good for you," I said. "And just so you know, I'll support whatever decisions you make."

* * *

Tracey and I talked about my date with Jay while making beds at work the next day.

She couldn't help but gloat. "I told you didn't I? I knew he wasn't mad at you. So'd you have makeup sex?"

"Oh, my God, Trace. Is that all you think about?"

She shrugged and stuck her bottom lip out the way Kayla did when she didn't get her own way. "Seems like it lately. I've been seeing Kyle for nearly three weeks and all he's done is kiss me."

"So, why don't you make the first move?"

"Because I don't think he's that kind of guy. He's sort of old-fashioned. He even opens the car door for me."

"What's wrong with that?"

"Nothing. I kind of like it, actually. I'm just not used to it."

We moved on to the next bed and worked in silence

until Tracey glanced at the door and said in a low voice, "Do you have a video camera?"

"Yeah, Mom got me one the Christmas after Kayla was born. Why?"

A devious look came over her face. "Maybe we could hide it in the bathing room."

"Are you serious?" I whispered, glancing nervously at the door. "What if we got caught? I'm pretty sure a hidden camera is illegal, especially in a bathing room."

"But think about it; Sheila's never here much earlier than seven and she leaves at one-thirty. That means the bathing room's empty for at least half an hour in the morning and an hour before our shift ends."

I stopped working and stared at her in astonishment. "You've actually thought about this, haven't you?"

She shrugged. "A little."

"Even if we did it and got something incriminating against Sheila, we can't use it if it's illegal."

"So, we make sure there's no way to trace it back to us and we send it to the police and the administrator anonymously. Once they've seen it, they can't ignore it."

"I don't know, Trace, it's risky. If anyone caught us or found out what we were doing, we'd be in big trouble. I'm already on Abby's bad side, so I'd probably lose my job. You could too."

"I know we'd be taking a risk, but maybe it's worth it. Have you come up with a better idea?"

"No," I mumbled.

"Exactly. So just think about it, okay?"

CHAPTER 24
THE LAST STRAW

AN INCIDENT TWO DAYS LATER made up my mind about the video camera.

I'd taken some of my residents to the auditorium for recreation time and was on my way back to Hall B to make beds. As I came around the corner, I heard loud voices coming from the bathing room.

"Stop it, stop it, I'm falling!"

"You won't fall, you're fine. Stop whining."

I paused outside the door to listen.

"I want down. Put me down."

I was sure it was Mrs. Martin, but I'd never heard her raise her voice before.

"I'm not letting you down until you stop yelling."

I pushed the door open slowly and peeked inside. Sheila stood facing the tub with her back to me. Mrs. Martin sat naked in the lift high above the floor, crying, "Put me down" over and over. She looked terrified.

Sheila left the poor woman hanging in the air, dripping wet, and walked casually to the storage cabinet. She hummed as she folded and straightened towels.

Mrs. Martin began to cry. Her body trembled

uncontrollably. I choked back the anger and pushed the door open wide. "Is everything okay in here? I thought I heard yelling."

Sheila jumped and turned toward me, quickly schooling her features to hide the guilt. "Everything's fine. Mrs. Martin just isn't very happy about having a bath today."

"So, you don't need help then?"

She turned and grabbed a towel off the pile she'd been folding. "Of course I don't need help," she said, marching to the tub. She pulled the controller from the pocket on the side of the lift and began to lower Mrs. Martin.

"Okay, good. Glad everything's okay." I closed the door gently and listened a moment longer. I heard nothing but the hum of the lift. I continued on to Hall B.

I found Tracey making Mrs. Amaral's bed and went to the other side to help. "Okay, I'm in."

"In how? What are you…? You mean the camera thing?"

I nodded and told her about what I'd seen.

Tracey's voice shook with anger. "That's exactly why we have to do this."

"I know. I still don't like it, but I don't see any other way. And I'm doing it myself. I don't want you dragged into it if I get caught."

"Uh, no, you're not. I'm already involved. Besides, you need me to be lookout."

"No, I don't. I'll find a way."

"I'm helping. That's all there is to it. We need to get together and plan this thing."

"Fine," I said, sighing in resignation. "How about

tonight?"

* * *

Mom picked Kayla up from school so I could go right to the hospital after work. I spent a couple of hours with Gran before going home to shower and help Mom make dinner. Tracey showed up while we were cooking. We had a glass of red wine while we chopped vegetables for the spaghetti sauce and the salad. Kayla climbed up on the stool beside Tracey. I handed her a cutting board and knife to chop mushrooms.

"Wow," Tracey said, "your mom let's you use a sharp knife, huh?"

"Only for things like mushrooms, 'cause they're easy to cut," Kayla replied matter-of-factly.

Tracey sighed and shook her head dramatically. "You must be really special 'cause my mom still won't let me use sharp knives and I'm twenty-five."

"You're funny," Kayla giggled. She went on to tell her all about school and her friends. Tracey listened avidly, inserting remarks and questions in all the right places.

After dinner, Mom left to go to the hospital. Tracey and I cleaned up the kitchen, while Kayla went into the living room to set up the Wii.

When we'd finished in the kitchen, we joined Kayla. I sat on the couch and finished my wine as I watched Tracey and Kayla battle. They bowled for a while and then moved on to boxing. The whole time, they bantered back and forth in friendly competition. It ended with Kayla landing a solid left hook and knocking Tracey out. She fell to the floor in mock unconsciousness. When Kayla bent over, Tracey grabbed her, pulled her to the floor and tickled her.

Kayla laughed until she shrieked, "Stop, stop! Can't breathe."

Tracey stopped and they lay breathless, side-by-side, on the floor.

"Okay, munchkin," I said, "now that you're all wound up, it's time to get ready for bed."

The lip came out. "But, Mommy, I don't have school tomorrow."

"I know you don't, but you have a busy day anyway. Nana's dropping you off at Amelia's house before lunch and you're staying there until I'm finished work."

That cheered her up and she ran off to get into her pajamas. Twenty minutes later, she was in bed sound asleep. I made a pot of tea and Tracey and I sat down to plot against Sheila.

"First of all," Tracey said, "I think we should go in ahead of time and scope out the room to find the best place to set up the camera."

I hadn't thought of that. Set-up would have to be quick, so we needed as much information as possible going into it. "Let's do it tomorrow during the Saturday matinee," I suggested.

Tracey nodded her agreement. "You have a spare memory card with nothing on it?"

I went to my room and came back with the video camera and battery. "I don't have a spare card, but I can load this one onto the computer and clear the card."

"You'll have to format, so the card's completely wiped," Tracey said. "And make sure you charge the battery."

"Okay, that takes care of the how," I said, "Now we

have to figure out the when."

Tracey thought for a moment. "We'll check the bath schedule for the week. I think our best bet is Mrs. W, since Sheila seems to enjoy picking on her so much. Hopefully one of her bath days co-ordinates with both of us working."

"And if Sheila's having a good day and we get nothing?" I asked.

"Really? Like that's gonna happen. Think about it. Sheila having a good day?"

We looked at each other and burst out laughing.

"Oh Trace," I said a moment later as I wiped tears from my eyes. "What are we getting ourselves into?"

* * *

Saturday was the perfect day to check out the bathing room. Neither Sheila nor Abby were there and it was a quiet afternoon, with some residents signed out or busy with visitors, and others watching the movie.

The morning seemed to drag by and with each passing hour I felt more on edge.

I waited until Tom and Anne showed up for their weekly visit with Edie. The last thing I needed was for Edie to become suspicious and involve herself in what could end up being a huge debacle.

I met Tracey outside the bathing room shortly after one. We moved the supply cart closer to the door. I pulled my keys out of my pocket and they slipped through my fingers onto the floor with a loud clang. The sound seemed to echo through the empty hallway and I froze.

Tracey bent down, picked them up and handed them to me. "You okay?"

I gulped nervously, nodded, unlocked the door and slipped into the room while Tracey pretended to be busy re-organizing the cart. I'd gone to my locker during my break and gotten my phone. I pulled it out of my pocket and snapped pictures of the room from every angle.

I noticed a cabinet on the wall in one corner with a dust-covered, fake plant on top. It would be a pain getting up and down, but it would be up high and out of sight. I opened the cabinet door. It was filled with cleaning supplies, rags, and other odds and ends. It was a possibility. I stood in front of it, facing the room, and took pictures to show the sight lines to the door and tub. I turned around, stood back and snapped one of the cabinet as well.

I pulled the stepstool out of the closet beside the shower room and placed it in front of the cabinet. I had to stand on the second step to reach the plant, but it was doable. I held my phone up in front of the plant and took a few pictures of the room from that angle.

I slipped my phone into my pocket, lifted the plant down and inspected it. The fake ivy was thick enough to hide a small camera. There was a piece of green foam inside that the stems were stuck into. The camera could sit on top of it. I put the plant back in its place and wiped my dusty hands on my pants. Judging by the thick layer of dust on the top of the cabinet, no one had been up there in years.

I stepped down, folded the stool, put it back in the closet and went to the door. I stood for a moment and listened. Tracey was whistling. I opened the door a crack. "All clear?" I whispered.

She rolled her eyes. "I wouldn't be whistling if it

wasn't."

"I know. I'm just paranoid."

I closed the door and locked it while Tracey put the supply cart back in place. We walked casually toward Hall B to make our rounds.

"Get any pics?" Tracey asked.

I nodded, looking around nervously to be sure no one could hear us.

"Okay, maybe we should do this at my place. More privacy. I'm going out with Kyle tonight. You free right after work?"

"No, I have to pick Kayla up and spend some time with her before I go to the hospital. I have tomorrow off."

Tracey laughed. "I'm working tomorrow. I'll call you later. We'll figure it out."

I popped my head into Mrs. Sellers' room. She was sleeping. Edie would be with Tom and Anne until two o'clock sharp, when Anne, as was her custom, would stand up and announce it was time to leave. Georgia had been signed out for the night and Sam, Rose and the twins were in the lounge, watching the Saturday afternoon movie. I glanced into the twins' room, certain it would be empty, and the next two as well. Once I had checked all the rooms, I met up with Tracey again and we headed to the lounge.

Tracey asked, "So, what are you up to tonight?"

"I have a date later too, with Jay."

The sound of Gene Kelly, singing and tap dancing through the rain, drifted out of the lounge.

"Hey," Tracey said, "I have an idea. Wanna go out together tonight? I mean, if the guys want to."

"I'd be okay with that. Ask Kyle first and let me know what he says, then I'll talk to Jay."

We walked into the lounge. Rose, Lily and Beth were there. Sam was not. "Where's Sam?" I asked the twins.

Lily and Rose stared at me blankly. Beth said, "Sam who?"

I sighed and left the lounge to look for him.

"Check the courtyard. All that rain in stereo probably gave him the urge," Tracey called after me.

She was right of course. I found Sam, wearing only his iPod and his underwear, dancing in the courtyard.

* * *

Kyle and Jay were fine with the idea of a double date. I'd had little free time to spend with Jay, so I felt a momentary twinge of regret when Tracey texted me to say it was a go. It didn't last long and as I got ready, I found myself feeling excited over the prospect of a night out with friends. It was a part of my youth I'd given up when I'd decided to keep Kayla. Not once had I regretted keeping her, but I sometimes regretted missing out.

Mom offered to take Kayla to McDonald's for dinner. It was a treat she only got about once a month, so she chattered excitedly about it all the way out the door. I barely even got a wave goodbye.

Tracey and Kyle were already at *The Queen's* when Jay and I arrived and had managed to get a booth. They shared a seat, so we slid onto the other bench together. "Wow, you're early," I whispered across the table to Tracey.

She grinned. "I know. It's Kyle's fault. He hates being late."

I introduced Jay to Kyle. They shook hands and immediately began to discuss the hockey game playing on the flat screen above the bar. I looked at Tracey and rolled my eyes.

"Men," she mouthed. She snuggled closer to Kyle and he put his arm around her shoulders. She looked so small next to him, yet they fit together so well.

The boys turned their attention to us after the waitress came around, and the four of us talked and laughed easily throughout dinner.

As usual, Tracey's bright smile and contagious laughter attracted attention from the men in the room. I wasn't the only one who noticed. As the night went on, Kyle sat up a little taller in his seat and his arm tightened possessively around her shoulders. Tracey, in her typical carefree way, was oblivious to the tension building in the room.

After the waitress finished clearing the dishes from the table, I put a hand on my stomach and groaned, "I'm way too full. I need to get up and move around. You guys want to go in the back room and play pool?"

Jay and Kyle looked at each other.

"There's a TV back there," I said.

Kyle shrugged one shoulder. "Sounds good to me."

We spent the next hour playing in teams of couples. Jay and I were sadly outmatched and lost all three games. We left the pub around ten-thirty, as it was starting to get busy. Tracey had to work the next morning so she and Kyle decided to call it a night. Jay and I walked to the café down the street for coffee. We sat at a quiet table in the corner and ordered two decaf-mochas.

"That was fun," Jay said. "Kyle seems like a nice guy."

"He is. I like him."

"Good job distracting him with pool. I was afraid he might hurt someone."

"You noticed that too, huh?"

"Uh-huh. He better get used to it or he's going to spend a lot of time being jealous and miserable."

We sat in the café and talked until closing time. Neither of us was ready for the night to end, so we strolled up and down the main street and talked some more. Jay took my hand. He twined his fingers through mine and didn't let go until we got to the car.

Conversation flowed easily on the drive to my house. I turned to Jay when we pulled into the driveway behind Mom's car. "Thanks, I had a nice night."

"Me too." He looked at my mouth, then reached out and ran his thumb gently across my bottom lip.

I shivered involuntarily and closed my eyes.

"Is your lip still sore?"

My eyes flew open. "Pardon?"

"Your lip is still a little bruised. Would it hurt if I kissed you?"

"Oh. No."

"Good, because I've been wanting to all night." The kiss was slow and gentle, and not nearly long enough. He pulled away. "How was that?"

"Mmm, hard to tell. I think we should try it again."

* * *

Tracey called me the next day when she got home from work and we agreed to meet later that evening to look at the pictures of the bathing room and make a plan. I stopped by her place on my way to the hospital. She gave me a quick tour. The apartment was a one-bedroom in an old, stone building. It had high ceilings, original wood trim, hardwood floors and a wall of floor-to-ceiling windows in the living room. She'd decorated it with bright colors and an eclectic collection of furniture and art. One piece of artwork caught my eye. It was a simple unframed canvas hanging above the fireplace. I wasn't normally a fan of abstract art, but the vibrant colors exploded off the canvas like a tidal wave of fire and water.

"This is amazing," I said. "I feel like I'm standing on the rocks overlooking the ocean and the world's on fire around me." Tracey looked at me oddly. For a moment I thought she might cry. "What's wrong?" I asked

"It's mine. I painted it."

"You—Oh, my God, Trace. It's beautiful."

She smiled and turned to look at the painting with me. "You're the first person who's ever seen it the way I do."

Tracey went to the kitchen to pour us some wine while I set the laptop up on the coffee table. She came in a few minutes later, handed me a glass of red wine and took a seat on the couch beside me.

I showed Tracey the pictures of the bathing room. She agreed the best place for the camera was on top of the cabinet, hidden in the fake ivy. Putting it up so high did create a problem, however.

"I'm putting it up there blind," I said. "We could end up with three hours of footage of the floor or the wall."

We were deep in thought for a moment. Finally, Tracey

had an idea. "We'll do a dry run tomorrow. Who knows, we might get something good. If not, at least we'll know if it's in the right place. Is the camera ready to go?"

"It is, but I'm not sure if I like that idea. The more we mess around in that room, the more chance of getting caught."

"Sarah, we're allowed to be in there, that's why we have a key. If somebody walks in, we say a resident lost something."

"Like what?"

"I don't know, like their comb, a slipper-something they take to the bathing room with them. You're worrying too much about somebody seeing us. No one's gonna care if we're in there, except maybe Sheila, and we'll be out way before she shows up for work."

Tracey was right, of course. I worried too much. It was my pessimistic inner voice telling me all the things that could go wrong.

We met the next morning in the parking lot, twenty minutes before our shift. Tracey got in my car and we went over our plan as we drank our morning coffee. I checked and double-checked my bag to make sure I had the camera.

After I zipped it up the second time, Tracey asked, "Sure you don't want me to go in and hide the camera?"

"No, I told you, I want you involved as little as possible."

"Then take a deep breath and calm yourself. It's not a friggin' bank job. You're not doing anything wrong and you'll be in and out in less than five minutes."

I took a couple deep breaths. "Okay, let's go," I said

before I could change my mind.

I pulled the camera out of my bag in the change room and put it in the big side pocket of my scrub shirt. I turned toward Tracey. "Can you see it?"

"Not really, it's pretty small. Put your hand in your pocket and hold onto it."

I did as she said.

She gave a satisfied nod and checked her phone before placing it on the shelf in her locker. "It's twenty after. Let's go."

A night shift support worker was on her way into the change room as we left. I smiled and hoped I didn't look as nervous as I felt. Tracey said a cheery good morning and held the door open for her. We walked through Hall B without seeing anyone and turned the corner into the next hall. I breathed a little easier when I saw that it was empty.

"Okay," Tracey whispered, unlocking the bathing room door and holding it open for me.

I walked hesitantly into the room and flicked on the light. Tracey closed the door gently behind me. A few seconds later, I heard her whistling. I took a deep steadying breath and hurried to the closet to get the stool. I unfolded it and put it in place, pulled the camera out of my pocket, turned it on and climbed onto the stool. Reaching up, I placed the camera in the pot on top of the foam block for a quick test shoot, then took it down and played it back. Satisfied the angle was right, I put it back up, making sure it was well hidden.

The sound of voices in the hallway stopped my heart. I stood perfectly still and listened. Tracey said something I couldn't make out. A moment later, it was quiet again. She whistled and tapped lightly on the door. I stepped down, grabbed the stool, stuffed it back into the closet and took one last look up at the plant to be sure the camera couldn't be seen. I flicked off the light and opened the door a crack.

Tracey stood there jingling the keys impatiently in one hand. She looked both ways down the hall and nodded. "Let's go," she said.

I hurried out and she locked the door. We walked at a casual pace back to Hall B. "We'll talk later," Tracey said before she veered off into Mrs. Martin's room.

I went about my work and was wheeling Mrs. Sellers into the auditorium for Pet Therapy when Tracey caught up to me again. She had Mrs. Amaral, who greeted me with her usual enthusiasm. We placed the women side by side behind the rows of chairs, where no one would trip over their wheelchairs.

Mrs. Amaral grabbed onto Tracey's hand before she could walk away. She gazed up at her pleadingly and said something in Portuguese.

Tracey crouched down to eye level to reassure her. "It's okay. I'll be back to get you soon. Tara's gonna show you the animals."

Mrs. Amaral loosened her grip. Tracey pulled her hand free and we went back to Hall B together to start tidying rooms and making beds.

Tracey glanced over her shoulder to be sure no one was behind us. "Did you get it set up," she asked in a hushed voice.

I nodded. "I heard voices. Who was in the hall with

you?"

"It was just Tina's resident, Mrs. Murray. She always gets up early and wanders around."

"It scared the crap out of me. I was still shaking an hour later."

Tracey smirked. "Yeah, you looked pretty scared when you came out."

We said hello to Carol as she passed us in the hall. She pushed Mrs. W in her wheelchair toward the auditorium. Three other residents followed along behind. She gave us a frosty nod as she walked by.

I waited until they were out of earshot to speak. "I'm not kidding, Trace. This whole thing gives me the jitters. I think we shouldn't talk about it at work at all. It's not worth being overheard."

"You're right. Sorry, I know it makes you nervous. We have to get the camera back today, though."

"I know. Meet me near the bathing room at twenty after two."

Chapter 25
The Preview

I CUT MY VISIT WITH GRAN short that night and went to Tracey's to watch the footage. We got comfortable on the couch with the laptop and glasses of wine before Tracey started the video. She skipped ahead until we saw the door open and Sheila enter the room. The camera was angled a little high and only caught Sheila from the waist up, but the tub and lift were in full view. We decided I could solve that problem by placing the back of the camera on the edge of the pot to angle it down slightly.

"This is weird," I said. "I feel like a voyeur."

"Oh, c'mon. We've seen most of them naked before anyway."

"I know, but this is different. It just feels wrong."

"You're right. It kind of does. But it's for the right reasons."

Sheila's voice was obnoxiously loud and condescending. She used crass names for various body parts and didn't seem to notice or care that she offended the residents. She left them hanging naked in the air, as I'd seen her do with Mrs. Martin. When a resident became upset or obstinate, her voice rose even more and she banged things in frustration.

Rose's bath was the last one recorded before the battery died. She was slow getting undressed because of her cast. Sheila finally became so impatient that she practically ripped the robe off Rose's body, causing her to lose her balance. Sheila grabbed onto her good arm and half-carried her to the lift.

When Rose complained the water was cold, Sheila told her to shut-up. She didn't wrap Rose's cast in plastic as she should have. She propped it on the side of the tub and barked at Rose every time she moved it.

She worked quickly and efficiently, scrubbing Rose's whole body except her privates. She dropped the cloth into the water in front of her and said, "Here you go. Wash your fish."

Rose lifted her injured arm off the tub as though to reach for the cloth.

"Not that arm, you retard!" Sheila plunged her arm into the water and came up with the cloth. She slapped it into Rose's good hand and walked away.

A tear rolled down Rose's cheek as she stared at the cloth. She was so cold her shivering caused little ripples in the water.

"Hurry it up," Sheila said. "Your time's almost up."

Another tear spilled over and Rose began to sob softly.

The screen went blank.

Tracey and I sat in stunned silence, staring at the laptop.

"Poor Rose," I said finally. "I can't believe I send her into that room twice a week to be treated that way."

Tracey was furious. She stood up and began to pace. "Oh, no. You're not allowed to feel guilty. You're the only one who's had the guts to stand up to that bitch."

"Do you think it's enough? Maybe we don't have to go back in for Mrs. W's bath."

"Oh no, we're gonna do this right."

My shoulders slumped. My stomach was in knots just thinking about having to sneak in there again.

Tracey sat down across from me. She leaned in close and put her hand on my knee. I'd never seen her look so intense. "It's not enough, Sarah." She jerked her thumb at the laptop. "That's no worse than what she did to Mrs. W that day in the dining room in front of everybody. And she only got a slap on the wrist for that. We need more."

I took a deep breath and thought of Rose, sobbing and shivering in the tub. "You're right."

Tracey smiled encouragingly and leaned back in her chair. "I checked the bath schedule today. Mrs. W's next bath is Thursday and Edie has one right after. I'm working Thursday. Are you?"

"I am."

"Perfect. Thursday it is."

* * *

Mom was home when I got there. She was sitting in the armchair in the living room, staring into the fireplace.

I sat down on the sofa, across from her. "You okay, Mom?"

She stared at me blankly for a moment. "Sarah. I didn't even hear you come in."

"I just got home, I stopped by Tracey's for a bit. I sent you a text to let you know I'd be late."

"My phone is… I'm not sure where it is."

I looked at her closely. Her eyes were sad and empty. The gleam of hope was gone. "What's wrong?"

Mom got up and stood by the fireplace, gazing up at the pictures on the mantle. She ran a finger lightly over a picture of Gran sitting in her old convertible, looking sun-kissed and windblown from the drive.

"I know she's not coming back. I've known it for a while, but I kept hoping she'd pull through somehow." She turned to face me, her expression full of guilt. "Today I found myself wondering why she's still alive. I thought, *If only she'd let go, I wouldn't have to decide.* My God, Sarah, I was sitting there, holding her hand, almost hoping for her to die! What kind of person am I?" Tears streamed down her face.

I went to her and pulled her into my arms. I could feel her body shaking. "You're a good person. That's why it's so hard for you to see her this way. It's hard for me too and I've found myself thinking the same thing. We're not hoping for her to die, we're hoping she'll find peace."

I slept fitfully that night. My head swam with thoughts of Gran and Sheila.

The next morning, I woke with a headache and puffy, dark circles under my eyes. Although I dreaded sneaking back into the bathing room, I almost wished Mrs. W's bath was that day. The waiting and suspense were unbearable. Worst of all, I couldn't get the image of Rose, sobbing and shivering, out of my head. Every time I sent a resident into the bathing room, I thought of her and felt a wave of guilt.

Tracey tried her best to reassure me, but by the end of the day, I was a mess. I hurried out to the parking lot at two-thirty sharp, without even waiting for Tracey.

When I got home, Mom was in the kitchen making a pot of tea. I pulled out a stool and sat at the island. "You're home from the hospital early."

Mom poured the tea. She placed a mug in front of me as well as a plate of cookies she and Kayla had made the night before. "I was hoping to catch you before you went to the school," she said, sitting down across from me. "I've made a decision."

"And?"

"I want Gran to come home. I think it's what she would want. I think it might be what she's waiting for."

I nodded. "I think it's a good idea."

Mom's shoulders sagged in relief. "My only concern is Kayla. How do you feel about her seeing Gran the way she is?"

"I think she'll be okay. Death is a part of life. It's something she has to learn eventually."

"I told Dr. Chang my decision today. He said if all goes well, she could be home by Thursday."

We'd need supplies for Gran if that were the case. "I have tomorrow off. Why don't we go shopping after we take Kayla to school and get the things we'll need for Gran?"

"That would be nice, Sarah. We certainly haven't had much time to spend together lately, have we?"

"You have your hands full with Gran right now."

Mom took my hand as I reached for my tea. "I know I haven't been there for you since your dad died." Her eyes filled with tears.

"Mom, you don't have to—"

"Yes. I do. I failed you. And I failed myself. I lost out on seeing you grow into a woman. I was so consumed by my own grief and pain that I didn't think about yours."

"I didn't exactly reach out to you either."

"You were a child! I was supposed to be the parent. I should have reached out. I was such a mess after your dad died. It was like a part of me died with him. For a long time I did want to die."

I squeezed her hand and blinked back tears of my own. "So did I. For a long time, all I could remember was how weak and helpless he was at the end, but the other day I smelled wood smoke and it reminded me of him and the trailer."

Mom smiled through her tears. "It was his favorite place."

"You'd lounge in your chair reading, while Dad and I fished."

"I fished too. Sometimes."

"Until you freaked out when you got that huge pike on the line and tipped the canoe and lost most of Dad's fishing gear."

We laughed and Mom shook her head at the memory. "He wasn't very happy with me, was he?"

"No, but he laughed about it later. I think my favorite time was in the evening, at the campfire. You and Dad would sit on that big log bench he built and I'd snuggle up under a blanket across your legs, with my head on a pillow on your lap."

"And I'd stroke your hair until you fell asleep," Mom said softly.

I nodded. "I remember trying so hard to keep my eyes open. I didn't want to miss anything."

"I'm so sorry I wasn't there for you," Mom said.

I squeezed her hand. "It was a bad time for all of us. Like Gran always says, you can't change the past. All you can do is learn from it and move on."

Mom smiled sadly. "Gran's always been full of good advice. Thank God she's been here for us these past ten years."

I lay awake that night thinking about our talk. It was the first time we'd spoken openly about my dad since his death. It had opened the floodgates and let long lost memories come pouring in; the smell of the campfire swirling around me, filling my senses, the warmth of the fire, the gentle rhythm of my mother's fingers in my hair, and the sound of my parents' subdued voices, lulling me to sleep.

I held those once-forgotten memories of my dad close, his face, etched with the lines of years of laughter, his voice, deep and musical. And the way he smelled, of sawdust, sweet fresh air and the earthy smell of sweat that comes from working outdoors.

I'd loved him more than I'd ever loved anyone until Kayla. I swore I'd never forget him; his face, his laughter, the wonderful smell of him.

The memories were overwhelming. There were so many, all at once, filling my head, my heart, my senses. My chest hurt. It felt as though someone had reached in, taken hold of my heart and was squeezing it. I struggled to breathe, sucked in a deep, quavering breath and buried my head in my pillow as the first sob tore from my throat. When the sobs subsided, I turned my soggy pillow over and cried myself quietly to sleep.

* * *

Mom and I spent the next morning shopping. Spending some uncomplicated time with her took my mind off Sheila and the camera for a while. Mom seemed more relaxed as well. The decision was made. It was one less thing weighing on her mind.

After stopping at a diner for lunch, we headed to the hospital to see Gran. Dr. Chang came in to confirm that she would be going home the next day. He explained what would happen, answered our questions, and left us with the nurse. She gave us some handouts to read and went over the basics of care with us. It was all information I was familiar with, but it would give Mom a better idea of what to expect.

I left Mom with Gran and headed home, stopping on a whim at the little market nearby to buy a bouquet of tulips. When I got home, I went to the kitchen, arranged the vibrant orange and yellow flowers in a vase and took them to Gran's room.

Before she'd come from the hospital after her first stroke, Mom and I had converted the dining room into a bedroom for her. The room was spacious with a big, bright window facing the backyard. It was near the kitchen and main floor bathroom and, most importantly, there were no stairs to worry about. It had been perfect for her while she recuperated.

I cleaned and organized the room and put away the supplies we'd bought. I moved the double bed into the corner against the wall to make room for the hospital bed we'd arranged to rent. The armchair was perfect in front of the window. I angled it so it would have a view of both Gran's bed and the yard. The nightstand and lamp went beside the chair. It would be a nice spot to sit with coffee and a book. I placed the flowers on the dresser beside the little flat screen TV. The walls looked a little stark, so I went to my room, got a piece of Kayla's artwork I'd framed and put it on the wall across from the bed.

I stood in the doorway and took a good look at the room. It was clean, bright and inviting. Gran might not be able to enjoy or appreciate it, but I knew it would make Mom happy.

I left to pick Kayla up from school and we went to the hospital to get Mom.

"Is Gran in there, Mommy?" Kayla asked when we pulled up in front of the main doors.

"Yes, she is."

"When can I go see her?"

"Well, Nana and I are going to talk to you about that when we get home."

"Why, 'cause I get to see her soon? Oh, look, there's Nana!" She beamed and waved her hand wildly out the window.

Mom opened Kayla's door and gave her a kiss before getting into the front seat. "How was school today?" she asked as we drove away.

Telling us about her day kept Kayla occupied all the way home, but the second we walked through the door she said, "Are we gonna talk about Gran now, Mommy?"

I gave Mom a questioning look.

She nodded.

"Sure, just give us a few minutes to get settled, okay?"

She skipped off to find something to do. Mom and I hung up our coats and went to the kitchen.

Mom put the kettle on and took the teapot down from its place on the shelf.

"Sorry to spring that on you," I said, taking two mugs down and placing them on the counter. "She asked about Gran when she saw the hospital and I realized, if Gran's coming home tomorrow, we have to prepare Kayla for it."

"It's okay, I thought of that today too."

Kayla came skipping into the kitchen and climbed onto a stool. "Could I have tea too?"

Mom gave her a reproving look. "It's 'may I', and you forgot your manners."

"May I have tea too, please?"

Mom took down a third mug. She filled it halfway with milk, added enough weak tea to make it warm, and put it in front of Kayla.

"Thank you, Nana," Kayla said, reaching for the sugar bowl.

"You're welcome."

I sat beside Kayla and put my hand on her arm as she reached for a second spoonful of sugar. "One's enough."

Her bottom lip came out slightly, but she didn't argue.

I waited until Mom had fixed her tea and taken a seat across from us before I said, "Are we ready to talk about Gran?"

"Do I get to see her?" Kayla asked.

"Yes, you do. She's coming home tomorrow."

Kayla clapped her hands in excitement and bounced up and down on her stool.

I took her hands and held them in mine. My expression was serious. "She's very sick, Kayla. She looks different than she did last time you saw her and she sleeps all the time."

"*All* the time? Doesn't she wake up to eat and drink?"

"No, she's too sick to eat and drink, so they feed her with a tube, kind of like a big, long straw."

"Will I be able to talk to her?"

"Of course," Mom said. "Your mom and I talk to her, and read to her, all the time."

"Gran can't talk," I explained, "but I'm sure she can hear us."

"If Gran can't talk, or eat, or wake up, does that mean she's ready to die now?"

I looked at Mom to see how she felt about that question. She gave her head a slight shake and I knew this one was up to me. "We think she is, sweetie. That's why she's coming home, so she can be comfortable in her own room and have us nearby. And speaking of her room, I cleaned it up today and got it ready. Would you like to come see?"

The three of us went into the room together. Mom put her hand to her mouth. Her eyes were full of tears when she looked at me. "It's perfect, Sarah. Thank you."

Kayla hopped up on the bed. "Why'd you move Gran's bed, Mommy?"

"There's a special bed coming for Gran tomorrow morning. Nana and I will take turns sleeping in this one so she won't be alone at night."

"That's good. I don't think Gran would wanna be all by

herself when she dies. Does dying hurt, Mommy?"

Mom quickly left the room. I sat on the bed and pulled Kayla onto my lap.

I left the room a long, difficult conversation later, feeling emotionally drained and fairly certain that talking to Kayla about sex a few years later would be a breeze.

* * *

Before I went to bed, I double checked the video camera and battery and put them in my bag. I felt sick to my stomach just thinking about what I had to do in the morning.

My phone went off as I was climbing into bed. It was a text from Tracey asking if I was ready.

As I'll ever be, I responded. So nervous.

Dont b! Ull b fine. Ud b a terrible spy

I slept fitfully and woke before the alarm. My stomach was so twisted up with nerves that I skipped breakfast. I filled a travel mug with strong, black coffee and was out the door well before six.

Tracey met me in the change room at six-fifteen. Five minutes later I was in the bathing room, setting up the camera. Shortly after six-thirty we were on the floor working.

Chapter 26
The Sh*t Hits the Fan

WHEN I ENTERED HER ROOM shortly after six-thirty, Edie was sitting in her chair, staring out the window into the fading darkness.

"Good morning, Edie," I said in a hushed voice.

Her hand flew to her chest. "Are ye trying to give me a heart attack, sneaking up on me like that?"

"Sorry, I wasn't trying to sneak. I was just trying not to wake Mrs. Sellers."

She twisted her hands in her lap. "Och, lass, I know that. I'm just a little out of sorts today."

"Are you feeling okay? You're not sick are you?"

"No, no, nothing like that. I didn't get a good night's sleep is all."

I was sure there was more to it than that. She seemed nervous about something. "Are you sure you're okay, Edie. Is there something you want to talk about?"

She hesitated, but shook her head. "No, thank you for your concern, but I'm fine and you've work to do. I'll not hold you up."

I didn't argue. I'd talk to her after breakfast when I wasn't so rushed for time. I unlocked her wardrobe. "Don't forget, you have a bath at seven-thirty this morning."

"Oh, don't you worry. I haven't forgotten."

* * *

It was nearly seven-thirty when I hurried back down the hall to Edie's room. She wasn't there. I was sure she'd gone to the bathing room, but I poked my head around the corner at the end of the hall to be sure. She was sitting on the bench outside the bathing room with her bag of clothing and toiletries beside her.

She looked up. I gave her a quick wave. She barely lifted her hand in return. Her face was pale and drawn. There was something wrong, more than she was letting on. I had a feeling she was hiding something. The twins' raised voices drifted down the hall. They were arguing again. I looked back toward Hall B. Albert was at the other end of the hall in a pair of plaid polyester pants and an undershirt, calling "Hairball!" over and over. He disappeared into Rose's room. I gave Edie one last concerned look, wishing I had time to talk to her. She smiled and waved her fingers upward as though to say "go". I sighed, gave her a grateful smile and hurried down the hall to find Albert.

Twenty minutes later I was on my way back from taking some of the residents to the lounge. It was a quarter to eight and I still needed to get Mrs. Sellers up and ready for breakfast. I was about to go into her room, when Sheila came running around the corner at the end of the hall. My mouth dropped open as I stopped and stared in disbelief.

Her hair was a damp, tangled mess. Streaks of black mascara ran down her blotchy face and her wet scrubs clung to her body. She waved her hands frantically as she hurried down the hall toward me, yelling, "She's crazy. Help me!"

Tracey came running out of Mr. Roberts' room. "What's going on?"

"I have no idea." Then it occurred to me. "Edie was in there with her!"

"Crazy...gun... help," Sheila gasped as she ran toward us.

I pushed past her and sprinted down the hall to the bathing room. "Edie?" I called, charging through the door. My heart pounded. I looked frantically around the room. Edie lay naked on the floor in front of the tub, in a puddle of water.

"Oh, my God!" I grabbed a towel off the bench beside the door and started toward her. I slipped on the wet floor, caught myself and went carefully to where she lay. Kneeling down in the water beside her, I covered her shivering body with the towel and picked up her hand.

"It's okay, Edie. I'm here." I placed two fingers on the inside of her wrist. Her pulse was strong. I held her hand in mine and continued to talk to her soothingly.

I could hear the sound of voices in the hall and people running. "Hear that, Edie? Help is on the way. We'll have you out of here in no time."

Her fingers twitched and her eyes fluttered open. "Tell you...later." She squeezed my hand and closed her eyes right before the door opened.

I could have sworn she winked.

The door opened a crack and Abby called out. "Sarah? Are you in here?"

"Right here. It's fine. Come in."

She opened the door wider and took a hesitant step into the room.

"Careful," I said. "The floor's wet."

She made her way cautiously across the floor. "Sheila said something about a gun."

"There's no gun."

The nurse in Abby took over. She crouched beside Edie to check her pulse. "I called 911. Help will be here soon."

Tina and Carol stood in the doorway. Behind them, a few residents had gathered curiously. I could hear Sheila in the hallway crying and prattling on hysterically about Edie and the mysterious gun.

"Tina, Carol," I said, "can you get these residents away from the door, please? And send someone in with blankets."

Carol took charge. "Okay, show's over. Let's go see if the dining room's open." The crowd dispersed and the door swung shut, blocking out the last of the noise.

Abby was carefully feeling Edie's limbs and joints, checking them for injuries, when the door opened again and Tracey came in with blankets. We draped them over Edie's trembling body and tucked them underneath as well as we could without moving her.

Abby spoke brusquely as she worked. "Nothing feels broken, but I'm worried about her head and back."

I took a towel off the shelf and mopped up as much water as I could from the floor around Edie. Tracey grabbed another towel and knelt down beside me to help. Within minutes we had the floor dry.

Tracey took my towel. She wrapped the wet towels in a dry one so they wouldn't drip. "I'll take these to the laundry and watch for the paramedics."

After Tracey left, I knelt beside Edie once more, and took her hand. "I'm still here, Edie."

Abby roamed around the room, checking every corner. She put on gloves and looked through the wastebasket. I watched her go into the shower room. She checked the shower area and the toilet stall. I even heard her take the lid off the toilet tank and replace it a few seconds later.

This is ridiculous, I thought. Where the hell does she think Edie got a gun?

She came back out a minute later and stood looking at me. Her eyes went to my pockets.

I let go of Edie's hand and stood up. "Check them."

"Pardon me?"

"I know what you're thinking. I don't want there to be a question in your mind about what really happened here today. Check my pockets."

She stepped forward, looked through all my pockets, nodded and stepped back.

I heard the sound of male voices and heavy footsteps approaching. "We both know there's no gun," I said quickly. "Maybe you should talk to Sheila again. And talk to Edie when she wakes up later. She's the only one who can or will tell you what really happened."

Abby had no time to respond. The door opened and we stepped back to let the paramedics do their job. The police questioned us. They also spent a long time in the bathing room after the paramedics took Edie away. I worried they might search the room after hearing Sheila rant about a gun.

Tracey had no such concerns. "They didn't find the

camera," she said as we crossed the parking lot after work. "Even if they searched the room they wouldn't look up there. Think about it. Edie's tiny. There's no way she could have put a gun way up there."

"Okay, but what if they did find it? There'll be footage of me leaving the room after I set it up."

"Sarah, stop worrying. We'll look first thing tomorrow."

I was torn between going straight home to see Gran or to the hospital to see Edie. I sat in my car indecisively for a few minutes before I finally called Mom and explained the situation.

"Sarah, everything's fine here. Go to the hospital and I'll see you when you get home with Kayla."

It felt strange to walk into the hospital and not go directly to Gran's old room in the ICU. I went to the third floor and stopped at the nurse's station to ask directions to Edie's room.

Tom was there, slumped over in a chair beside Edie's bed, holding her hand. He straightened up when I walked into the room. "Sarah!"

"Hi, Tom. I'm sorry, I didn't know you were here. I can come back later."

"No, it's okay." He waved me in. "She's still asleep, but she'll be happy you stopped by."

I stood next to him and looked down at Edie. She was a little pale, but her breathing sounded good. "How's she doing? Has she woken up at all?"

"The doctor said they couldn't find anything wrong with her. They aren't sure why she won't wake up. They ran some blood tests and they're just waiting on the results. Do you know what happened? All the doctor could tell me was that the paramedics who brought her in thought she slipped and fell in some water."

"That's what it looked like. She went into the bathing room around seven-thirty. Sheila, the support worker who gives the residents their baths, came running out about twenty minutes later, calling for help. I went in and found your mom lying on the floor."

Tom was quiet for a moment as he digested what I'd said. "Would you let a resident walk on a wet floor?"

"No, I wouldn't. Maybe Sh—"

A loud voice behind us made me jump. "What is she doing here?"

Tom cringed and looked at me apologetically. I turned to face Anne. "I came to see Edie, of course."

"You have some nerve showing up here. If you girls had been doing your jobs properly this never would have happened. Tom and I are seriously considering talking to our lawyer about a lawsuit."

"That's your prerogative." I looked at Tom. "Thanks for letting me see her. I'll be going now." I turned to walk away.

"Sarah, wait. Stay," Tom said. His voice shook, but he sounded determined.

"What are you doing?" Anne growled from between clenched teeth.

Tom stood up and faced her. "Wh-what do you think I'm doing? You spent our whole marriage telling me what to do. You treated my mother like a second-class citizen and I stood by and let you." With each word his voice grew louder and he stood taller. "I can't do it anymore. It's done, over. I want you to leave. I'll stay at a hotel tonight and come get my things tomorrow."

"You—you don't mean it, Tom. You're not thinking straight. You need to—"

"No!" he yelled. He lowered his voice, but spoke firmly, with conviction. "That's the thing. I don't *need* to do anything anymore if I don't want to. Now go."

Anne stared at Tom in disbelief. Finally, without a word, she turned, pushed past me and strode angrily out the door.

I didn't say anything, but inside I was cheering. Edie was right, Anne was a tyrant and poor Tom had been a doormat long enough.

Tom sank into the chair and put his head in his hands. His shoulders shook silently.

I stood there awkwardly for a moment, unsure of what to do. "Uh, is there any way I can help?"

His shoulders shook harder and he began to make awful, choking noises.

I moved closer and put my hand on his shoulder. "It'll be okay, Tom. You—"

He looked up at me. My mouth fell open. He was laughing. He took a deep, shuddering breath and blew it out hard. "Tissue, please."

I looked around, spotted them on the little bedside table and handed the box to Tom.

He mopped the dampness from his face. "I'm so sorry you had to see that, but I've been wanting to do that for as long as I can remember."

"There's no need to apologize to me. You just do whatever you have to do."

"I plan on it, from now on."

"Tom, is that you, lad?" Edie's weak voice was barely a whisper.

Tom's face lit up. He stood and took his mother's hand. "I'm here, Mom."

"Is Anne with you?"

"No. I sent her away."

Edie struggled to keep her eyes open. "You what?"

"I sent her away. For good."

"Oh, my. Well, it's about time."

"I know, Mom. We'll talk about it later. Sarah's here now."

I moved closer and smiled down at Edie through tears of relief. It was so good to hear her voice.

"Here now. There'll be none of that," she said, struggling to sit up.

I reached over the side rail and pushed a button to raise the head of the bed. Tom went to the other side. We each took an arm and pulled her upright. I fussed with her, arranging the pillows and straightening the blankets, until she slapped my hand away.

"Enough, now, lass. I'm not an invalid." She slumped back against the pillows in exhaustion. "Although I could use some water if you don't mind."

Tom went out into the hallway to find a nurse. She came in with him a few minutes later, carrying a pitcher of ice water and a cup with a bendable straw.

"Well, hello, Mrs. MacAdams, It's nice to see you awake. That was some sleep you had." She poured a cup of water and handed it to Edie. "Are you able to do it yourself?"

Edie sighed loudly. "As I told these two, I'm not an invalid." She guided the straw into her mouth and took a long drink.

"No, of course you're not," the nurse said. She took the cup from Edie, placed it on the tray table and clipped the call bell to the blanket where Edie could easily reach it. "Here's your call bell. If you need anything, push the button and I'll be here as soon as I can."

Edie managed a tired smile and stifled a yawn. "Thank you, lass."

As soon as the nurse left, Edie said, "Tom, dear, do you mind leaving me and Sarah for a bit. We need to talk."

He cleared his throat. "Uh, sure. I'll go down to the café and get a coffee."

After Tom left, I sat in the chair beside the bed, leaned forward eagerly and said, "I have to pick Kayla up at three-thirty. You've got half an hour to tell me everything."

* * *

I pulled up to the school just as the bell rang.

"Remember what I said," I told Kayla on the drive home. "Gran might not look the way you remember. She's hooked up to all those tubes and machines I told you about. It might look a little scary at first."

"I know, Mommy. And I have to be quiet, right?"

"A little bit, yes, but only when you're in her room."

"'kay, I'll use my inside voice in Gran's room."

I smiled. Kayla rarely had an "inside" voice unless she

was sick or sleeping.

Her excitement seemed to fade when we walked into the house. We took off our boots, hung up our jackets and went down the hall to Gran's room. Kayla stopped outside the door and stood twirling her hair around her finger nervously.

I went to her and put my arm around her shoulder. "Are you ready?"

She looked up and shook her head hesitantly. Her eyes were full of apprehension.

"I'll be with you the whole time."

"I'm scared, Mommy."

"Oh, sweetie. She's still the same Gran you've always loved. She still loves you, even if she can't say it, and she's been waiting a long time to hear your voice again."

Kayla looked thoughtful for a minute. She took a deep breath. "Okay, Mommy. Hold my hand and we'll go together."

It didn't take Kayla long to get over her fear. After the initial shock of seeing Gran unconscious and surrounded by tubes and wires, Kayla spoke to her as though she'd never left. I got the stool from the laundry room and put it on the floor beside the bed so Kayla was able to climb up beside Gran. She spent most of the rest of the day in there, coloring, doing puzzles and watching TV.

* * *

That evening, after Kayla was asleep, I went in to Gran's room to talk to Mom. She was sitting in the chair beside the window, staring out into the darkness. I doubted she'd left Gran's side for more than a few minutes all day. I flopped down on the double bed and stifled a yawn. "I thought it went well today with Kayla," I said.

"It did. You look exhausted."

"I am. It was a tough day."

Mom nodded sympathetically. "Do you want to talk about it?"

I rolled onto my stomach and looked at her. "Later. It was a tough day for both of us. You arranged for help with Gran in the mornings, right?"

"The nurse will be here every day," she replied, looking away.

"Mom, we've talked about this. You need to have a support worker come in and help out so you can take a break every day."

"I can do it myself. Most of the time I'm just sitting here reading or watching TV anyway."

"That's not the point and you know it. It's emotionally exhausting. How much good are you to Gran if you can't function?"

"We'll try this for a few days. If I think I need help, I'll arrange it." She put up her hand when I tried to argue. "No, I appreciate your concern for me, Sarah, but I want to do this."

I smiled. Mom was taking charge and acting like the mother in our relationship for the first time in ten years. I was proud of her. "Fine. We'll talk about it again in a few days."

I helped Mom with Gran's nightly care. I washed her face and smoothed on moisturizing cream. We put lotion on her arms and legs and massaged it into her feet, hands and elbows. I rubbed balm gently onto her dry, cracked lips, repositioned her and placed pillows where needed. While we worked, I told Mom the details of what had happened that day.

"Do you think it's possible she had a gun?" Mom asked. "Why would Sheila say such a thing if it wasn't true?"

"I'm not sure. I don't think she had a gun. I was the first one in the room, I would've seen it. Abby checked the whole room, even the toilet tank." I snorted at the thought. "There was something going on that Edie's not telling me, though."

"What do you mean?"

"I'm not sure. Edie was off this morning. Something wasn't right. I'm wondering if she antagonized Sheila into losing her temper."

"Why in the world would she do a thing like that?"

"Edie and I had talked about Sheila. Edie had this idea that she could push Sheila into doing something so we'd have proof of her mistreating residents. I told her not to, but…" I sighed and pulled the blankets up over Gran. "I wish I had talked to her this morning."

Mom reached across the bed and patted my hand. "It's not your fault, sweetheart. You couldn't have known what was on her mind."

When we finished with Gran I went to my room to get ready for bed. There was a message on my phone from Jay. I called him and we talked for nearly an hour. We didn't talk about Edie. I hadn't felt much better after my conversation with Mom and talking to Jay about other things was a welcome distraction.

Before we hung up, he said, "I know you're working all

weekend, but I'd like to see you, even if it's just for coffee. I missed you this week."

My stomach fluttered at his words and I realized I'd missed him too.

* * *

The next morning, Tracey stood guard while I went into the bathing room to get the camera. All my worrying had been for nothing. The camera was right where I'd left it. The halls were quiet and we saw no one. I took the camera to the change room, put it in my locker and went to work.

Tina was in the staff room when I went in for my morning break. She was unusually friendly and babbled excitedly about the incident the day before. "Abby told Carol that the doctors said Edie was drugged. Sleeping pills apparently. Not enough to kill her, but enough to knock her out for a while."

"But how?" I asked. "Residents don't have access to drugs."

"I know. That's why people are wondering if it was Sheila."

Not Sheila, I thought. "Really?" I said, pretending surprise. "Sheila drugged Edie? Why would she do that?"

"Who knows? She obviously lost it. I mean, she was ranting on like a mad woman about Edie having a gun." She laughed. "Imagine, that sweet, old woman holding Sheila at gunpoint. Just the thought of it is crazy."

"What do you think happened then?"

"I have no idea. Maybe Edie slipped on the wet floor and fell and Sheila panicked. Or maybe Sheila really did go crazy. Maybe she drugged Edie before her bath. I guess we won't know anything until Edie starts talking. She's awake, you know."

"Mmhmm, I heard that."

"But she says she doesn't remember anything."

I shook my head in mock wonder. "Imagine that."

* * *

It was strange not having Edie around. Georgia was a little lost without her and didn't know what to do with herself. I tried to keep her busy. I left her and Rose in the lounge sorting a basket of socks. Later, I took them to the auditorium for Time for Tots.

Connie had filled Lloyd in about the situation with Edie and he'd called to say he would be picking Georgia up early. I was in the main hall after lunch, helping her get settled into an armchair to wait, when the police walked in. Abby was on her way back from Hall A with her medication cart. The two officers intercepted her outside the nurse's station. I couldn't hear what they were saying, but I saw Abby nod her head stiffly before turning to lead them toward Hall B. She stopped when she spotted me and waved me over.

I reminded Georgia to wait there for Lloyd and walked over to the group. My heart pounded against my chest.

"Sarah," Abby said. "These officers have some questions about the incident yesterday."

I remembered Officer Moore from the day before.

"Hello Sarah," she said with a smile. "This is Officer Fletcher." She turned to Abby. "Is there somewhere private we can go to talk?"

Abby hesitated. "I think the staff room is empty."

"Great. I'm sure Sarah can take us there. Thanks for

your help."

Abby nodded shortly, took her cart and wheeled it into the medical supply room. She didn't look happy about being so politely dismissed.

I led the officers into the staff room. Officer Fletcher closed the door and they sat across the table from me. I put my thumb to my mouth, caught myself and folded my hands tightly in my lap.

They asked me the same questions officer Moore had asked the day before. They also asked me some pointed questions about Sheila and Edie.

"You told me yesterday that Edie is your resident," Officer Moore said. "How was she yesterday morning?"

"She was a little off. I asked if she was okay and she said she hadn't slept very well."

"Was she on any medication for that?"

"I don't think so, but I'm not responsible for the residents' medications. You'd have to talk to the nurse about that."

"Did you see Sheila yesterday morning before the incident?"

"No. The first time I saw her was when she ran out of the bathing room."

"Are you a support worker?"

"Yes."

"Is Sheila a support worker as well?"

"Yes, she is."

"And do you or any of the other support workers have access to the room where the residents' medications are stored?"

"No. Only the nurses have access to that room."

"Did you, at any point, yesterday morning, see a gun?"

"No!"

They asked me again to tell them what I remembered about the incident. They took notes and interjected some new questions while I recounted the story.

"Okay," Officer Moore said when I'd finished, "that's all we need for now. Thanks again for your co-operation."

I looked at the clock as I stood up to leave. It was one-thirty. We'd only been in the room for ten minutes. It had felt like forever.

"Oh, one more thing, Sarah," Officer Moore said as they followed me out the door.

I turned to her. "Yes?"

"Is Tracey Armstrong working today?"

"She is."

"If you could get her for us please, we need to speak to her as well."

I turned to go to Hall B. My mind raced. Why did they want to talk to Tracey? *Of course she was there, in the bathing room with me and Abby.* I took a deep breath to calm myself and glanced over to see if Georgia had left yet.

Lloyd was there, helping his grandmother out of her seat. He looked from me to the police and back questioningly. I gave my head a slight shake, smiled reassuringly and hurried to Hall B to find Tracey. She was in Mrs. Amaral's room, helping her settle in for a nap.

"Hey, Trace. The police want to talk to you."

"Oh boy! Are they hot?"

"Well, Fletcher's tall and not bad looking. Moore's only

about five foot four, but she's really fit."

"Hey, I haven't completely ruled out women. It would double my chances."

I rolled my eyes and nodded toward Mrs. Amaral. "They're waiting for you in the staff room. Do you need help finishing up in here?"

"No, I'm good," she said, pulling the bedrail up and locking it into place. Mrs. Amaral was already snoring.

Tracey and I walked toward the main hall together. "Find me later," I said just before I turned into the lounge. "Let me know how the questioning goes."

"Will do."

"Oh," I called after her. "And just so you know, you are not sleeping with me if you ever stay over."

The sound of her laughter followed me down the hall.

We met up again in the change room when our shift was over.

"How did it go with the police?" I asked as we walked out of Dementia.

"Fine. They asked questions, I answered them. I have nothing to hide."

I looked at her with a raised brow. "Really? Nothing?"

"We're not talking about that here, remember? But we will tonight. What time are you coming over?"

"After I put Kayla to bed and help Mom with Gran."

We walked into Long-Term Care. Marg looked up and our eyes met. She smiled. I blinked in surprise, wondering for a moment if I'd imagined it, then raised a hand and smiled in return. "Did you see that?" I asked Tracey.

"Sure did. Apparently she's happy Sheila's gone, too."

Tracey and I parted ways in the parking lot. "See you tonight," Tracey called as she walked to her car. "It's your turn to bring the wine."

* * *

Kayla and I spent a couple hours in Gran's room, talking to her and playing cards. Before I left the room, I repositioned her.

"Why do you have to do that, Mommy?"

"Because Gran can't move herself, so we have to do it for her. If she's in one position too long she could get bedsores and they're really painful."

I gave Kayla one of the small pillows. "Here, help me put this under her feet. The pillows help keep her heels and elbows from rubbing against the sheets."

We placed pillows under her elbows as well. Kayla helped me pull the blankets up to Gran's chest. I pulled the bedrail up and locked it in place. "I'm going to help Nana make dinner. Are you coming?"

She picked her favorite storybook up off the nightstand and climbed onto the chair. "No, I'll stay here and keep Gran company."

Mom had already put the chicken in the oven. We cut up sweet potatoes, put them into the bottom of the roast pan, and made a salad. When we'd finished, I went to my room to call Jay.

"Are you okay?" he asked right away. "My dad said the police were talking to you."

"I'm fine. There was an incident at work yesterday and the police were following up."

"Uh-oh. Was anyone hurt?"

"Edie took a fall. She's in the hospital, but she seems okay. I stopped in to see her yesterday after work."

"I'm sorry to hear that. Will you have time for a coffee tonight?"

I frowned in disappointment. "I can't, I promised Tracey I'd spend the evening with her. Do you have plans tomorrow night?"

"That depends. Are you asking me out on a date?"

I laughed and we made plans to meet for coffee the next night.

I'd barely put down the phone when it vibrated. It was Tracey. I picked it up. "Hey, Trace, can I call you back? I'm about to eat dinner."

"No, Sarah, it's important."

I knew right away something was wrong. "What is it? What happened?"

She was quiet for a moment before I heard her take a deep, tremulous breath. "It's Edie."

I closed my eyes. My whole body went cold. *Please, let her be okay.*

"Connie just texted me. She said they heard from the hospital about an hour ago that Edie had a heart attack."

I swallowed hard and blinked back the tears. "Is she…?"

"She died, Sarah. I'm so sorry."

Oh, my God. I couldn't breathe. It felt like my chest was caving in on my heart.

"Sarah, you still there?"

I choked on the pain and guilt, but managed a sound of confirmation.

"Why don't we put off watching the video? We don't

have to do it tonight."

I could barely talk past the lump in my throat. "No. I want to. I need to see it."

I hung up and sat in my room in a daze. I heard Mom call me for dinner, but couldn't seem to make my body move. She came to my door a few minutes later, stopping short when she saw my face. "Sarah, what's wrong?"

I put my face in my hands and started to cry. Mom hurried across the room and sat on the bed beside me. She put her arm around me and pulled me close. I buried my head in her shoulder and sobbed quietly.

She waited until the sobs subsided to an occasional hiccup before saying, "Do you want to talk about it?"

I took a deep, shuddering breath and sat up straight. Mom handed me a tissue. I explained it to her as I wiped my face dry. "Tracey called to tell me... my resident, Edie, died."

"Oh, sweetheart, I'm so sorry. I know how special she was to you."

"Thanks. I'm not feeling hungry anymore. If you don't mind, I think I'll go to Tracey's early."

CHAPTER 27
A NIGHT AT THE MOVIES

I PACED BACK AND FORTH with a glass of red wine in my hand, trying to make sense of the situation as Tracey set up her laptop. "I knew something was going on. Edie wasn't herself yesterday morning. I should have talked to her. I could have stopped her."

"Sarah, it's not your fault. She had a heart attack. There's no way you could've stopped that from happening."

"But maybe it was the pills or the stress that caused the heart attack. We have the footage of Mrs. W. Edie didn't have to do what she did, damn it!" I sat down hard on the sofa beside Tracey, nearly spilling my wine. I set my glass on the coffee table and hung my head in my hands.

Tracey put her arm around my shoulders. "Stop blaming yourself. Edie did what she felt she had to do. Now we need to make sure it wasn't all for nothing."

I sat up and wiped the tears from my face. "I know. I just…I can't believe I'm never going to see her again."

"I know, hon. She was one of the special ones. You ready?"

I nodded, picked up my wine, and sat forward with my arms on my knees to watch the video.

The first image to appear was of me putting away the stool and leaving the bathing room. There was nearly half an hour of an empty room before Sheila came on shift, so Tracey skipped ahead to the footage of Mrs. W's bath.

Sheila came in and started the bath water running. She worked methodically and efficiently, gathering everything she needed.

The door opened and she went to hold it for Carol, who wheeled Mrs. W into the room. They exchanged pleasantries before Sheila asked, "How is she this morning?"

"Cranky and complaining as usual," Carol replied. They laughed as though sharing some private joke. Carol helped undress and transfer Mrs. W into the bath seat before she left.

Sheila raised the lift and lowered the seat into the tub. The moment Mrs. W's feet touched the water, she began to squirm and whimper. The water covered her legs and came up over the seat. She yelled and grabbed onto the side of the lift as her body was slowly immersed.

"Stop your yelling," Sheila said. She continued to lower the seat until the water was up to Mrs. W's chest.

Her body trembled. "Co, co, co, co," she stammered.

"Complaining already. I guess Carol was right," Sheila said, grabbing the washcloth and dipping it in the water. She rubbed some soap on it and washed Mrs. W's face. "Maybe, if you would behave, you could have a nice warm bath. But you can't can you? You're just like my mother. All you do is whine and complain. You don't appreciate what I do for you." She grabbed Mrs. W's hair and yanked her head back so she had to look at her. "She didn't either. She treated me like a piece of shit when I was a kid. But she regretted it when she was old and helpless and needed me to take care of her." She gave one final yank before she let go, causing Mrs. W to cry out loudly. Sheila gave her a sharp cuff across the back of the head. "You shut your dirty mouth or I'll give you a reason to scream."

I heard Tracey's gasp of horror and glanced over at her. She was staring at the screen with her hand over her mouth. "You don't have to watch this with me," I said.

"No, I have to. It's kind of like watching a horror movie. I don't wanna to see what happens next, but I can't look away."

I felt the same way. I just hoped it didn't get worse. I took a gulp of wine and turned back to the laptop.

Sheila went on to wash the rest of Mrs. W's body. She scrubbed so hard, the poor woman cried out and tried to move away. Sheila ignored her as she scrubbed and ranted. "I know why your kids never come to see you. You treated them like shit. I know you did. I overheard your daughters talking when they brought you in here. You were a mean, nasty woman and you deserve everything you get."

Sheila pulled the plug. She was quiet while she washed Mrs. W's hair. She left her sitting with shampoo in her hair while she went to the sink, filled a paper cup with water and stood sipping it. Mrs. W sat in the cold tub, shivering and crying. Globs of shampoo crept down her forehead and slid into her eyes. She squeezed her eyes shut and swiped at them frantically.

"Oh, what's wrong?" Sheila asked in a nauseatingly sweet voice. "Do you have soap in your eyes?" She laughed, tossed her cup in the garbage and strolled casually back to the tub. She turned on the hand held showerhead and proceeded to rinse the shampoo from Mrs. W's hair. Steam rose from the tub. Mrs. W cried out loudly and lurched in pain when the hot water hit her.

"What? Now you're complaining it's too hot?" Sheila said, once more slapping her across the head. "You're never happy, are you? Now stop your complaining."

Mrs. W sat quietly, despite the stream of hot, soapy water running down her face.

"Put your head back," Sheila ordered.

Mrs. W tilted her head back slightly.

Sheila sighed loudly. She put her hand on Mrs. W's forehead and pushed her head back roughly. "I *said* to put your head *back*," she gritted through clenched teeth.

Mrs. W roared in pain and anger and flailed an arm wildly in Sheila's direction. Sheila ducked out of the way. She grabbed the arm and twisted it down until her face was inches from Mrs. W's. "Don't you ever try to hit me, you dirty, nasty, Polack bitch. Do you understand me?"

Mrs. W whimpered.

Sheila made a sound of disgust and dropped her arm. "It's time to get out." She raised the lift and left Mrs. W hanging in the air while she went to get a towel.

Mrs. W continued to moan and whimper. She shifted in the wet seat, causing her big body to slip sideways, gave a terrified shriek and grabbed onto the lift.

Sheila sighed loudly and walked back to the tub with towel in hand. "Yelling doesn't make me want to put you down. If you want down, you need to sit there quietly and behave." She walked away again, picked up Mrs. W's toiletry bag and laid everything out neatly on the counter.

Mrs. W closed her eyes, wrapped her arms around her body and sat shivering and whimpering quietly. Her skin was covered in goose bumps and her lips were tinged with blue. Finally, when Mrs. W's teeth began to chatter, Sheila went back to the tub and lowered her to the floor. She worked in seething silence, drying her with short, terse strokes, then tossed the towel into the laundry bag and picked up Mrs. W's comb.

Mrs. W whimpered.

Sheila bent down and held the comb in front of Mrs. W's face. "What's wrong? Don't you like having your hair combed?" She laughed and walked around the lift to stand behind her, comb in hand. Mrs. W's hair hung past her shoulders in a thick mess of curly, grey tangles. Sheila lifted the comb and ripped through a section of hair.

Mrs. W cried out in pain and reached up, grasping at the comb.

Sheila grabbed her hand and held it tightly as she leaned forward to speak softly into her ear. "Behave yourself, old woman, or I'll tie your hands together and torture you like the Nazis did."

Mrs. W's body became rigid. She squeezed her eyes shut and sat without moving.

Sheila clucked her tongue and let go of Mrs. W's hand. She continued to pull the comb roughly through the tangled mess as she spoke. "Did you watch them rape your mother? Did they rape you? Poor little girl. Such a horrible life you had. Is that why you're such a nasty old bitch?"

A tear slid down Mrs. W's cheek, then another. She winced in pain every time she felt the yank of the comb, but remained quiet. Sheila stopped talking and finished combing Mrs. W's hair in silence.

A few minutes later, Carol came in to help Sheila get Mrs. W dressed and back into her chair. As they left the room, Sheila called out, "Have a good morning, Mrs. W. See you at breakfast."

* * *

Tracey paused the video. She closed her eyes and took a deep, tremulous breath. We sat in stunned silence for a moment, digesting what we'd seen. When Tracey opened her eyes again they glittered with angry tears. "My God, Sarah. How long has she been doing this to these poor people? This is what we've been sending them to every day."

I couldn't speak. I was choking on guilt and tears.

We took a short break. I'd barely touched my first glass of wine, so Tracey topped hers up and left the bottle on the coffee table. She went to the kitchen and came out a few minutes later with a plate of crackers, cheese and grapes. She set it down beside the wine and popped a grape in her mouth.

My stomach growled.

Tracey put a piece of cheese between two crackers and handed it to me as she sat down.

"No, thanks."

She gave me a stern look. "I know you're hungry. Eat something."

"I can't. My stomach can't handle food when I'm upset."

She snorted and took a bite of the little sandwich. "I wish I had that problem. I eat more when I'm stressed out. No wonder you're so skinny." She shoved the second bite into her mouth and picked up her laptop. "Okay, here goes," she mumbled around the mouthful of food. "You sure you're ready to see this? It could be bad."

"I'm ready. Let's get it over with."

* * *

Sheila cleaned and sanitized the tub, then turned on the water for Edie's bath. While the tub filled, she cleaned the lift seat and wiped up the floor. Finally, she went to the door to get Edie. She ushered her in, closed the door and went back to the tub to turn off the water.

My heart clenched when Edie's face appeared on the screen. I choked back a sob and felt Tracey's consoling hand on my back.

Edie placed her bag on the bench beside the door, then turned and stared at Sheila's back balefully. Her face was pale. She lifted a trembling hand from her side and slid it into her robe pocket.

Sheila turned and squinted at Edie. The lines between her brows deepened as she scowled. "Why are you just standing there? Take your housecoat off and get ready. I don't have all day." She turned her back without another thought.

Edie locked the door.

Shelia turned with an angry yell, "You know we're not allowed to lock—"

Edie pulled her hand out of her pocket and pointed a gun at Sheila.

"Oh, my God," I said.

Tracey gasped in surprise and looked at me incredulously. She paused the video. "Whoa! Did *not* see that coming. Did you know about this?"

"Of course not!"

"But you said you talked to Edie...."

"I did, but she didn't tell me much. She said she didn't want me to have to lie, so the less I knew the better. She told me she took sleeping pills and that she 'set Sheila up'. I wasn't even sure what it all meant until now. She was exhausted. Her words were jumbled and she kept nodding off in the middle of sentences."

Tracey peered at me skeptically. "Fine. You're off the hook."

I rolled my eyes. "Gee, thanks."

She flopped back onto the couch and started the video again.

"What the hell? What are you doing?" Sheila asked in disbelief. "Where the hell did you get a gun?"

Edie laughed. Her cheeks bloomed with color. Her pale blue eyes flashed with anger. She sounded so wicked, my sweet little Edie, and the gun looked so comfortable in her hand, as though it belonged there. "It's your turn to have a bath today," she said, waving the gun carelessly. "Strip."

"Pardon me?" Sheila gasped. Her face was an awesome combination of panic and outrage.

Edie lifted the gun with both hands until it was level with Sheila's chest. Her frail little hands trembled slightly with the effort, but her face was deadly serious. "I said strip. Now!"

Sheila shook her head in disbelief, but wisely kept her mouth shut and began to slowly undress. She removed her shoes and socks, pulled off her scrubs, folded them and placed them carefully on top of her shoes. She stood facing Edie defiantly in her underwear and bra.

Edie was having none of it. Her voice dropped to a low, threatening tone. She enunciated each word carefully and slowly, as though speaking to a disobedient child. "I know how to use this. My second husband was a cop and he taught me everything he knew about guns. I suggest you do what I say. I've nothing to lose. Now, take off the rest and get into the lift."

Sheila hesitated, as though thinking and weighing her options. After a moment, her shoulders sagged and her eyes welled up with tears of defeat. She finished undressing, glanced at the chair, then at Edie, who simply waved the gun toward the lift. Sheila went to the chair, pulled herself in and buckled the restraint.

Edie edged closer, careful to keep a good distance between herself and Sheila, and picked up the controller. She raised the lift as high as it would go, then moved it sideways, until Sheila was directly over the tub. She lowered the seat slowly into the tub.

Sheila gasped as the water covered her legs. She twisted and turned in the seat and sucked in her breath when the water lapped at the sensitive skin of her stomach. Her hands fumbled for the seat belt around her waist.

Edie waved the gun in Sheila's direction. "Don't touch it. Put your hands up on the sides of the tub."

Sheila did as she was told. "It's cold!"

"Well, you ran the bath, didn't you? Did you care that I would've been cold? Of course not, you nasty bitch! You don't care about anyone but yourself! That's why it's come to this." She laughed. "No time for a proper bath today, but that's okay, I didn't care to see you wash your "fish" anyway."

Up went the lift again, into the air as high as it would go, then out and away from the tub. Now Sheila hung, naked, dripping wet and exposed, five feet above the hard tile floor.

"Put me down!" Sheila demanded. When Edie ignored her, she went back to pleading. "Please, Edie, put me down. Just let me go and I promise I won't tell anyone."

Edie snorted and rolled her eyes. "Well now, we both know that's a lie." She put the controller down, slid the gun into her pocket and walked away, leaving Sheila hanging in the air. She plucked a towel off the shelf on the wall behind her, picked Sheila's clothes up off the floor and placed everything on the bench beside her own things.

Sheila squirmed uncomfortably. She gripped the edges of the seat so tightly her knuckles turned white. "Edie," she whined, "don't leave me up here. I'm cold."

Edie ignored her. She went across the room to the sink, filled a paper cup with water, reached into the other robe pocket and pulled out a handful of pills. I couldn't tell how many, but she took them all, drank the water, and tossed the cup into the garbage. She walked over to the tub where Sheila still whimpered and whined, picked up the controller and looked up at her. "It's not very nice is it, being cold and helpless, humiliated and degraded?"

Sheila shook her head. A tear slid down her cheek and she swiped it angrily away. "You won't get away with this," she hissed.

"As I said, I've nothing to lose." Edie pushed the button and released it. She did this over and over again, causing the lift to jolt and the seat to sway crazily back and forth. Sheila squealed with fright. She panicked, sucking in huge, gasping breaths interspersed with wretched sobs. Her wet body slid about crazily in the slippery, plastic seat.

Finally, Edie stopped and pulled the gun out again. With it in one hand and the controller in the other, she pushed and held the button, bringing the seat all the way down. She dropped the controller and stepped back quickly. Her caution was unnecessary, Sheila was curled up in the seat, shaking and crying. Edie looked at her in disgust. She sighed loudly. I got the strange feeling she'd been hoping for more of a fight, but it came as no surprise that beneath her tough exterior, Sheila was a coward.

"Go on with you then," Edie said. "Get your clothes on. They're on the bench, and there's a towel there as well."

Sheila glanced up quickly at Edie. Her face flooded with relief as the words registered. Her hands shook as she fumbled with the belt around her waist. Finally free, she scrambled out of the chair and rushed across the room, slipping and nearly falling on the wet floor. She snatched the towel off the bench and hurriedly dried her trembling body.

Edie kept the gun in her hand and one eye on Sheila as she walked to the sink and took a small pitcher off the shelf below. She went back to the tub, filled the container with water, and placed it carefully on the lift chair. She watched as Sheila struggled to pull the clothes onto her wet, flabby body. When Sheila bent to pick up her shoes and socks, Edie said, "Turn around."

Sheila turned to face her. Streaks of mascara lined her cheeks. Her eyes were puffy and red from crying and her lower lip trembled slightly.

"Sit down and put them on," Edie commanded. She stood silently while Sheila struggled with shaking hands to tie her shoes. "Now stand up, turn around and face the door. Good. Now, don't move until I say so."

Edie shrugged out of her bathrobe and hung it on a hook on the wall near the tub. She went back to the lift, laid the gun on the seat and picked up the pitcher full of water. Her hands shook, but she managed to lift the pitcher to her chest and pour water over her body. She put the pitcher back on the seat, picked up the gun and stood, proud and regal in all her wrinkled, naked glory, looking at Sheila.

Water dripped from Edie's body onto the floor, forming a puddle at her feet. She was exhausted. I could see it in her face and in the slight trembling of her hands. Her eyes were becoming cloudy with the effects of the drug she'd taken. "Get out," she said in a weary voice.

Sheila bolted out the door.

Edie moved as quickly as her eighty-three year old body would allow. Holding onto the tub with one hand, she lowered herself to the floor. On her knees now, she stretched her arm into the maze of pipes and hoses beneath the tub that housed the lift mechanics and placed the gun somewhere inside. She lay down, naked, in that cold puddle of water. It was eerily quiet in the room. She shifted slightly and closed her eyes right before the door burst open and I rushed in.

I felt a sudden, cold chill as I watched the screen and waited for the chaos I knew was coming. It was so strange to watch it now and see it from a different perspective. I could see that her whole body had been trembling. I'd wanted so badly to move her out of the cold puddle of water. It was painful to see the worry on my face, to remember how terrified I'd been that she would die as I sat holding her hand, waiting for help.

Then I saw it, the slight movement of her hand before she opened her eyes and whispered, "Tell you later." I watched her face carefully as I leaned in closer to the screen. She winked and closed her eyes seconds before the door cracked open and Abby called my name.

"I knew it! I knew I saw her wink."

Tracey stopped the video. "Do you think she knew about the camera?"

"I don't know. I mean, how could she have?"

"Maybe she heard us talking."

I nodded slowly, recalling the way she'd acted that morning before her bath. "I'm sure she knew something. I thought she wasn't feeling well when I saw her that morning, but now that I look back on it, she seemed nervous. I wouldn't doubt she eavesdropped if she had the chance. Turns out she was a lot smarter than anyone gave her credit for. I'm pretty sure the reason she sneaked out that day was to go get the gun."

"Well, if she did, that means she was planning this for weeks."

"Or months," I added. "Don't forget she sneaked out in December too. And she told me a while ago that she had things to do before she got out of Dementia."

Tracey laughed. "Boy, she really had guts, didn't she? I hope I'm like her when I get old."

I stared down at my hands, remembering the conversation I'd had with Edie about Abby. "Remember when I told you that Abby said I was wrong about Edie not having dementia?"

"Uh-huh."

"I talked to Edie about it. She admitted that she made Abby think she had it. She said she had to be there to help me get Sheila." I swallowed hard and felt my bottom lip tremble.

"Stop it," Tracey said.

I glanced up, surprised by her fierceness.

"Stop feeling guilty. Nobody made her do this."

"But she didn't have to die." A tear slid down my face.

Tracey shook her head sadly. "No, she shouldn't have. All that crap about everything happening for a reason is bullshit. But, it wasn't your fault. You made her happy, Sarah. You made her life better."

I smiled through the tears. "She made mine better too. God, I miss her."

She squeezed my hand comfortingly. "I know you do. At least now you know what happened." She tapped the camera. "We'll edit this and get the footage of Mrs. W to the police. Everything'll be fine."

* * *

Nothing was fine, of course. Edie was dead, and aside from the fact that I already missed her terribly, she'd left loose ends that now needed to be tied up before they were discovered and undid all she had done. Tracey and I went to the bathing room a few minutes before our shift the next morning. The door was open and Debbie from housekeeping was in the shower area mopping the floor.

Tracey poked her head inside. "Morning, Deb. You're here late. It's almost six-thirty."

Debbie scowled. "I know. One of the residents had an accident. They brought him in here to shower him off and he had another accident. So, now I'm stuck cleaning it up."

There was nothing we could do but wait until later to look for the gun. We went to Hall B to start waking residents. Without thinking, I walked into Edie's room first. The light from the hallway spilled into the room and across her empty bed. The pain snaked through my chest and I felt my throat tighten. I hurried out of the room before the tears started.

The morning dragged by. It was agonizing waiting until the bathing room was empty and no one nearby so I could go in and get the gun. I hoped it was still in there. Tracey and I had watched the rest of the video the night before. We'd seen the police searching the room, but the camcorder battery had died partway through.

After lunch, Tracey and I helped our residents get comfortable in the lounge for the Saturday matinee, then made our way quickly to the bathing room. Tracey made herself look busy outside the door while I slipped inside.

I hurried to the tub, pulled a pair of gloves out of my

pocket and put them on. My heart was pounding as I got down on my knees and reached into the spot where I'd seen Edie place the gun. My hand moved blindly over the cables, but found nothing.

I heard voices and pulled my hand out quickly. They continued on down the hallway and faded to silence. My hands shook. A bead of sweat slid down my temple. I reached in again and put my hand deep down inside the pipes and cables. Finally, I felt something move. I wrapped my hand around it and pulled it out. It was smaller than I'd expected, but surprisingly heavy. I glanced at it briefly to be sure the safety was on and slipped it into my pocket. My hand shook so badly I was afraid I'd end up shooting myself. I laughed under my breath at the thought. How the hell would I explain that?

I closed my eyes, took a deep breath to calm myself, stood up and went to the door to listen. All I heard was Tracey's off-key whistling. I switched off the light, opened the door slowly and peeked down the hallway in both directions.

Tracey shoved the pile of washcloths she'd been folding onto the top shelf of the supply cart. She pulled her keys out of her pocket. "Did you find it?"

I patted my pocket.

"Take your gloves off," Tracey whispered.

I peeled them off and tossed them into the garbage on the end of the supply cart. Tracey locked the bathing room door and we walked around the corner to Hall B.

"I'll do the final room check and meet you in the main hall," Tracey said. She veered off into the first room.

I strode down the hallway, through the main hall, to the change room and straight to my locker, where I took out my duffle bag. I went into a bathroom stall, closed and locked the door and collapsed onto the toilet as my legs gave out. I began to shake uncontrollably. My chest felt so tight it was hard to breathe. I rested my elbows on my knees, dropped my head down between my legs and tried to calm my breathing.

Finally, I felt my body begin to relax and my breathing go back to normal. I sat up slowly and touched my hand to my pocket. The weight of the gun hung heavily against my hip. It terrified me. I pulled out a fresh pair of gloves, put them on and slid my hand into the pocket. I shuddered when I felt the cold, hard metal through the glove, but forced myself to wrap my hand around the butt and pull it out.

I'd never shot a gun, but had watched my dad load, unload, and clean his hunting rifles. I opened the chamber, intending to empty the bullets. It was empty. "Oh, Edie," I whispered, "you crazy, brave, wonderful old lady."

I wiped the gun clean and wrapped it in the paper bag used for disposing of sanitary products. My hands shook so badly I almost dropped it. I was tempted to toss it in the garbage right then and be done with it, but I couldn't risk someone finding it there and connecting it with Edie. I would stop at the coffee shop on the way home and drop it in one of the garbage cans in the parking lot. I tucked it inside a sweater, shoved it into the bottom of my bag beneath my purse and jacket and stood up to leave.

The change room door squeaked as it swung open and I heard voices. I stood frozen in place while they talked and banged locker doors. Finally, their voices faded. I waited until I heard the door click shut before I left the stall. I peeled the gloves off my sweaty hands and tossed them in the garbage. Touching the gun had left me feeling dirty, so I went to the sink and scrubbed my hands with hot soapy water. My face was burning. I pulled a handful of paper towel from the dispenser, ran cold water over it and held it against my hot skin.

I straightened up and took a good, long look at myself in the mirror. My skin was flushed. There were dark circles under my eyes. Understandable, since I hadn't slept much the night before. I took a few deep breaths, left the room with my bag over my shoulder and went to the nurse's station to do my paperwork.

I passed Sam in the main hall, strolling along with his earbuds in, humming softly. I gave him a wave. He barely spared me a glance, simply nodded in acknowledgement and continued on.

It was nearly two-thirty by the time I finished documenting. I picked up my bag, intending to leave, but found myself heading toward Hall B instead. I glanced into the lounge as I passed. Lily was on the couch, enthralled with the singing and dancing on the big flat screen. Beth was beside her sister, head resting on Lily's shoulder as she dozed peacefully. Rose sat at the table in the corner stringing beads and tapping her toe to the music on the TV.

I continued on to Hall B. Somewhere, in the distance, Sam began to sing. His deep, gravelly voice filled the hall with the sorrowful words of Hank Williams' "I'm so Lonesome I Could Cry." His voice quavered with an emotion that echoed the sadness of the lyrics. My chest tightened and I quickened my pace. All the emotions of the past few days welled up, threatening to choke me.

I walked into the last room at the end of the hall. Mrs. Sellers was in bed, asleep. I stood staring at Edie's things; her bed, so neatly made by her only two days before, the picture of Tom and Anne on the table beside it, the tartan wool blanket that so proudly proclaimed her Scottish heritage, draped over the back of her chair.

Tomorrow, Tom would come in, gather her things and take them away. Maria would strip the bed and housekeeping would clean and sanitize everything in sight. I'd come back to work on Monday and all traces of Edie would be gone.

I turned and left the room with tears streaming down my face. Sam's lonely voice and the image of Edie, sitting in her chair by the window each morning, waiting for me, would surely haunt my dreams that night.

Chapter 28
Afterward

IT HAD BEEN NEARLY TWO months since Edie had died. Tranquility was not the same without her. There was a new resident in her room, a new chair by the window, new photos on the nightstand. It didn't matter. I still walked into the last room on the right in Hall B and thought of it as Edie's.

Georgia became so depressed after Edie left that she wandered the halls aimlessly, looking for someone she often didn't remember. I tried my best to cheer her up and keep her busy, but she was inconsolable. Lloyd was overcome with guilt when he realized how miserable she was and he brought her home to stay. The family took turns helping out and a support worker went in every day.

Jay spent every Sunday afternoon with Georgia. Sometimes we visited her together. She didn't always remember me, although she still called me Sahara. She seemed more content being home, surrounded by her family.

Jay had become an important part of my life in a short time. I was still tentative and slow to open up, but he was patient and seemed content to let me set the pace. I hadn't told him yet, but I'd decided, when the time was right, I would introduce him to Mom and Kayla. I still hadn't told him the truth about Edie, the video, or the gun. I doubted I ever would. Some secrets are meant to stay secrets forever.

Tracey swore to never tell anyone what happened that day and she helped me edit the video. We deleted the footage of Edie and anonymously sent the video of Mrs. W's bath to the police and Tranquility's administrator.

The police came in with a warrant, seized medical records and documentation charts and questioned everyone who had ever worked with Sheila. I'd been the first on-scene that day in the bathing room, but the police seemed more interested in the other incidents I'd recorded, such as Lily's red wrist and the bruises on Mrs. W's neck.

Sheila no longer worked at Tranquility. She'd been arrested shortly after Edie died and was out on bail awaiting trial. Maria had taken over as the new "Bath Lady." Abby had been demoted and moved to nightshift in Palliative Care and Emily was now the nurse in charge of Dementia. Having Sheila and Abby gone would make my last few months at Tranquility far more enjoyable.

I was both nervous and excited about nursing school. Tracey had applied as well, but after the deadline and had been waitlisted. In her typical carefree, optimistic way she shrugged it off saying, "Oh well, if I don't get in there's always next year."

She was still seeing Kyle. It was the longest relationship she'd ever had. When she wasn't with him, she was often at our house. We'd become her surrogate family. She'd become the sister I'd always wanted and the aunt Kayla never had. She and Mom had also become close and I knew it made

Tracey reevaluate her relationship with her own mother. She'd been home to visit twice in the last month and had even made an effort to get along with her stepdad.

My own relationship with my mom continued to grow and evolve. I think being able to speak openly about my dad's death helped her to heal and finally find peace and closure. She also started dating. Dr. Chang took her out to dinner one night, but she quickly put an end to it, deciding a relationship with him would be too complicated considering the circumstances. Lately, however, she'd been seeing more of Andrew, the widower from the mall. She came home from her dates glowing.

She was falling more easily into the role of mother. Sometimes too easily and at the worst of times, which often ended up being embarrassing and awkward, but I knew she was only trying to make up for lost time.

Since Gran had come home to die, I'd seen strength in my mother I never knew she had. She made decisions I didn't think she was capable of making. One of those decisions was to take Gran off life support.

Dr. Chang came to the house with a palliative team. Gran was sedated, the feeding tube removed and all fluids stopped. Morphine was continued to keep her comfortable and sedated. A few hours later, she was taken off the ventilator.

They'd gone over it with us, so we knew what to expect. She could stop breathing as soon as ventilation was stopped, or continue to breathe on her own indefinitely.

Mom was at Gran's side when the ventilator was shut down and removed. After Gran's comfort was seen to, the medical team gathered up all the equipment and left.

I took Kayla into the room when they were gone. I'd arranged for a few days off work and pulled Kayla out of school so we could be there. Mom was sitting in the armchair beside the bed, holding Gran's hand. Kayla climbed up onto Mom's lap and sat quietly, studying Gran's face. "Is she dead, Mommy?"

I crouched down next to her. "No, sweetie. Listen, you can hear her breathing."

"She's quiet now," Mom said. "She sounded rough a few minutes ago."

Kayla placed her tiny hand on Mom's cheek. "Don't be so sad, Nana. Mommy said when Gran dies she's gonna go to a really nice place with Grampa and Daddy."

Mom swiped away the tears that were now sliding down her cheeks. "I know, sweetie, but I'll still miss her."

"Me too. Are you gonna die too, Nana?"

Mom put her hand to her mouth and looked away. "Yes," she finally replied, smiling down at Kayla through her tears, "but not for a long time. I still need to see you grow up, finish school and maybe get married and give me a grandbaby to love as much as Gran loves you."

Kayla smiled and gave my mom a hug before she jumped off her lap. She seemed content with the answer. She climbed up on the bed beside Gran and took her hand gently in her own. "It's okay, Gran. Mommy told me 'bout that place. We'll miss you, but if you wanna go there, it's okay. We'll always love you, even if you're not here." She leaned over and kissed Gran's cheek, then jumped down and ran out of the room yelling, "I'm gonna watch TV now, okay,

Mommy?" I smiled wryly at Mom, who looked a little shell-shocked, and said, "That went better than I expected."

* * *

Gran's raspy breathing startled me out of my thoughts. The events of the past months had been playing out in my head like a movie as I sat with her and waited for the end. I'd sent Mom upstairs to help Kayla get ready for bed. It was the only way I could get her to take a break from sitting with Gran.

With each passing hour, it became more of a struggle for Gran to breathe. I knew she'd been sedated enough that she wasn't in any pain, but it was still hard to watch her fight to stay alive. She'd hung on longer than anyone thought she would. It didn't surprise me that she was as stubborn now as she'd always been. She was a fighter and now she was fighting for every breath not to be her last.

I thought of my dad and my last memory of him, lying in a hospital bed, hooked up to tubes and machines. For a long time, that was how I'd remembered him. I hated him for leaving me. I hated him for leaving my mom sad and empty and incapable of being a mother. Now, finally, I felt like I'd forgiven him. I'd moved past the hurt and anger and started remembering the good things.

I pulled a tissue from the box on the nightstand and wiped the dampness from my face. "I still miss him, Gran," I said aloud. "I still get that tight, achy feeling around my heart when I think of him. I think that ache is good, though. It means I won't forget."

Gran moaned. She was restless suddenly and her breath rattled. I turned her gently on her side, placed pillows under her arm, against her back and between her knees. The rattling stopped and she rested easy again.

I sank back into the armchair, took a sip of lukewarm tea and glanced at the photo on the nightstand beside me. It was one I'd taken the Christmas before of Gran, Mom and Kayla, cuddled together on the couch after turkey dinner watching TV. They looked sleepy and contented; bellies full of good food, heads filled with wonderful new memories, hearts full of each other. It was the final photo I took that day, the special photo of our last Christmas together.

I rested my head against the back of the chair, closed my eyes, and listened to the birds sing their farewells to the setting sun. The sound of Kayla's laughter drifted down the stairs. The ache in my chest eased a little. It was good to be alive.

THE END

Thanks so much for reading Tranquility. Please take a moment to leave an honest review of my work on Amazon and/or Goodreads. If you enjoyed Tranquility feel free to pass it around so others can read it too!

About The Author

LAURIE GARDINER GREW UP ON A farm in a small Northern Ontario community in Canada. She left home at seventeen to experience life in the city and now lives in Cambridge, Ontario with her husband of twenty-seven years. Raising three kids, teaching fitness and operating a home daycare left little time for writing, but she did have some poetry published in various anthologies over the years. In 1997, her short story "'Til Death Do Us Part" placed first in the Cambridge Writers Collective anthology.

At the age of forty, Laurie went back to school and began a new career as a personal support worker. Though she ended up working in homecare, it was a placement in the dementia unit of a long-term care facility that inspired her to write her first novel, Tranquility.

Laurie is currently enrolled in the Creative Writing Program through the local community college and is working on her second novel.

www.facebook.com/

www.lauriegardiner.me/

amazon.com/author/lauriegardiner

www.goodreads.com/author/show/12065017.Laurie_Gardiner

https://twitter.com/LaurieGardiner1

Also By

"Retribution" in A Journey of Words

"Thief" in A Haunting of Words

"Don't Forget Me" in A Contract of Words

Coming Soon

"There's No Sunshine in Hell" in A Flash of Words

For more information and to see all of her works, check out her website

https://lauriegardiner.me/

Printed in Great Britain
by Amazon

10905129R10194